1288551 6

CW01214364

North Yorkshire County Council Library Service
Renew online at www.northyorks.gov.uk/libraries

MK 20

WITHDRAWN

Lesley Field

CONTEMPORARY NOVELS

Look out for the next books in the Saunders series

Book 2 SAUNDERS – ENDINGS AND BEGINNINGS

Book 3 SAUNDERS – SISTERS AND LOVERS

* * * *

HISTORICAL NOVELS

Coming 2018/19 the third and fourth books in the Duchess in Danger Series.

DANGEROUS DESIRE

DANGEROUS ENCOUNTER

Saunders – Lies and Deception

Saunders - Lies & Deception © 2018

by

Lesley Field

All rights reserved. No part of this book may be reproduced or transmitted in any form or by any means, electronic or mechanical, including photocopying, recording, or by any information storage and retrieval system, without permission in writing from the publisher, and the author

The characters and events portrayed in this book are fictitious. Any similarity to real persons, living or dead, or events, is coincidental and not intended by the author.

First Print Edition August 2018

Published as an e-book on 29th May 2018

by MuseItUp Publishing

Cover by World of Panorama

Lesley Field

This dedication I have saved for the Saunders series.

I dedicate the whole Saunders series to my parents, William (Bill) and Elizabeth (Betty), for everything they did for me. I know they would have been so proud of what I have achieved.

To Neil for preparing the print version and cover for Saunders – Lies & Deception

ACKNOWLEDGEMENTS

Karen Sorensen, Mayor of Banff, for her friendship. Also for the coffee's we share during our visits.

To the people of Banff for giving me so much joy and pleasure over the years.

To Karin, for the many visits we have had with her at the Cabins.

To Madrona Beach Resort, Parksville, Vancouver Island.

To Radium Hot Springs, Radium, BC

To my editor Lea Schizas for her wonderful editing of the e-book version, not to mention her patience.

Again a big thank you to MuseItUp for giving me the opportunity to continue writing for them.

Lesley Field

Forward by the Author

I set my contemporary romances in Canada and thought you may wonder why.

It was my dad's family who gave me the love for Canada. My father (and also my mother) grew up in the mining communities in the Durham area in the UK, both coming from large families.

There is a family story (true or not I don't know) that my father's eldest sister Lizzie, lied about her age to obtain passage to America. When she arrived at the port, the ship had sailed. That was the thing that saved the Canadian side of the family. The ship she missed was the Titanic. But eventually she reached America. At some point she travelled into Canada and later sent for her sister Florrie. After her marriage she and her husband farmed in Saskatchewan. She had several children and all were named after her own siblings.

My parents almost immigrated to Canada before I was born, but then changed their minds. So I could have been born Canadian.

I first visited Canada in 1977 with my mum (sadly my dad had passed away) but we met for the first time my Aunties Lizzie and Florrie. We visited Canada again in 1984.

In 1986 I re-married and took my husband, Neil, to Canada in 1989. I am fortunate that my husband loves the country just as much as I do and we are now regular visitors. I call it my heart home, every time I leave, a part of me remains. Banff is special to me and we love to spend Canada Day with the people there.

I have lots of relatives in Canada, some who know me, but lots who don't. One day I may get around to searching you all out, so beware.

SAUNDERS - LIES & DECEPTION

Lesley Field

Prelude

Banff, Canada, 1984

Sarah slipped into the telephone booth and entered Annie's number. She hated this secrecy but it was necessary in view of the promise she had made. Hearing the phone ringing she waited eagerly to hear her friend's voice.

"Hi, Annie, it's Sarah. How are you? Sorry it's been longer than usual but I've had this dreadful cold and just haven't felt well." She garbled the message out quickly, not wanting her friend to think she'd forgotten her. "No, I'm fine now, just sorry I haven't been in touch earlier," she said, answering her friend's anxious questions.

As she listened, the tone of Annie's voice changed. Her heart missed a beat when she heard her friend's news. "Oh no, Annie, how bad is it?" She listened to the response. "Yes, I know I will. I have to come back. I'll see if I can get on a flight as soon as possible. I'm not sure how I'm going to explain it to Jeff, but I'll find a way. Can Corey and I stay with you and Bob?" She talked some more then thanked her friend for the offer of accommodation.

Putting the phone down, she walked slowly back to Mountain View in somewhat of a daze trying to figure out how to explain to Jeff that she needed to return to England for a short while. She could feel the tears threatening at the shock of the news, but for now, she had to keep them at bay and keep her emotions under control.

Walking back into the hotel she went to the office knowing Jeff would be in there waiting for her. They were going to have coffee together before she picked up Corey from playgroup. Opening the office door, she halted in the entrance. He wasn't alone, his mother was with him.

"Sorry, darling, I thought you were alone," she turned, intending to leave.

"No, its okay," he said, grinning broadly. "It's time for a break anyway. You don't mind, Mom, if Sarah and I go for coffee now?"

Sarah glanced at her mother-in-law, Sylvia Saunders; no matter how hard she tried, she couldn't feel any warmth toward her. There was something predatory about her. She looked very much the wife of a rich man, or the widow of one, which is exactly what she was. Her elongated face seemed to pull any pleasantness out of her features. The long straight nose gave her a haughty look, as if she was looking down at you, which of course she probably was, thought Sarah. There wasn't a hair out of place on her head, the dark grey hair was pulled severely back and fastened in her customary bun at the back of her neck.

She looked at Sarah, and there was no attempt to disguise the disappointment on her face that her son had, in her view, married beneath him. Her lips tightened, and Sarah thought the bright red lipstick looked almost like a danger sign, a warning to others to keep out of her way. She moved to the side as Jeff stood and walked around the desk to join her. She was trying to appear normal but as soon as he got close, it became clear that she'd not succeeded and he'd noticed she was upset.

"Sarah, what is it? Is something wrong with Corey?" he asked, instantly concerned.

She shook her head and tried to blink the tears away. "No, he's fine as far as I know. It's just that I've had some upsetting news about..." she hesitated for a brief second before continuing, "one of my close friends. She's dying and I would really like to go and see her while I can, but it would mean going back to England for a short while."

By this time, Jeff had reached her and pulled her close. "Of course you must go back if it's so important to you, darling. I know what it's like to lose someone close." He was referring to his late father, and dropped a kiss on top of her head.

She looked up at him. "So you would be okay with me going back. It will only be for a short while. I don't think she has long to live." Her lips trembled as she spoke the words.

"Of course I don't. You must do what you feel is right."

"Oh thank you, darling. I'll go check the airlines and see if I can get tickets for Corey and me as soon as possible."

* * * *

Sylvia Saunders stood quietly watching this exchange. So the thorn in her side was running back to England. If only she would stay there, the thought almost made her smile. She had been opposed to this marriage since the start but for once had been unable to make her son see her point of view. If only she had been here when Sarah had first turned up, she would have made quite certain that the involvement had never had a chance to happen. When she thought of the suitable young women Jeff could have married, young girls she could have moulded into the kind of daughter-in-law who would have been only too willing to concede to her mother-in-law, it made her even more determined to find a flaw in this interloper.

She was still considering this when she heard Sarah mention about taking Corey with her and that comment made her interrupt the conversation. "Is it wise to take Corey with you? If you are visiting your friend who's sick, would it be advisable to take a small child into a sick area? It might be better to leave him here, that way you can visit your friend without any worry about Corey." The thought of Sarah taking her precious grandson out of the country was something that she would not tolerate. But she would have to play this carefully.

Sarah looked horrified at the suggestion. "But he's only three, I can't leave him."

"Oh don't be melodramatic, Sarah," said Sylvia, an edge of irritation in her voice. "His daddy is here and me. It's not like you're leaving him with strangers."

Jeff cut into his mother's words. "Perhaps I should come with you, then I can look after Corey while you visit your friend," he suggested, believing he'd found the perfect solution.

Before Sarah could answer, Sylvia spoke. "Oh, darling, that sounds such a sensible idea, but I need to go to Vancouver next week, and I'm not sure how long I will be, you know we can't leave Tom to run things on his own. So, sadly, this is one time when business will have to come first." She watched as Sarah and Jeff digested what she'd said. Her son looked disappointed but Sarah, well, she thought she saw a glimpse of something…possibly relief in her face, just for a fraction of a second.

Jeff didn't respond to this information. He knew nothing about his mother going to Vancouver, but then again perhaps she'd just arranged it. Being co-owner of a hotel had its advantages but this was one of the disadvantages, they couldn't both be away at the same time.

"It's okay," said Sarah, reaching up and kissing her husband's cheek. "I understand business has to come first sometimes and, as your mother says, you can't leave Tom on his own. I'll take Corey with me and we'll manage."

"Oh no, Sarah, that would be too much for you," said Sylvia. "If you are upset now, my dear, think how upset you will be when you are with your friend, and how that will upset Corey. No, it's probably best if he stays here with his daddy. He can go to his playgroup and be with his friends while Jeff is working, then when I come back from my trip, I'll be here to look after him as well." She smiled at Sarah as she said the words. "I'll leave you to talk it over. I know you will decide what is best for Corey." As she closed the door, she only hoped that her son would agree with her on this. If not she would have to find another tactic.

Sarah was instantly worried. Sylvia calling her, my dear, was unusual but she did seem to be trying to sort things out to make it easier for her. Sarah hadn't been able to see anything in her face to give a clue as to what she was thinking; so thought perhaps she should give her the benefit of the doubt. But what about Jeff. Looking at her husband she asked him what he thought would be the best thing to do. She could see he was torn and knew he'd wanted to come with her, and she would have loved to have him by her side, but it would complicate matters. But was he happy about their son going with her, or would he agree with his mother? For once Sarah couldn't disagree with Sylvia's suggestion, but she hated the thought of leaving Corey.

"I don't know, Sarah, mother's right in a way about Corey staying here with me and his friends, but I know he'll miss you like crazy. I don't like to think of him being upset. Then again, if you are upset in England he'll pick up on it, which will upset him anyway. So whichever way, he will have only one parent and will likely be upset. Perhaps it's better if he does stay here with familiar things. But look, we can discuss this later if you wish. You stay here and check out flights on the computer then we'll take it from there. I'll go and see what mother is up to, unless you want me to stay and help."

"No, I can manage. It will give me time to think what will be best, then we can talk later." He kissed her lightly on the lips before leaving.

Sarah stared at the screen in front of her. She could get a flight out tomorrow, late afternoon; it was the only seat left. All she had to do was decide whether to take Corey with her or leave him at home with Jeff. Her heart was telling her to take him, but her head was saying that, for once, what Sylvia said made sense. What fun was it going to be for him in a sick room with a dying person, and thinking sensibly, could she risk taking him with her? Her head made the decision. She called the airline and booked the seat for one person.

Going through into reception, she saw Jeff manning the desk. He smiled then asked if she had managed to sort things out. "Yes. I've decided that it's probably best if Corey stays here with you. I won't be more than a couple of weeks, perhaps three, but I'll be home as soon as I possibly can."

Standing around the corner of reception, and out of sight, Sylvia listened to the couple's conversation, a smile curling her lips, pleased that her grandson was staying here. Waiting a few moments, she walked into the reception area and casually asked if they had managed to sort anything out. She saw no point in letting them know what she'd overheard.

Listening to what had been arranged she agreed that it was a sensible decision to leave Corey at home, then suggested that Jeff take the rest of the day off and spend it with his family, since they were going to be apart for a few weeks.

Collecting Corey from playgroup they wandered down to Centenary Park, and Sarah watched as Jeff kicked a small ball round with their son. She'd been surprised at Sylvia's offer but had no intention of looking anything other than the pleased daughter-in-law at her considerate thought. In her wildest dreams, she couldn't have imagined herself being this happy. She had a gorgeous husband, an equally adorable son, and her life was getting better as each day passed. Her decision to come to Canada had been the right one, but now it was impossible not to be sad as this had taken her away from the other person she loved, and that person was now dying. The worst part of it all was that she couldn't share this with Jeff, or with anyone. This was her secret, the one she had sworn to keep.

She waved at Jeff then laughed as he ran to collect the ball that Corey had somehow managed to kick some distance away. Their son, seeming to realise he was on his own, decided to make a bid for freedom and set off at a pace toward the river. Sarah was on her feet in an instant and had gathered up the giggling little boy before he'd got half way to his goal.

Jeff came running up to them as Sarah swung Corey round and up in the air. Gathering him close, she felt the tears threatening. She was going to miss him and Jeff. The thought of being without them, even for a short while, was like a knife being thrust through her. For a moment, she considered cancelling her trip, but no sooner had the thought entered her head, than it was dismissed. She had to go back, had to see the one person who had given her her freedom, just one last time.

Handing Corey to his daddy, she wiped her eyes with the back of her hand. Jeff seeing this pulled her to him with his free hand and kissed her forehead. "The time will soon pass, darling, it's not like its forever."

"I know." The reply was automatic, but what she didn't say was that she was scared. Going back to something she had escaped from frightened her. A shiver went through her. There was a premonition that something bad was about to happen, but didn't know what, or even where the feeling had come from.

"Come on, let's go and eat. We'll have a nice steak with a bottle of wine and Corey can have some fries as a treat, then we'll go home and you can pack. How does that sound, sweetheart?"

"It sounds wonderful." she said, trying to dispel the gloomy feelings.

Lying in bed that night, wrapped in her husband's arms, she gave herself up to his lovemaking, knowing it would be some time before either of them enjoyed this again. He woke her again through the night telling her he didn't know how he was going to manage without her delightful body for such a long time. She laughed and told him that a few weeks apart would only make their reunion that much better, but in her heart she knew that this separation was going to tear her apart.

Calling in at Mountain View on their way to the airport, Sarah said goodbye to Tom, the Manager, while Jeff had a word with his mother. Going through to the office, she smiled as their son ran across the room calling out, "Daddy," only to be picked up and swung high in the air. Watching them together her heart was full of love for them both. They were so alike, same blonde hair and blue eyes. The older of the blue eyes looked across to her and her insides almost melted. He could turn her to jelly with a look, and knew what he'd meant last night; she didn't know how she was going to manage without him for the next few weeks.

Sylvia watched the interchange between them and pursed her lips. How her son could be so distracted by this slip of a girl, was beyond her. But she had given her a wonderful grandson so reluctantly credited her with that. Bidding farewell to the couple she hugged her grandson, then turned back to the desk as they left. Picking up her address book she lifted the phone and rang the selected number.

It was answered after four rings. "Claytons Investigations, how can I help?"

Saunders – Lies and Deception

"Clay, its Sylvia Saunders. I have a job for you and I hope your passport is up to date."

Lesley Field

Chapter One

Sarah excused herself to her fellow traveller, squeezing past him to go to the toilet. The plane was still cruising at thirty-seven thousand feet but she knew that it wouldn't be long before they started their descent into Calgary. It was this thought that had her rushing to the bathroom, not because she needed to go, but because of the sick feeling in her stomach.

Locking the door behind her, she sat in the tiny confined space, holding her head in her hands. What on earth am I doing? She asked herself, not for the first time. She'd allowed her friends, Annie and Bob, to persuade her to take this journey, now she was within hours of her destination and the doubts that had been plaguing her for the last eight hours or more were working overtime. Pulling herself together she washed her hands and then tidied her hair. That made her laugh, as the hair she combed certainly wasn't her own. Well it was, but not the colour it should be. A quick wash-in colour had changed her dark auburn hair to almost black. She hardly recognised herself. The colour made her look pale, but it was a necessary camouflage; something she hoped would keep her from being recognised.

Settled back in her seat, she picked up her magazine and continued to glance through the pages until the plane started to descend, then she gazed out of the window. How many times had she imagined this moment, played the scenario over and over in her mind in the early years. She would be eager and excited as the plane landed, anxious to get through customs, and when she did she would hurry into the arrivals hall and they would be there. Her handsome young husband would be waiting, standing tall and slim with his blonde hair falling slightly over his brow and their son, with the same blonde hair as his daddy, would hold out his chubby little arms to her. She would run to them and they would hug and kiss. She would tell them that she had missed them so badly and would never leave them again.

Pulling her mind back to the present she realised they were bittersweet memories, but not even memories, she thought, because memories were recollections of things that had happened, and the reunion she had so longed for had never taken place. She swallowed hard on the lump that had come into her throat, and could feel the sting of tears in her eyes. Looking out of the window she tried to see the mountains but they were lost in the haze of clouds. Her stomach churned as the plane started to come into land. She was about to face her demons, but hopefully wouldn't meet them. She had done as they'd asked and stayed away, but now this was her last chance to see her son before he took the huge step into matrimony.

As soon as they stopped taxiing, there was a mad rush of people scrabbling to get luggage out of the overhead bins. Sarah wasn't in a rush. Her small backpack was under the seat in front and all she needed was her fleece from the bin. Waiting until the people from the seats alongside her had gone, she reached up, pulled her fleece down, then put it on. Walking along the aisle, she smiled and thanked the crew as she passed and said goodbye, not that she had needed any attention during the flight, her thoughts had more than kept her occupied.

She waited patiently in the long line of people waiting to go through the ritual of passport control and then customs. She was eager to be outside, but at the same time scared of her own reactions. Following the other passengers, she was soon heading toward the baggage hall. Walking into the Main Hall she couldn't help but remember the last time she'd been here. There had been tears, mostly hers as she had said goodbye to her family. Closing her eyes for a moment she wished it was possible to turn back time. To find them waiting for her, but she knew that was a fool's dream. Pushing the trolley containing her one suitcase, and with her small backpack over her shoulder, she followed the signs directing her to the shuttle bus that would take her back to the place she had once thought of as home.

Her case was soon placed in the luggage compartment while she quickly disposed of the trolley. Climbing on board, she walked halfway along the bus before settling into a window seat that would later, hopefully, give her a view of the hotel she wanted to see. She wasn't sure if she would recognise it. It could have changed over the years, but at least she could look.

As they drove along the highway she listened to the excited chatter of her fellow passengers. Looking at them from behind her dark glasses she could see they were mainly young people probably going to work in the town for the summer. There were a few obvious tourists looking eagerly out of the window at the unfamiliar scenery.

For Sarah, the scenery was familiar; she had travelled this highway many times with her family. The last time they did it was because she had to go away and leave them, but it was only going to be for a short time. She remembered how they had been laughing and singing as they drove to the airport mainly to stop them from feeling sad. If she had known then what was to happen she would have insisted Jeff turn the car around and go back, but she didn't, so she left. Now she was back and for a very special reason, but nothing could wipe away the pain or the tears of the past eighteen years.

As they travelled further along the highway toward Banff, the mountains could be seen in the distance moving ever closer as they gradually left the farmlands behind. She felt her heartbeat increase and a familiar sense of excitement began to wash over her, although this time it was tinged with a feeling of fear and apprehension. They passed the turnings to the town of Canmore and Sarah knew from the signposts that it wouldn't be long before they drove through the Park Gate. Then shortly after that they would turn off the highway and head toward Banff. She recalled the first time she had arrived in this country, a young naïve girl of seventeen with her head filled full of dreams all planted and encouraged by her mum. She had never been abroad before, and she'd been both excited and terrified at the same time.

She would never forget the exact moment she first set eyes on the one person who would steal her heart, and then cruelly cast her aside at the time she needed him the most. Remembering brought pain, as she had learned over the years, so she closed her heart to the thoughts that kept coming back to haunt her. In England it was easier to forget, and she needed to do that because the pain was almost too much to bear. But now she was back, and couldn't help but wonder if this visit was going to tear her fragile world apart.

Bringing her thoughts back to the present she eagerly looked out of the window as the bus turned off the highway then onto the road that would lead into the main Avenue. She heard the gasps of the other passengers as they saw the elk grazing by the side of the road. She smiled, remembering how they would often see the elk in the town site, and in a way it was reassuring to see something so familiar.

The bus was now travelling down Banff Avenue and she was looking ahead to where she remembered the hotel was. It was still there. Her heart missed a beat as the bus passed by, and she suddenly felt sick. Although some changes appeared to have been made, she was able to see it still looked pretty much as it did all those years ago. Settling back in her seat she clasped her hands together and breathed deeply to calm herself before they pulled into the bus station.

Getting off the bus she put her backpack on and, pulling her case behind, walked the short distance to where she was staying. She found her accommodation easily from the instructions given, and was greeted by an elderly couple who showed her into the unit. Having been assured that she was fine but a bit tired, they left saying she was to let them know if she needed anything. Closing the door she leaned against the wood. She was finally here, on her own, back in Banff, somewhere she thought she would never see again.

Waking the next morning, she couldn't wait to get up and dressed, for she had a mission today that excited but also scared her. Lifting a clean pair of warm pants from the small closet she quickly dressed, thankful of the shower she'd had the night before.

Eating the somewhat dry sandwiches she had picked up at the airport the previous day, she had a glass of water before collecting her bag and stepping outside. I must remember to pick up some provisions including milk before I return. Locking the door to the unit, she walked along the passageway into the bright sunshine. Being late May the air was cool despite the brightness of the sun, making her thankful the fleece she wore kept her warm. Standing for a moment, she closed her eyes and drank in the smell of the clean air. Then covering her eyes with dark glasses she set off toward Banff Avenue and the hotel she saw yesterday.

As she approached the front of the hotel she looked discreetly through the windows. Although the exterior looked pretty much the same inside it had changed somewhat. There appeared to be some kind of coffee area at the front, which would give her the perfect place to sit, or hide said a small voice in her head. Walking as casually as she could through the doors she glanced around. Seeing no familiar faces she made her way to one of the tables by the window. Selecting a chair that gave her a perfect view of the reception desk, she waited.

A young girl approached, "Hi, can I get you something to drink?"

"Just a coffee please," said Sarah quietly.

She had long finished her coffee and ordered a second cup so as not to look too conspicuous. Halfway through the second cup the door leading from reception to the office opened. Lifting her head, she gasped as the object of her whole trip came out and spoke to the young girl on the desk. There was no mistaking who he was; his blue eyes and blonde hair were so familiar she would have recognised him anywhere. His likeness to his father was unreal. Her heart thundered in her chest as she looked at him, and a longing that she had tried to suppress over the years ripped through her body. This was her son, her darling, Corey, the person she had given birth to and whom she loved beyond anything else. She watched from behind dark glasses, a lump formed in her throat. She could feel the stinging of gathering tears. She willed him to stay. She couldn't believe her luck when the young girl disappeared and he remained on the desk in her place.

It had been a calculated guess on her part that he would learn the family business in the same hands on way his father had and, despite tomorrow being his wedding day, had a feeling she would find him here. If she had been wrong she would have been disappointed, although she would have the opportunity to see him tomorrow. But now having seen him, dare she risk seeing him again tomorrow? Every part of her said yes, but would she have the courage to do so, and then walk away?

She continued to watch as he dealt with the people waiting at the desk, speaking in a soft Canadian accent and with a smile that reached his eyes. She could see the young girls vying to catch his eye, hoping no doubt that he may ask them out. But she knew he wouldn't do that as his heart belonged elsewhere. She only hoped that, unlike his father, he would stay true to her. Tucked away in the corner watching his every move, she remembered the toddler she had left and looked at the fine young man he had turned into. She had to credit Jeff with this, and no doubt Sylvia, for she, his mother, had taken no part in it. Had not been allowed to, barred from her son and unable to give the love she had for him. But now she needed to savour this precious time so she could remember it in the years to come.

The young girl returned and asked if she wanted anything else but she shook her head and paid for the coffees as quickly as possible. Content just to sit with the magazine partly raised, she watched him over the top of the page. Her hands trembled but she couldn't stop them. Her emotions were so intense it was all she could do not to jump up and hold him in her arms and tell him who she was.

She heard the main entrance door open and watched as an older woman entered and walked up to the desk. She was small and slim with dark hair tied loosely at the nape of her neck. Smiling, she leaned across the desk and gently touched his face. He walked out from behind the desk and, bending slightly, hugged her and kissed her on the cheek. Sarah could clearly see the love and respect they had for each other. She didn't know her, and she should hate her for she was sure this was the person who had taken the place in his heart that should belong to her. I should go, she thought, but couldn't bear to tear herself away. The realisation that she had left it too late to return, that she probably shouldn't have come at all, did little to help her emotions.

No, I have every right to see my son, she told herself sharply.

She had kept her end of the agreement up to now, but his life was about to change. She had a right to see him, to see for herself that he was happy. She had never had anything from him, or his father, over the years so had no way of knowing what his thoughts were toward her. Tomorrow was her son's wedding day and she didn't want to cause any trouble that would spoil it for him. To see him now as a young man was more than she had dared to hope for. But it was bittersweet knowing that someone else had loved and guided him as he grew up.

In that moment she hated Sylvia Saunders more than ever, and Jeff? Yes, she hated him too for he was part of it all. She thought of what they had had, all of it thrown away. Yes, she hated him, of course she did; she had too? Tears gathered in her eyes. It was too much; she needed to leave before she drew attention to herself.

Reaching for her bag she stood and crossed the hotel lobby toward the door, the door that would take her back out onto the street and away from him. She wasn't worried that he might see her as he wouldn't recognise her. Her eyes were so blinded by tears she didn't see the tall figure coming through the door until she almost bumped into him.

"Sorry, ma'am," said a soft voice. "Are you okay?"

Sarah felt her heart somersault and she swiftly nodded her head but made no attempt to raise it. She didn't dare turn around until she was outside. She recognised the voice straightaway and would have known it anywhere. It was the voice that used to whisper such words of love to her. But words were all they turned out to be, she thought bitterly.

Hurrying outside she felt sick and her body trembled. She felt as though she had been hit by a bolt of lightning. How, after all this time, could he still have this effect on her? Once on the forecourt she risked looking back through the glass-fronted lobby. She could see him striding toward the desk and the dark haired woman moved to greet him. She saw his outstretched arm gather her close, kissing her on the cheek. This gesture was like a knife being thrust through Sarah's heart. She wanted to scream that he was once her husband, and was supposed to love her forever. She swallowed hard to suppress the sob that threatened to tear the soul out of her, realizing that she no longer had a place in the world her son, and the man who used to be her husband, had created.

Painful though it was, she had been right to come and see her son before he took the big step into married life. Did she have regrets about leaving him and his father all those years ago? Yes, a million regrets. Would she do it again? No, she wouldn't, she'd be the one standing next to his father now, nestled into his side, and not the dark haired woman who was now presumably his wife.

Life had been empty without them both and it would remain so. There was no place for her here now. But she was older and, hopefully, wiser and no one could stop her from wishing her son the happiness she had once shared with his father. Quickly wiping the tears that had escaped from beneath her dark glasses, she waited quietly on the seat outside the hotel, a place that had once been so familiar to her, until her legs were strong enough to carry her back to her accommodation.

Once back in her lodgings she put away the few shopping items and then sat down and reflected on what had happened. She had been apprehensive about what she was doing and also scared. She had so much here that belonged to her, but at the same time, she had nothing. Making herself a drink she sat on the small sofa reflecting on the mission she had set herself for today. She had seen her son but the excitement she had felt this morning when getting ready was now replaced with a deep sadness, and a yearning for the lost years that could never be recovered. All those special days and moments in her son's life that she'd not been able to share. Shaking her head to stop her train of thought she tried to keep cheerful by reminding herself that there was still tomorrow to look forward to…at least there would be if she didn't lose her nerve at the last minute.

Chapter Two

The next morning, the sun was shining and the sky was so blue. She had always been fascinated by the blueness of the sky and had never seen one so blue since she had left. But today, only a true blue Canadian sky would be right for her son on his wedding day. After the agony of yesterday she had thought for one crazy moment to spare herself any further pain. To spend the day at one of her favourite places, the top of Sulphur Mountain, away from the town site. Away from what was taking place below, but she couldn't. She had come such a long way for this. The longing to see him again, and his bride, was too great. So later that morning, she found herself sitting on a bench watching the people in their best outfits going into the church opposite.

Finding out the time of the ceremony had been easy. Although she couldn't be there standing next to his father, she could see it all from a distance. She wore a pair of smart black pants with a cream top so as not to look too out of place, but she could do nothing about the fleece, since it was the only jacket she had. Carrying this over her arm, she had walked the short distance to the church and was now watching the vicar greeting everyone at the door. Then she saw him striding toward the vicar, her son. She was so proud of him. He was tall and slim like his father, although probably a couple of inches shorter than him. The dark trousers and morning coat made him look so handsome. He resembled his father so much that memories of her own wedding day came flooding back. Heartbreak ripped through her as she thought of what could have been.

She noticed the young man at his side whom she presumed to be his best man and wondered if he was a friend or, a sickening thought hit her, was he a brother. Oh no, I never considered that his father could have had more children. She felt sickened at the thought of him with someone else, raising their children the way they should have raised their son. She watched as they disappeared into the church and then she saw his father following close behind. His blonde hair was blowing slightly in the breeze. He looked so handsome in his morning suit. Her pulse raced. Watching him walk into church on his own she realised that his wife was probably already inside waiting for him to join her, so they could sit at the front together as parents of the groom. It should have been me, she thought, holding back a sob.

Other people arrived and, although common sense told her she should leave, she was drawn across the road as if by some inexplicable cord. Before she knew what was happening she found herself walking up the path toward the church. Her subconscious told her this was madness, she ignored it, convincing herself it wouldn't do any harm to sit at the back. Following an elderly couple inside, she slipped quickly into a pew on the right. Sitting down, she glanced around. It felt so right to be there.

Lesley Field

Someone had placed an Order of Service in her hand and she held it tightly. It would be a reminder of this day, something for her to have forever. Looking at the names embossed on the front, she gently ran her fingers over them. Laura Elizabeth Connaught and Corey James Saunders. She remembered the day she and Jeff had chosen his names, Corey being Jeff's choice and Sarah choosing Jeff's middle name of James.

A flurry of excitement outside brought her back to the present just as the organ started playing. Sarah turned to look at the person who would have been her daughter-in-law as she stood waiting for her cue to start the walk toward her groom, and her future. She is beautiful, thought Sarah, looking at the slender young woman, her dark hair falling in soft curls around her face, and a smile that would light up a room. How she would love to meet her, and have them both in her life, but that was not meant to be. The next thirty minutes or so would have to last her for the rest of her life.

Looking toward the front, she watched her son turn, saw the smile that spread across his face as his bride started the slow walk down the aisle toward him. She remembered an identical look on his father's face when she'd taken the same walk all those years ago.

The service was beautiful and, as she listened to the Vicar's words as he started the service, "Dearly beloved we are gathered together ..." her mind drifted back to her own wedding day, a day just like today when she had felt so happy that she thought she would burst.

Jeff had believed she had no family so there was only his family and friends at the service. His family were well known and whilst a lot of the people there were strangers, she hadn't cared, she'd been so happy. She remembered the small but beautiful ceremony where everyone was smiling, apart from Jeff's mother who never seemed to lose the slight stern look on her face no matter what the occasion. Sylvia Saunders had never considered Sarah good enough for her precious son. For a start, she wasn't local and therefore considered to be a stranger, and an unknown quantity. Sylvia liked to be in control, and you can't be in control of something you don't fully know or understand.

Sarah was certain that she and Jeff would never have been able to start a relationship had Sylvia been around when she'd first arrived in Banff, but Sylvia had been on vacation. By the time she returned, it was too late, they were inseparable. She had done all that she could to prevent the marriage but had failed. Sarah knew she was tolerated, but eventually she'd scored a few points when she presented Sylvia with a beautiful grandson. But Sarah was always aware of the tension between them. That she was never good enough for Jeff. Would things have been different if Sylvia had liked her? She doubted it.

Sarah's mind came back to the present. The hymns were sung, and she joined in with the unfamiliar words, so happy to be able to share the moment when this beautiful young woman became her son's wife. The bridal party moved to sign the Register and people sat patiently waiting for the formalities to end, so they could see the happy couple together for the first time. Sarah realised that she should slip out now. She had shared this beautiful moment but now needed to leave. As she was about to do so the photographer moved into position, ready for the photos of the happy couple coming down the aisle, blocking the end of the pew. Okay, don't panic, it will be all right. No one is likely to recognise me, she thought, thankful again for the temporary change in her hair colouring.

Trying to remain calm she waited, and then the organ started playing. Everyone stood up. She watched her son and his beautiful bride walk down the aisle. You look so handsome and so proud, Corey, my darling. The young newlyweds looked at each other, happiness radiating from them. She saw the love between them and wanted to cry. That was the way she and Jeff used to look at each other...like no one else existed.

Lost in the moment, her eyes followed the young couple as they walked toward her, and then they were alongside. Tears filled her eyes, and she blinked to clear them. She began to turn her head back toward the front before she made a fool of herself, but suddenly found herself looking straight into a pair of blue eyes that she once knew so well. Eyes that had once caused her to tremble with desire; that had looked so tenderly at her as they made love. Shock filled every part of her body but she steeled herself to keep calm. She saw the look on Jeff's face, puzzlement, and then a slow realisation before he turned his head swiftly to the front, but not before she saw the clenching of his jaw. In that moment she knew he had recognised her. She kept her head lowered, having no wish to see his wife or, God forbid, his mother. She couldn't face a confrontation with Sylvia. The last one they had was more than enough to last a lifetime, and it had taken away from her everything she held dear.

How she got back to her lodgings she didn't know. She half walked, half ran on legs that would hardly hold her up. Sitting on a small chair, with her arms wrapped around her shaking body, she listened to the gentle hum from the kettle as she waited to make a coffee. She needed time to think about what to do because the last thing she wanted was a meeting with Jeff. She had chosen not to stay in the centre of the town site, where the main hotels were, to avoid places where she was likely to bump into him. The family's hotel, Mountain View Inn, was on Banff Avenue, but far enough away, and there was no need to go near it again. Going there yesterday was a risk, but one she'd considered worth taking at the time. But after today's encounter she would have to be extra careful.

After all this time she thought she would have some control over her feelings for him, but she was wrong. How could she still feel this way about him after he'd ripped her world into shreds? Seeing him again face to face tore her apart and the longing for him was overwhelming, feelings that had been buried for so long had erupted inside her like a volcano. The strength of the feelings made her feel sick. But the look on his face told her quite clearly she was the last person he expected, or wanted to see.

Tossing and turning that night; all she could see in her broken dreams was Jeff's face. Waking early she thought about staying inside to avoid any further encounter, but this was the first time she'd been back in Canada and in Banff since leaving eighteen years ago. Places had changed and there was a lot more tourism than there used to be. Today was Sunday so there would be lots of people and families out enjoying the weekend, so she could mingle in with the crowds.

You can't stay inside for the next five days until you are due to fly home. Having decided, she took a book from the few provided in her unit and ventured to the edge of town to Centenary Park, once a favourite place for her to take Corey when he was a baby, while Jeff was working. She walked down to the park and, as expected, it was full with families enjoying the sunshine. There was a grassy spot under one of the trees and she sat down on the grass and opened her book. It was peaceful here, just the shouts of children as they played and the smell of the grass and trees, it was almost enough to lull her to sleep.

Saunders – Lies and Deception

As the time passed, she tired of reading, and found herself watching the families from behind her dark glasses. Her thoughts drifted back to the times she would wheel Corey down here in his buggy and then spread a rug on the ground where he would run around shrieking, as a toddler does, while she chased him. Then exhausted they would fall back on the rug, both of them giggling, and she would hug him so hard. Her life was perfect; too perfect she used to think. She was always a bit scared that something would spoil it, but was never prepared for what did happen.

She watched a young mom chasing her little boy round and round in circles until the toddler fell over dizzy. Mom then picked him up and held him high above her head and then close to her chest. Sarah realised that tears were running down her cheeks and swiftly wiped them away with a tissue. It was a bad idea to come here, but it was bittersweet. She was feeling emotions that she hadn't felt in a long time. Feelings of love for her son that she had buried so deep in an attempt to forget them. But now, not only could she feel the emotions she had felt when she held Corey, she could remember the soft powdery smell of him. She couldn't do this, it was too overwhelming, the pain was too intense. In England these feelings could be buried but here, in a place where everything was suddenly so familiar, it was impossible. A sob caught in her throat, she jumped up and began walking quickly back toward Banff Avenue.

Lesley Field

It was early evening and the town was bathed in the sinking sun. It looked so beautiful with Cascade Mountain as a backdrop. She used to love standing at the end of the Avenue, close to the bridge, just looking back at the town site, it was one of her favourite views. Tourists were out and about looking in the shops for souvenirs. Suddenly, she realised that was exactly what she was, a tourist, not part of the Banff community as she used to be, but someone who was just passing through. The realisation hit her hard. Going into one of the small restaurants for dinner she requested a table away from the window and sat alone with her thoughts. This isn't home anymore, but then I knew that. But being here it feels like it is. When the time comes for me to leave it's going to be hard. Last time was bad enough, and it was only going to be for a short time. Now when I leave, I won't return. I'll never see all of this again. She sighed and pushed the half empty plate away.

She would have gone straight back to England when Jeff had seen her, but that wasn't an option as she couldn't change her flight. There was no other choice but to wait it out until Thursday when she would be able to get the airport shuttle back to Calgary.

Leaving the restaurant, she risked going to the supermarket and bought some bread, ham and cheese to make sandwiches for the next few days. Walking along the side streets she made her way back to the Johnson's. They had a lovely little house and had turned the basement into a self-contained unit they could rent out and, as they told her, it helped to supplement their pensions. It had all that Sarah needed, a combined living/kitchen area with a separate bedroom and a small shower room. There was a TV in the living area, and a toaster, microwave, electric kettle and a fridge/freezer in the kitchen. For Sarah it was a refuge where she could come and go when she wanted through her own entrance, with no awkward questions about what she had been doing.

* * * *

Walking back from the departure area, Jeff smiled as a familiar face beamed at him across the hall.

"Hi, Jeff, it's been a while. You just arriving or meeting someone?" said Max, thrusting out his hand and clasping his friend's in a strong grip.

"Neither, Max. Good to see you. Just been dropping off Corey and his new bride. They're off to Hawaii on honeymoon."

"Oh, of course, I remember someone saying he was getting married. Can't believe how the years have flown. So are you in a rush to get back, or do you have time for a coffee, or something stronger if you want?"

Jeff looked at his watch. He really wanted to get back, but it was ages since he'd seen Max and it seemed churlish to turn down the chance of a catch up. "Sure, coffee would be good."

"Great. I'll just let the team know where I'll be," said Max, pulling a walkie-talkie from his belt.

Jeff listened as Max detailed his whereabouts and when he'd finished asked him how the security business was.

"Oh you know, need eyes everywhere. Since 9/11 everything has changed but I still enjoy the job so I guess I'll keep doing it until they decide to retire me, or replace me with a younger chap to take over as head of security."

Reaching the small coffee area Jeff found a couple of chairs near to the window and waited while Max brought the coffees over.

They talked about general things to do with their jobs and eventually got onto the subject of ice hockey. But even this subject couldn't keep Jeff's mind off the events of the previous day, and he knew Max realised that he was somewhat distracted when he enquired if he was alright. He assured him he was but could see Max wasn't convinced.

"Are you sure, Jeff? Not a problem with the newlyweds?"

"No, they're fine. Couldn't be better, in fact. It's nothing to worry about, just something that happened yesterday, but I'll sort it."

"Well, it must be more than something to distract you from ice hockey, and to have you on edge. And don't say you're not, because I can see you are. Trained to spot these things, you know."

His half-hearted attempt at a joke made Jeff smile. But also made him realise that his friend wasn't going to give up the inquisition, and if he were truthful, it would be a relief to talk to someone about it. Running a hand through his hair, he said, "Corey's mom was at the church yesterday." The words just came out. He'd had them bottled up since yesterday and he just told it as it was.

Max looked shocked. He knew how his friend's wife had walked out on him and Corey and how affected his friend had been at the time.

"Bloody hell, mate, no wonder you look anxious. Didn't expect that. Do you know what she wants?"

Jeff shook his head. "No, I haven't a clue. I was too shocked when I saw her to do anything, and anyway, how could I right in the middle of the wedding."

"Did Corey see her?"

"No, thank God, although he wouldn't have recognised her. But I'm worried that she may still be here when Corey and Laura get back from Hawaii, and I just don't know what effect her being here is going to have on both of our lives. I just hope she's gone by the time the kids get back."

Max looked thoughtful for a moment. "What's her full name?"

"Sarah Catherine Saunders." Just saying her name had brought a sick feeling into his throat. Then he remembered that she could be going under her maiden name. "Or she could be under the name of O'Connor."

He wondered why his friend wanted to know this but before he could ask the question Max told him to wait saying he wouldn't be long. He returned some time with a slip of paper in his hand.

"Well there's no need to worry, Jeff, because according to our records she's due to fly out this coming Thursday, and I presume that's long before Corey and his wife will be home, unless they're having the shortest honeymoon ever," he said with a short laugh.

Jeff laughed with him, relieved at the information but also at the thought of Corey and a short honeymoon. "No short trip, Max, three weeks apparently, or at least that's what he told me. Said it was one of the perks of being the boss's son. But I do appreciate this information. The last thing I want is Corey upset, particularly not now when things are going so well, and he's so happy."

Jeff arrived back at the hotel thankful that the Sunday traffic hadn't been too bad. He was hot and tired but unexpectedly he had managed to find out some information about Sarah even though this was by chance. Seeing her had shaken him more than he cared to admit. He had thought of her yesterday, hard not to when it was their son who was getting married, but to suddenly see her in the church after all these years was something he hadn't expected, and how the hell had she known, he'd asked himself. How he'd managed to get through the rest of his son's wedding day he wasn't sure but he wasn't prepared to let anything or anyone spoil the special day for the newlyweds.

Saunders – Lies and Deception

He checked with reception on his way through and left instructions that he was not to be disturbed. Closing the door to his office he slumped down into the chair behind his desk. His thoughts went back to his meeting with his friend Max and the information he'd given him and was even more grateful for the slip of paper he'd handed telling him this was the address given on her landing card. Looking at the paper he had seen the address Rocky View, Wolf Street, Banff. Now sitting in his office Jeff was contemplating what to do next. Should he simply ignore she was here, or confront her? Part of him wished he had never seen her, but part of him was furious and wanted to know why she was here now after deserting them all those years ago. He thought back to the very first time she had come into his life, walking through the doors of the hotel and asking for a job. He was still a trainee manager and wasn't normally allowed to hire and fire but this slip of a girl with her auburn hair, green eyes and pale complexion was different, and she had stirred something inside him, well certainly something in his pants.

He remembered going into the back office to check on vacancies but really it was to compose himself. He knew they had a vacancy as someone had let them down, but wondered if she wanted to be changing beds, etc. After a few minutes, he had gone back out and told her about the job. She'd been only too pleased to accept it. He'd casually looked at her papers but knowing the checks that were made before these were issued he knew she should be okay. After telling her what time to be there the next day she had left.

Even now, after all this time he could remember how he had watched her walk away. How he had liked the way her hips swayed, and like most young men his age, his eyes had been drawn to the cute little bum and the way it moved. After she had left he had filled in the paperwork for her employment and then, and only then, had he hoped he'd done the right thing. His mother usually vetted staff but she was away and in her absence the manager Tom McCall was supposed to do this. To clear his conscience he'd phoned Tom at home and told him what he had done but said that she had looked a good worker and honest, then pointing out they did need someone quickly. He recalled Tom joking with him about offering her the job and passing some remark about betting she was really ugly as well. He couldn't prevent the smile as he remembered Tom's words.

Bringing his mind back to the present he realised that he had to see her and find out not only why she was here, but why she had changed from the person she was, into someone who had walked away from her family without so much as a backward glance. Leaning forward, he switched on his computer and, pulling the slip of paper from his pocket, entered the address where she was staying in the search engine. The owners of the property Mr &

Mrs Johnson were a couple that he knew slightly as long standing residents.

He read the description of the property and noted the mention of a private entrance. So he could go and see her without having to explain himself to Peter and Freda Johnson. Without giving himself time to think he picked up his keys and went out to the parking lot, jumped into his car and drove down to Wolf Street. He drove slowly and, stopping short of the property, parked the land cruiser, bearing the Plate 'Saunders 1," on the opposite side of the road.

He was about to get out when he saw her coming along the Street, her eyes hidden behind dark glasses, and carrying what appeared to be a bag of shopping. Settling back in his seat, he watched as she turned into the gate and then walked down the side of the house before disappearing through presumably the rear entrance. She still had the same way of walking and he was shocked by his reaction to seeing her again. God, he felt a stirring in parts of his body he hadn't felt for years. He was disgusted with himself for feeling that way after what she'd done, and knew that he couldn't do this now. He needed some breathing space so quickly started the engine and drove away deciding that the meeting could wait until he felt more in control.

Chapter Three

The following day brought the same blue sky and sunshine so Sarah decided to venture out of the town site and take the rover bus, then go to the top of Sulphur Mountain. Having made some sandwiches she collected a bottle of water from the fridge before packing them in her small backpack. The walk to the main street was heavenly. There is nothing like the clear air in Banff, she thought inhaling deeply. She waited at the stop for the bus and then found a seat by the window to watch the scenery changing as it made its way to the Gondola Terminal.

She stood shocked at the scene in front of her. Gone was the simple terminal of years ago. In its place was a large complex, complete with gift shop, café and all that the tourists would need. Also gone were the prices of eighteen years ago, and Sarah considered whether going to the top was a good idea in view of the cost. But she had to. It was a pilgrimage that she had promised herself when making the decision to come back here. If she didn't she would regret it for the rest of her life. And I have enough regrets already. Carefully handing over the required Canadian dollars, the ticket was soon held tightly in her hand. She used to love coming up here with Jeff, sometimes they would hike up and then take the gondola down, but she loved it at the top.

It was wonderful going up in the gondola car. Seated on her own meant she was able to move from one seat to the other to fully enjoy the views of the surrounding mountains. The town site was getting smaller and smaller as the gondola made its way up the mountain. She could see Banff Springs Hotel and watched as it got smaller. Laughing, she held onto the rail when the car swung about as it moved over the support tower junctions. The top was getting ever closer and she could feel the excitement rising in her stomach. Finally the car swung into the top station then, as it slowed to almost a stop, the door opened and she quickly jumped out, revelling in the thrill of being back.

Once outside the station, she was surprised at the number of tourists, but also at the walkways that had been constructed so people could walk safely from the gondola station to the top outcrop. Sarah walked out to the outcrop from where she knew visitors could look back down the mountain to the town site. Finding a spot to sit, she was able to savour the moment, the sheer joy of being here, and enjoy the view. She had been up here many times with Jeff and they had made love on more than one occasion on the mountain. In fact, they both believed that this was where Corey was conceived, not in the comfort of their own king-sized bed, but up here, in the heat of passion with a rug on the ground. They had laughed about it later and Jeff had sworn it must have been the gradient they were on at the time but they didn't care, a baby was going to make their lives complete.

Lesley Field

Sarah's mind was back all those years ago in Jeff's arms on this mountain, feeling his arms around her, and could smell his aftershave. Actually, she could smell aftershave. She sat upright and opened her eyes. The first thing she saw was a pair of shoes and as she raised her head, she realised that someone was crouching down in front of her.

* * * *

Jeff had been watching Sarah for quite a while as she sat with her knees drawn up to her chin looking out across the mountains. Having chickened out of a confrontation the night before he'd decided that he needed to track her down today. Driving along Banff Avenue he had spotted her waiting at the bus stop. Checking his mirror he saw the rover bus just behind in the traffic. Pulling into a convenient parking space, he waited until she had boarded. The last thing he wanted was a showdown in the main street. It was easy just to follow the bus, and he had a pretty good idea where she was going. He pulled into a parking bay at the Gondola Station and watched as she went inside. He gave her time to buy her ticket and go to the top before he followed. Watching from a distance gave him a feeling of being in control of the situation. She clearly had no idea that he knew where she was.

Lounging against the wooden railings he'd let his eyes roam over her, taking in every detail that he could see. She looked small sitting there but he knew her long legs would still take her to the five foot seven she was when they first met. She seemed thinner than he remembered but her figure looked just as good. He recalled how she would fit perfectly under his chin and how her body moulded to his. What had been done with her hair he didn't know, but he hoped that the silky dark auburn hair would be somewhere underneath. He could almost feel its silkiness sliding through his fingers. With her hair tied up in a ponytail she appeared younger than her years but they were both older now.

He would have recognised her anywhere. Disguising her hair might have worked, but her eyes would always give her away, as they did in the church. She was still beautiful. A soft creamy complexion had replaced the golden tanned girl he knew. Again, he was shaken by his own reaction to her. Pulling himself together he thought of how he'd felt when she hadn't come back. How angry he had been. Concentrating on that anger was the only way for him to get through this meeting. Waiting until most of the tourists had moved away he slowly walked toward her and crouched down, waiting until she realised that someone was there. He saw the dreamy look on her face change as she sensed someone else's presence close to her. He couldn't see her eyes for the dark glasses as she raised her head. She was looking straight at him now and he leaned toward her, taking off his own dark glasses as he did and spoke very quietly.

"Mrs Saunders, I presume?" He could have kicked himself the minute the words were out. The last thing he wanted to do was to suggest any link between them, so using her married name was stupid but he couldn't take it back now. All he could do was wait for her reaction.

Her mouth opened to speak but no words came out. She just stared at him in apparent shock.

"Oh come on, Sarah," he softly goaded. "Surely you can say something. How about an answer to a couple of questions like…where the hell have you been for eighteen years and…why are you here now? Or perhaps your appearance at the church on Saturday has already answered that one."

Recovering somewhat she managed to get out, "I came to see Corey, but no one was supposed to see me."

"That was obvious since you have been scurrying around Banff like a fugitive," he threw back at her.

"You've seen me?"

"Of course I have. You surely didn't think you could stay here and I wouldn't find you," he replied, trying to keep the anger out of his voice.

"I don't want to cause trouble, Jeff. I just wanted to see Corey."

"Well you saw him and it's a good job he didn't see you, not that he would have known who you were. After all, he was only three years old when you abandoned him and me."

She saw the coldness in his eyes. "I did not abandon you. You knew I was coming back."

Giving a wry laugh he replied, "Yeah, yeah, when, some day, some year? I could take a month or even two but when the phone calls stopped and you didn't come back after three months it was too much. Mother even went to England to bring you back, but you wouldn't come home then, not even when you knew Corey was seriously ill."

Jeff's voice had become raised and people nearby began glancing in their direction. Seeing the attention they were drawing he said quietly, "Come on, Sarah, we can't talk here." He stood up.

His six foot two frame towered above her as he waited for her to get to her feet. "Hurry up. I have no intention of becoming a spectacle for other people." Seeing her start to get to her feet he turned and strode back along the boardwalk toward the gondola station.

The moment he approached the boarding gate to descend down the mountain, Jeff realised his mistake when he turned round and saw she had disappeared. Glancing around he had a good idea where she would be but wasn't prepared to stand outside the ladies washroom until she decided to come out. He took the gondola back down the mountain and then, collecting some bottled water from one of the machines, made his way back to his car. He could wait this out in comfort. There was only one way down the mountain. She could, of course, walk back down, but on her own in bear country, Jeff knew she wouldn't consider that option. He put on some music, adjusted his mirrors so he could see people coming out of the station and settled down to wait.

Sarah got to her feet in a daze. She hadn't expected a confrontation with him, particularly here of all places, but all she could think about was what he had said, about Corey being seriously ill. She wanted to ask him what he meant, but he was now striding back along the boardwalk toward the gondola station. Needing time to think, to pull herself together and regain some composure, she held back. When Jeff turned toward the departure gate, she did the only thing she could think of and quickly ducked the other way, taking refuge in the ladies washroom.

She stayed in the washroom for about half an hour, watching the hand on her watch move ever so slowly before she dared to come out. She cautiously looked around but couldn't see Jeff so quickly made her way to the boarding gate. As she waited for a gondola, she was trembling. Part of her wanted to stay at the top and hide away, but part of her couldn't wait to get off the mountain. What she had hoped would be a day to remember, was turning out to be anything but. More likely this would be a day she wouldn't forget. There was no pleasure in the journey down. He would be waiting at the bottom, but when she came out there was no sign of him. Hoping that he had given up and gone she made her way cautiously to the stop hoping the bus wouldn't be too long.

Jeff saw her the minute she came out of the building, watching as she looked around to see if he was there. He waited until she reached the bus stop before starting the engine. Backing the land cruiser out of its parking space he then drove off, around the top car park before coming back down and stopping in front of her.

Putting down his window he said between gritted teeth, "Get in, Sarah."

"No," she said abruptly, startled by his sudden appearance.

He sighed in exasperation. "If you want to make this difficult do so by all means but you either get in the car, or I get out and put you in. Your choice."

Sarah glanced at the people who were walking toward the bus stop. Should she make a scene? She thought about it, but then looked back at Jeff's stern face and realised that he meant what he said. She guessed some explanation was owed, although didn't know why; after all it was he who didn't want her to come back. Didn't want her in his life or their son's life anymore. But what he'd said about Corey being ill and her not coming back had shocked her, and she needed an explanation.

She moved toward the car and got inside, pulling the door shut behind her.

"Wise choice," said Jeff, pulling quickly away from the stop before she had a chance to change her mind.

As he turned back toward the town site she asked, "Where are we going?"

"You'll see in good time, but hopefully somewhere we won't be disturbed."

His voice sounded menacing but while Sarah was worried she wasn't scared. Jeff wouldn't hurt her, or at least she didn't think he would. He drove quickly around the outskirts of the town and headed toward the highway, making Sarah wonder where he was planning on going. Just before the highway he turned left and Sarah knew then where they were heading as this road ran alongside the Vermilion Lakes, a popular place for spotting wildlife. Jeff drove past the lakes and she thought they would stop in the car park area particularly as there was a sign across the road to say it was closed ahead. But he drove around the sign and stopped some distance further on in a small clearing. Her heart pounded as he switched off the engine then turned his body so he was looking straight at her.

He hadn't said anything further since answering her question, there'd just been a stony silence in the car, and Sarah was now waiting for the full force of his anger. Oh, he was angry, she knew that by the steely look on his face and the way his jaw was set. Such a lovely jaw, she thought, her mind drifting off for a split second before being pulled back to the present by his words.

"Well, I'm waiting."

"For what, Jeff?" She heard the wobble in her voice and took a deep breath to steady herself. "I told you I came to see Corey."

"Why now?" he asked. "Why, after all this time? Do you want to hurt him all over again?"

"No," she cried out. "I would never hurt him. I found out he was getting married and I just knew I had to come to see him; just once to make sure that he is happy."

"Happy!!" The word exploded out of his mouth. "What the hell do you care about his happiness, or anything about him? No contact, no nothing from you all these years. If you wanted to leave me, okay, although some hint that you were unhappy would have been good, but to desert your own child, that was unforgivable."

His voice was filled with disgust and Sarah couldn't understand what he was saying; he seemed furious that she had left, not that she was back. But he was the one who didn't want her back. None of it made any sense, and anyway, what had he meant before about Corey being ill. She needed to find out.

"What did you mean about not coming back when Corey was ill?"

"Oh come off it, Sarah. You knew that was why mother came looking for you to bring you back. I was going to come but Corey was seriously ill with pneumonia and was asking for his mommy, so how could I leave him as well. Then mother offered to find you and bring you back."

Sarah slumped back in the seat. She couldn't take this in. Her darling baby had been so ill and she hadn't known, had never known until now.

"What, got no answer to that, Sarah, so busy living it up in England that you couldn't even come back to see if Corey survived?"

Sarah turned to face him. "I didn't know, not till now." Her voice came out in a strained sound, and she felt her eyes fill with tears.

Jeff was about to reply with a cutting remark but held back when he saw her face. She was pale and looked so genuinely shocked, that for a moment he hesitated, not knowing whether to believe her or not. But no, he couldn't believe her; she had to be lying. There could be no other explanation for it.
"Sorry, Sarah, tears won't wash. Mother told me she had seen you but that she couldn't persuade you to come home, not even for Corey."
Sarah's mind was whirling and taking her back to a time that she had tried to forget. Yes, Sylvia had found her but she hadn't said anything about Corey, except that he was happy with his daddy and they had gone away on holiday. Her main topic was that Jeff was furious that she had not come home and had said that if she cared so little for him and Corey then she could stay in England. She'd protested at that, but Sylvia was having none of it. Oh come now, Sarah, a wife who won't return home, is a wife who has something to hide. Then later, Sylvia had taken great pleasure in informing her that she had found out about Sarah's background and that she had relayed all the sordid details to Jeff who had been horrified at her family's activities and her deceit. At the time, she'd found it hard to believe what she was saying, but remembering that she hadn't been able

to speak to Jeff for a couple of weeks, she had suddenly felt insecure.

She still hadn't wanted to believe that he would dismiss her without any explanation until on one of her final visits Sylvia had produced divorce papers, already signed by Jeff, that she said he'd had couriered over. She had delighted in telling Sarah that she had been instructed to have them signed by her so that Jeff and Corey could get on with the rest of their lives without any stigma from her past.

Did you really think, you silly girl, that he would stand by and allow his son's future, and our good name to be tarnished by someone from a criminal background? She had argued that she was not involved in any criminal acts, but Sylvia had just laughed.

Maybe you were, maybe you weren't, but things can be made to look as though you were. And you wouldn't want your son to see his mother's name in the papers now, would you?

She remembered how she'd argued, but I wasn't, and you couldn't prove I was, but Sylvia had only smiled.

My dear girl, one can do anything if you know the right people and have enough money. So be sensible, let go, and let my son and grandson get on with their lives. And what if I won't, she'd protested...I don't really think you would survive well in prison, Sarah. So I suggest that you sign the papers and let that be an end to it all.

Her parting shot the last time Sarah had seen her was that Jeff didn't want her to contact him or Corey anymore and if she did he would do all that he could to stop her from being allowed to stay in Canada if she tried to come back. Remembering the conversation made Sarah feel sick, even now, after all this time. And now Jeff seemed to think that he could ride roughshod over her again, but not this time, she was older, wiser and a little bit tougher than the twenty-one-year old he once knew.

She wiped her hand across her eyes clearing the tears away. "If you think for one moment, Jeffrey Saunders, that I would not have done everything I could to get back, especially had I known Corey was ill, then you didn't know me at all. And if you think that I am going to sit here and have you rant at me for something I know nothing about, then you can think again. If you don't believe what I'm saying ask your mother, and do it in my presence so I can hear what she has to say, and then I can tell her to her face that she's lying."

Having said her piece, Sarah flung open the passenger door and jumped down from the car. Staring at him through the open door, her hands on her hips and her eyes blazing, she looked at him waiting for an answer.

Jeff watched her, not saying a word, but weighing up very carefully what she'd said. She seemed so small and defiant that he would have laughed if things hadn't been so serious. None of what she said made any sense to him, this was not what he'd been told and had spent the last eighteen years believing. His mother had seen her, had spoken to her and not only would she not come home, she hadn't bothered to contact either of them over the years. If what she is saying is true then he needed to get to the bottom of it, and to do that they needed to talk rationally and calmly.

"Get back in the car, Sarah," he said abruptly.

"No, not until you agree to ask your mother."

"I can't do that."

"Why? Are you worried about what she will say?"

"No I'm not worried, but I can't ask her, Sarah, because she died two years ago."

Sarah looked at him in disbelief. "Do you expect me to believe that?"

"Actually, yes I do. She was involved in a road accident driving back from Calgary late one night, so you see I can't ask her anything."

Seeing the serious look on his face she knew what he was saying was true. Her first thought was for her son. "How did Corey take it?" she knew that, as a toddler, he'd loved his grandmother.

"How do you think? He was heartbroken. Mother idolised him and he her. Now will you get back in the car?"

"No, I need to think. I have legs, I can walk."

Looking beyond where she was standing he reached forward in the car. "I don't think so, Sarah. I would suggest that you get back in the car now. In fact that's not a suggestion more an instruction and you should start to move slowly toward the car, now."

Sarah heard the change in the tone of his voice and saw his hand reach into the open glove box and slowly take out a spray container.

"Come on, Sarah, don't be foolish, get in."

It crossed her mind that he might be trying to fool her into getting back into the car, but he looked deadly serious, and they were in bear country. "There's a bear, isn't there?" she said quietly.

"No, not a bear, but something you don't really want to encounter close up."

Hesitating for a fraction she did as instructed and moved slowly toward the open door, climbing back in before pulling the door closed behind her. Only then did she dare to look behind her and saw at the edge of the clearing a coyote, or it could be a wolf, she never could quite tell the difference. It was just standing and staring at the car, and while she was now safely inside, she would have been in a dangerous situation if it had decided to run at her. The thought made her shiver and she was glad of the protection the car gave her. They both waited, saying nothing but watching until it gradually lost interest in them and turned and walked back into the trees.

Jeff finally broke the silence between them. "Okay, Sarah, I don't know what to make of what you've said. Things just don't make any sense at all but one thing is for sure, you are not going anywhere until this has all been sorted out and I have got to the truth."

Sarah was suddenly tired and weary. Seeing him again was too much and resurrected emotions that she had tried to bury over the years. What he had told her about Corey had shaken her and now she wanted nothing more than to go back to where she was staying. She needed time to take it all in.

"Take me back to town, Jeff...please?" she added.

"Okay," he said, seeing her strained face, "But this conversation isn't finished."

She nodded and sighed. "As you wish."

Lesley Field

Chapter Four

Waking up the next morning, having had little sleep, she knew it was late All she'd been able to think of was what Jeff had told her yesterday. She had never seen him angry before, but then there had never been any cause for anger between them. The look in his eyes has haunted her, where once there had been love, there was now a hardness and coldness. She had stayed up late, too late, thinking about him and the first time they met.

When she'd arrived in Canada as a seventeen year old her head was full of the description and pictures of Banff she had scoured the local library for. This need to visit the place came from her mother. It was she who had told her tales of the prospectors and the wonderful Rocky Mountains. It was her mother who had given her what money she had saved, then told her to go and follow her dream and not to look back. So she had done that and arrived in Calgary, the closest airport to the mountains her mother had told her so much about. Then following her fellow passengers she'd boarded a shuttle bus from the airport to Banff.

She had pre-booked into the local Youth Hostel as she had to have somewhere to stay that was cheap and central to the town for the work she hoped to find. The room had been smaller than the one she was in now but had been clean. It was strange how she could remember it all. She'd taken a day to find her way around before starting to look for a job. The employment card in her pocket meant she could stay and work initially for up to twelve months which seemed a lifetime to Sarah.

She had tried a few hotels for work but they were all fully staffed. Then she went into the Mountain View Inn and found herself at the reception desk looking into the bluest pair of eyes she'd ever seen. A voice asked if they could help her and Sarah had dragged her gaze away from the eyes to the face, bronzed from the outdoor life and, oh so handsome he'd taken her breath away. The straight nose and firm lips ended in a strong jaw that she'd had an urge to stroke. She remembered feeling herself starting to blush at her thoughts and asking if they had any job vacancies. He'd left her for a short time and then came back with the news that they did have a vacancy for a housemaid, which meant cleaning rooms and changing linen, etc. After telling her the going rate, which Sarah knew was what she could expect to get, and checking her employment card he had offered the job to her. She hadn't needed to be asked twice and had accepted straightaway. Having been told to report at the hotel for seven the following morning she had reluctantly turned away from the gorgeous young man telling herself that at least she would be working in the same place as him. Walking out she had felt on top of the world and so excited at the prospect of being able to stay.

It was three days before they'd met again. She'd been into work early and the housekeeper had told her she could finish early. Walking through the reception area, as she was leaving, he was on the desk. He called out to her asking if they were working her hard enough. She had told him that she was enjoying it. Then someone had come out of the office and he turned to speak to them, so Sarah had taken this as her cue to go and walked out into the warm air of the early summer afternoon. She had instantly loved this town with a passion she could not believe but fully understood what her mother had meant. Looking at the blue sky she'd decided to walk down to the centre of town before going back to her lodgings.

She'd been lost in thought when she heard someone calling her name. Turning around she found him hurrying after her.

"Hi, fancy a coffee, or something a bit colder?" he had asked as he'd reached her.

Coffee had sounded good so they'd walked downtown and he took her into a small coffee house. As he held the door for her she had brushed against his arm—it was like an electric shock. She knew he had felt it as well by the way his body flinched. He had found them a table, then after formerly introducing himself, Jeff had ordered coffee. They'd sat talking, tentatively at first, then chatting and joking both losing track of time.

Sarah was always conscious of her mother's words before she left: Tell no one more than they need to know and nothing about your life or family here. Go and forge a new life and live it to the full. So remembering this she had reluctantly told Jeff that she had no real family in England and was on her own. Offering some further explanation she had told him that she had lost contact with her parents a long time ago, had lived in foster homes, before coming to Canada to try and start a new life. Well the bit about a new life had been true and she could almost call Annie's house her foster home, she remembered telling herself at the time.

Over the following weeks, they had become close and the other staff soon became aware they were an item, despite their furtive attempts to cover it up. Sarah had discovered early on in their relationship that he was not just the trainee assistant manager, as she first thought, but that his family actually owned the hotel. Sarah had let the jibes about landing the boss's son go over her head. She knew they weren't malicious, everyone loved Jeff and thought they were well suited as a couple.

The one person whom Sarah hadn't yet met was Jeff's mother, Sylvia Saunders, who, according to the gossips, was co-owner of the hotel with Jeff. Jeffrey Saunders senior had passed away a few years earlier and had left the hotel to his wife and son. She remembered how she hadn't been looking forward to meeting her, as she had heard stories about her from the other staff, and even Jeff had seemed a bit anxious about her reaction to their relationship.

Sylvia Saunders had arrived back at the hotel in what the other girls had described as her usual form. Checking everything in minute detail and it wasn't long before she had picked up on the romance between her son and a new staff member. Sarah had been called into her office and given the third degree about herself and her background. No mention had been made of Jeff, much to Sarah's relief, and she'd walked quickly toward the door, having been dismissed with a perfunctory, you can go. Just as she had been about to open the door Sylvia had called after her in a very casual way. Don't get too comfortable with my son; it won't last. All young men need to sow their wild oats, so for now I'll let it go. But I'm watching.

Sarah could still remember being shocked at the coldness in her voice and the underlying threat. Deana, one of the other housemaids, was waiting nearby when she got out and had asked how it went. Sarah had told her it was awful, that she thought she had actually threatened to break Jeff and her up. She'd asked Deana how she could be Jeff's mother as he was nothing like her, but was told that he was like his father who apparently everyone loved. But he had died.

The summer months had turned into the fall and then the snows heralded the onset of winter. The hotel seemed even busier in the winter months with skiers. Sarah was glad to have been kept on. Her relationship with Jeff was stronger than ever, despite several attempts by his mother to stop them being together by suddenly remembering a meeting he had to attend or someone he had to see. She'd been wary of his mother and although they had taken their relationship to the edge, she had not been able to fully commit to that final step of them being together. Jeff had said it didn't matter, he could wait, but Sarah had known it was difficult for him. Her own mother had always told her to be sure of the person before she gave away the most precious gift she had to give. Sarah was sure that Jeff was the person she wanted to be with but were his feelings for her as strong. He could have anyone, so why her? And his mother's words haunted her.

One particular night when his mother was out of town at a conference, things had almost spiralled out of control. Jeff had taken her back to the family home on the outskirts of the town. They had grabbed a takeaway on the way and after eating he had put on some soft music. The fire was burning and Jeff had pulled her down onto the rug. They started kissing and things began to get more passionate. She could still remember the feelings she'd had when Jeff had carefully undone the buttons on her shirt before gently pushing it off her shoulders. She had shivered in anticipation of his next move.

She let her thoughts take her back and could almost feel him caressing her hair with one hand whilst showering kisses on her face. His other hand gently slid down the zip on her jeans then ran over her flat stomach before moving down into the soft hair of her groin. She had gasped in pleasure. They were both breathing heavily as he began to ease her jeans down, lifting her bottom so the material could slide over her hips. Then her jeans were gone and she was lying in his arms with only a flimsy bra and briefs between them. As quickly as he had shed her clothes he had disposed of his own before laying alongside her keeping only his boxers on. They hadn't gone this far before but Sarah had felt something different between them that night.

Memories and emotions gripped her. Memories of him rolling on top of her, of feeling the hardness of him pressing into her stomach. He had groaned, you don't know what you do to me, Sarah. She had laughed nervously she could feel what she did to him. He had chided her about thinking it funny to turn him on the way she did. No, not funny but amazing that I can. Then he'd moved his lower body off hers. His hand had trailed down across the flatness of her stomach before his thumbs hooked underneath the band on her briefs and pulled them down, before quickly disposing of them. His hands had run back up along the inside of her thighs until she felt him in the moist area between her legs. God, Sarah, I need you, and want you so much. She could still remember the way her body had trembled, the way it had arched underneath his hands. The way she had wanted him.

She had really thought she was going to be able to give herself to him completely that night. But just as he'd started to move on top of her, when the hardness of him began moving toward her; she heard herself telling him no. No, Jeff, I'm sorry, I can't do it. We need to stop. He had frozen at her words. She had kept repeating sorry to him over and over again, but as always he understood and told her it didn't matter, they could wait. That night they had come very close, too close for him. He had quickly excused himself and retreated into the bathroom. Sorry, I need to see to myself.

It wasn't hard to remember how upset she had been, when he had left. They had come so close. She had really thought that tonight would have been the moment they both wanted. But his mother's voice had suddenly penetrated her thoughts, and that was it, the moment was gone. She had pulled her clothes back on while waiting for him to come back. Then they had sat by the fire holding each other, saying little, but sensing the others thoughts. So instead of having the night of her dreams he had taken her back to the apartment she shared with two other girls, and gently kissed her goodnight.

Perhaps that was when he'd made the decision that they were meant to be together, but the relationship between them had changed that night, as she had found herself being propelled toward a new and wonderful life. How Jeff had stood up to his mother over their marriage she never knew, and hadn't dared to ask, but by the time her employment card needed renewing they were engaged and planning a wedding. Then before another twelve months had gone by they had Corey, which made life perfect for them.

Remembering all of that, and how it had felt to be with him, had kept her out of her bed. Then when she finally did try to sleep all she could think about was Corey being ill. So now, not only was she late and tired the very reason for her present state was due to collect her in, oh my god, she thought, thirty minutes.

Throwing back the covers she grabbed her clothes before heading for the shower. Switching on the kettle for a badly needed cup of coffee she let it boil while she quickly showered. Coming out of the small bathroom with the towel wrapped around herself she stood at the unit drinking the coffee while attempting to dry herself. Just when it seemed she was going to be okay for time there was a knocking on her unit door. Damn, she thought, he's early, but there was no option but to open the door.

Neither spoke then Sarah stated the obvious.

"You're early."

"Yes, I know." No other explanation, just that.

"Well, you had better come in. Unless of course you're worried about what your wife might think."

Hesitating slightly before he replied he said, "No, I'm not worried, my wife knows exactly where I am."

That reference to his wife cut through Sarah like a knife but she didn't allow it to show. Stepping back to let him in, she said as calmly as she could, "I won't be long," before escaping back into the bathroom and pushing the door to with her foot.

Left alone, he breathed deeply. He'd been about to knock again when the door opened and he found himself confronted by a slender figure wrapped in a pink towel. Christ, he thought, just what I need after spending most of the previous night trying to get the image of her out of my mind. She'd left him standing near the door but as he waited he wandered into the room. Small apartment with a living/seating area, a kitchenette and a separate bedroom and bathroom off.

He looked around taking in the homely pictures and the mirror on the wall. He drew his breath in sharply wishing he hadn't seen the mirror as it gave him a view into the bathroom where the door was slightly ajar. He could see the full view of her back as she towelled herself dry and he watched, willing her to turn around. When she did start to turn he saw the small breasts that he had once lovingly caressed coming into his view. He couldn't do this. "I'll wait outside in the car," he called out. "Don't be long."

Once outside, Jeff climbed in the driving seat and started the engine. He turned the air conditioning up to full blast. He was disgusted with himself. He was supposed to be a married man. How could she affect him this way, after all this time, and after what she'd done?

In ignorance of the reason, Sarah was relieved that Jeff had decided to wait outside. His presence in the room seemed to suffocate her. She quickly finished dressing, pulling on a pair of old blue jeans with a plain t-shirt and a denim shirt on top. Thrusting her feet into a pair of trainers she grabbed her fleece from the chair and dashed outside. She didn't want to keep him waiting; this meeting was going to be bad enough without her antagonising him before it started.

The car was parked outside with its engine running so she climbed into the passenger seat. Gosh it was cold, she thought, wishing she'd put the fleece on instead of carrying it. He must have noticed her shiver as he leaned forward and turned the air down. They drove in silence for some time. Sarah didn't dare ask where they were going. The stern look on his face prevented her from making any conversation.

She began to recognise some of the scenery and before long realised they were going toward Lake Minnewanka, a name they had laughed about many times in the past, although she much preferred its original name of 'The Lake of the Water Spirit,' nevertheless she couldn't help the small smile that crept across her face.

* * * *

Jeff caught sight of her smile and realised she knew where they were headed. His own lips began to twitch before he reminded himself why they were there and quickly suppressed the threatened smile.

He'd come up with a few places they could go to sort this out, but this was the one that offered the least distractions, apart from the name, of course. He turned left into the car park and switched off the engine.

"Come on," he said, climbing out and, as Sarah quickly followed him, he grabbed a rucksack from the trunk and set off toward the lake.

He headed out along the boardwalk toward where a small motor launch was moored. Climbing on board, without a backwards glance, he went down below to deposit the rucksack. Coming back on deck he found Sarah standing on the dock.

"You can come aboard," he said. "I promise I won't bite." Holding out his hand to steady her as she stepped cautiously onto the deck, he then jumped off and untied the rope mooring the boat to the dock. Coming back on board he went to the wheel and started the engine.

Before long they were leaving the dock behind and heading out toward the centre before turning to head down the lake. They travelled along the lake for some time, neither of them saying anything. Jeff was concentrating on driving the boat, but cast a quick glance at Sarah. From the look on her face it was clear she had no wish to start the conversation she knew was to come. Some time later, they turned in toward a tiny inlet and Jeff stopped the engine, before throwing out a small anchor.

"Well," he said, "this looks a good enough place. No one to interrupt and no way either of us can walk away. If you want to be useful you could go below and make a coffee. There's hot water in the flask, coffee and mugs are in the top cupboard, and there's fresh milk in the fridge."

Having been given her orders, and thankful to delay the conversation, Sarah went down the few steps into the cabin below. Everything was where he said it would be. With the coffee made she was about to take it back on deck when Jeff came down below. The small space seemed even smaller as he lowered himself into one of the seats, taking a mug of coffee from her as he did.

"Okay, Sarah, I think it's time for straight talking, so let's start at the beginning with why you had to go back to England, because your friend was very ill, leaving your husband and young son. Why exactly was this friend so important to you?"

Sarah knew it was time to tell Jeff the truth but didn't know how he was going to react. Taking a deep breath, she started to talk.

"I didn't go back to England because my friend was ill." But before she could say any more Jeff spoke out.

"Ah, I knew it. Mother told me that you had been unable to cope with the thought of another child. Remember we had discussed a brother or sister for Corey, but you told mother that you felt trapped with a young child in a strange country. That the prospect of another was too much, and that's why you had to leave."

Sarah gasped. "No, that's not the reason I left. Anyway, I don't know why you are reacting like this. After all, it was you who didn't want me back, you who wanted a divorce because of what your mother found out about my past. So don't expect me to tell you what you already know."

Now it was Jeff's turn to be shocked. What the hell was she talking about? Telling himself to remain calm he looked at Sarah and said quietly, "Indulge me."

"Okay, Jeff, if that's the way you want to play it, but if you want to know the whole story let me tell it without interruption. Then you can do and say what you want."

"Okay," he said, still reeling from mention of her past and divorce.

Taking a deep breath she started talking again.

"I left because I'd phoned a friend, my best friend Annie and she gave me a message, not to say that she was sick, but to say my mother was sick."

"Mother! You told me you had no contact with your family."

"I know, and I hated lying about that but I did it because it's what my mother wanted. Jeff, it's very hard and painful for me to tell this story, and I don't think I can do it if you keep interrupting."

Jeff held his hands up. "Okay, go on."

Realising that it would be better to start right at the beginning she began again.

"My mother was the only child of a local store manager and his wife. They were what was known in England as middle class. She was brought up in a fairly strict household, but like most teenagers she began to rebel as she got older. She got in with a rough crowd and through them met this older man, George. He was divorced with two sons who lived with their mother. George lived on the edge of the criminal fraternity but my mother was infatuated with him, and despite everything her parents threatened her with, she wouldn't stop seeing him. Eventually the inevitable happened and she fell pregnant, with me. Her parents were horrified, having an illegitimate child in those days was unthinkable, especially in her parents' circle of friends. They wanted to send her away and for the child to be adopted, but my mother wouldn't hear of it, so her parents told her to leave as they couldn't bear the shame." She took a sip of coffee before continuing.

"To give him his due, George stood by her and offered to marry her, so she had me and I was raised in a small house on a council estate. I didn't have too hard a time as I was growing up, my mother saw to that, but when I was about thirteen George's sons from his previous marriage began to come around. They would bring whisky for their dad and get him involved in various scams. My mother did all that she could to protect me from what was going on, but it wasn't unusual for the police to come knocking on the door." Her voice dropped as she recalled this bad time in her life.

"By the time I was fifteen, George's sons began to take notice of me. My mother was scared of them and would send me to my room if she knew they were coming. I wanted to further my education but my dad said no, I had to get out and earn some money. So I had to leave school and find a job. I was lucky, I'd been taught typing at school so was able to get a job as a clerk at the local hospital, and that was where I met Annie. We clicked straight away and I was happy to have a friend since I had none where we lived. Annie would help me with my typing and show me how to do various tasks at work. She's about ten years older than me and was like a big sister. She hadn't been married long when I first met her and her husband Bob worked on the oil rigs so he was away a lot of the time.

"I used to stay at their house when I could, and my mum encouraged me to do this. She wanted me to get away from home and used to tell me of the things she had done as a child. Although her parents were strict she hadn't wanted for anything. I think she felt guilty at being unable to give me that kind of childhood. I think she regretted falling out with her parents, but wasn't brave enough to go back," she added wistfully. "Sorry, I got distracted. Anyway, she would often tell me about the special holiday they took her on to Canada, when they'd gone to visit some distant relative, and of the time they spent in Banff. I loved hearing her describe the mountains to me. If we were in town we would go into the library and look at the pictures in the travel books of the Rocky Mountains. Mum said that she would love me to go there, to see it all for myself one day, and that was when she started to work on her plan, as we eventually called it." She stopped speaking and took another mouthful of coffee before continuing.

"She wanted me away from home and as far away from my half-brothers as possible. They hung around in a gang and were always in trouble with the police. Then they started bringing other gang members to the house to see dad. They would ply him with drink and then start making suggestive comments to me about how much I could make on the streets with me being pretty. Mum had been scared before but I was older now, and she was really frightened for me. Told me I needed to get away as soon as I could. She'd saved some money and wanted me to change my name so I had no connection with them. Once that was done, I was to get a passport in my new name and to go abroad. She wanted me to find a new life. I knew where she meant, she'd almost brainwashed me about Canada, but everything she told me was true," she said, glancing across at him.

"Mum had been planning this for a long time and was determined that she wanted me to go, no matter how much it would hurt her not to see me again. I resisted at first, I didn't want to leave her, but she became so upset. I could see that this was what she really wanted for me. I tried to persuade her to come with me, but she wouldn't. Said she had made a bad decision when she was young which shouldn't reflect on me. She was scared I was going to be forced into something I didn't want."

"When I finally agreed, I couldn't believe how easy it was to change my name, but I wanted to keep some connection with my mum, so I chose the name O'Connor, as it was her maiden name. We put my address as Annie's, saying I was her lodger, which in a way was true as I stayed there so often. So all the paperwork including my passport were sent to her home and, once I had those, I was able to apply for an employment card so that I could work in Canada. Annie knew all about the problems at home and helped me as much as she could." She paused and wiped a hand across her eyes. Remembering her mum was painful, even after all these years.

"My leaving home was supposed to take place just after mum's birthday. Annie and I had arranged to take her out for lunch on the pretence it was a birthday treat, in case my dad asked, but really it was a farewell lunch. But it never happened because one night my half-brothers came around unexpectedly with some others from their gang. I was in the back yard alone when one of their so-called friends grabbed me and pressed himself against me, then he tried to get inside my blouse. I was terrified and screamed out. Fortunately, mum came running out and pulled him off me, but that was it as far as mum was concerned. She told me I had to get away, and soon." She shut her eyes and took a deep breath. Remembering that night still made her feel sick.

"I went to work the following morning as usual and told my dad that I was staying at Annie's that night as she was on her own. That gave me the excuse of taking a small case with me. The next day, I met my mum at lunchtime. That was when she gave me what money she had managed to save, but also some she had taken from my dad. She was planning to tell him that I had to work late that day and would stay with Annie again that night. This would prevent him from asking awkward questions. Two days later I was able to get a flight to Calgary and effectively started a new life. That lunchtime was the last time I saw my mum, until I went back eighteen years ago."

She caught the sob and held it back, then glanced at Jeff. His face was unreadable and he was looking intensively at her, so she continued.

"I was so happy with you, and then when Corey came along life was wonderful. I loved you both so much. Everything was perfect. But when Annie told me my mum was dying, I had to go back and see her. I wanted to tell her about my new life, and also that she had a grandson. I know you knew nothing about Annie, she never called the apartment because I was too scared to give her the number, in case anyone else got hold of it. I would phone her from a phone booth every couple of months and it was then that she told me about my mum. Annie is secretary to one of the Consultants at the hospital and she had seen my mum in the Oncology Department. Mum had told her not to tell me, but Annie knew it was something she couldn't keep to herself. So I went back using my old British passport. I left my Canadian one at home, and I only took cash with me, I couldn't risk taking my bankcards. Only Annie knew about my life here and I didn't want anyone else to find out except my mum."

She paused for breath before speaking again. But risked glancing up. He was still staring at her. His straight face and jaw rigid were off-putting. But she had come this far and there was no turning back.

"When I got back to England I stayed with Annie and Bob, they were wonderful, running me around. By this time my mum was in the hospital and had only been given four to six weeks. Whether it was because I went back to see her I don't know, but against all the odds she lived for just over three months. The last two months she spent in a hospice, and during the whole time I was there my dad never visited her once, so I had no contact with him. After mum passed away the hospice had to inform him, technically he was her next of kin, so he could make the funeral arrangements.

"I saw him for the first time at the funeral. He was there with my half-brothers but I sat with Annie and Bob and kept away from them. After the cremation he came up to me, wanted me to look after him and give him money. I hope you are coming home to look after me, girlie. You owe me for taking my money. I told him no, I wasn't, and I hadn't taken any money from him. No, you didn't, but your mum did and since she never paid it back, you owe me now. I had some money but not on me. Although I didn't owe him anything, I was worried he would turn up at Annie's and cause trouble, so I agreed to meet him the next day in the centre of town, said I would give him what I had. That was my mistake." She took another sip of coffee. "Have you nothing to say?"

"You told me not to speak until you'd finished. So unless this tale is at an end, continue."

His reference to it being a tale almost made her stop. She wanted to scream at him that it wasn't a tale, but his face told her that would be a bad move. So she continued.

"When he turned up he was with his sons but since we were in a public place I felt reasonably safe. I gave him what money I had but while I had my bag open one of his sons grabbed it. He took my passport then found my plane ticket and my wedding ring. I'd taken it off, as I didn't want them to know I was married. He flung the bag back at me, said he would keep them to sell. I was distraught, Jeff, but I didn't dare say it was my wedding ring. They went off laughing and I just stood there, unable to believe what a fool I'd been. I should have known better than to meet him at all."

"After meeting them I'd been going to go to the travel agents to arrange a flight home but I couldn't do that, as I no longer had my ticket or passport. I had to go back to Annie's so we could try and work out what to do. I could get another passport but that would take time, and I could buy another ticket except I had no money to pay for this, although Annie offered the money, but I couldn't do anything about my wedding ring. I didn't want to lie to you, tell you I had lost them and ask you to send me some money and my Canadian passport, but I realised that was what I was going to have to do."

"So why didn't you?"

"Annie suggested that I take a couple of days to pull myself together before phoning you. I was also worried about phoning, as I hadn't been able to speak to you for two or three weeks because I was told you'd gone away. Waiting had seemed a good idea at the time, but then your mother turned up before I had a chance to do anything. I'll give her credit," she said with a wry laugh, "she'd been putting in some work and had tracked me down to Annie's and took the greatest delight in telling me that she also knew all about my family's background. You know she actually said she'd hired a private investigator to follow me as soon as I had left Canada and to delve into my past. So you see, Jeff, I came from a world far apart from yours, and your mother found that out. I think she was pleased to have found out something to hold over me."

She ventured the last comment and waited for his reaction. But there was none. Looking briefly at him he hadn't moved but his mouth was set in a tight line, and his blue eyes looked like steel. "Go on," his voice was taught.

"When she first came to see me the only thing she said about you and Corey was that Corey was happy, but you were furious that I had stayed away so long and had said to her that if I cared so little about you both perhaps I should stay in England. I told her that wasn't true and I wanted to speak to you, but she told me you had taken Corey away and didn't have a contact number. I didn't believe her, but what could I do thousands of miles away. She came to see me a few more times telling me that you were still away but said she had told you all about my dubious past, and, as she nicely put it, you know I can remember her words. I still hear her voice even after all these years…Now Jeffrey knows all about your background he's horrified and appalled that he's been lied to. He doesn't want your criminal background affecting the family name or Corey's future in any way. He has no wish to remain married to someone with that background. He wants a divorce. I wouldn't believe her at first. I knew she never thought I was good enough for you, but I believed in us as a family. When she turned up a few days later and produced divorce papers already signed by you, my world came crashing down. She told me you'd had them couriered over as you wanted the matter sorted out before she returned home." She stifled a sob before continuing.

"Have you any idea what it did to me to see those papers signed by you? But I told her I wasn't signing anything, and I had rights as far as Corey was concerned. I was his mother." She could feel the tears building as she remembered what happened next in that meeting. "Then she told me I had no right to Corey, that if I went back you would seek sole custody on the grounds that I was an unfit mother and had deserted you both. Told me she had the money and influence to make certain that I lost any claim to him. She even threatened to bring up my family's unsavoury past, said that it would be quite easy to get someone to swear a statement to say I had been involved in their activities. She told me everyone had a price and, the way it was said, I knew she meant every word of what she threatened. The thought of you thinking of me as a criminal was just too much to take. I knew that she'd won. That I had lost everything I loved."

She scrubbed her hand across her eyes before continuing. "She told me you wanted me to just disappear, but I wasn't going to lose my son forever. I told her I wouldn't sign anything until I had her word that I could keep in contact with Corey, especially on his birthday and at Christmas."

Sarah remembered the look on Sylvia's face when she has stood up to her on this point. I'm not signing anything until you promise me this one thing. It's not a great deal to ask considering what you are asking me to give up. She'd been surprised when Sylvia had finally agreed, but wasn't going to question her motives.

"She was very reluctant to agree but said it should be through a box number, pointing out you would no doubt move over the years. It broke my heart to sign those documents. I had just lost my mum and now I had lost the two most important people in my life. I couldn't believe that I would never see either of you again, that you didn't want me to come home, but I swear to you, Jeff, she didn't say anything at all about Corey being ill. The first I knew of this was when you told me yesterday. After I'd signed the papers she left and I never saw her again. I had to try and make some kind of life for myself and I would never have done that without Annie and Bob's help. The only consolation I had was that my mother had died knowing that she had a grandson and believing that I was happy. If she had known the sacrifice I'd had to pay for seeing her, she would have been distraught."

She could have gone on to tell him how she had been ill and had cried herself to sleep night after night. That she would wake in the night sobbing and calling out his name only for Annie to be the one to hold and comfort her, but saw no point if he wasn't going to believe her. Sarah stopped speaking, she was emotionally drained. It was a big deal for her to tell anyone about her previous life. She wiped a hand across her eyes to clear away the tears.

Jeff didn't say a word when she fell silent, just continued staring at her, his eyes boring into her, then got up and went back on deck. Sarah waited; not sure what he would do. Would he believe her? She just didn't know. After what seemed an eternity she ventured up the steps and peered out onto the deck. He was sitting with his back to her with his head in his hands. She didn't dare go further, so went back below to wait.

Chapter Five

Jeff was stunned by what he had just heard. That Sarah had lied to him about her mother and her past he could understand, in a way. But what she'd said about his own mother's involvement was another matter. This was not what his mother had told him. Yes, she informed him she'd found Sarah, had spoken to her, but said that she was living with friends and quite happy. Nothing had ever been said to him about her family, about her mother dying or about divorce papers. He had never signed or sent any such papers to his mother in England. His mother had been quite definite in saying that Sarah had not wanted to come back, had felt out of place in Banff, and certainly had not wanted to be trapped there with another child. That had been the hardest thing to hear. But what about the threats Sarah said she'd made, about her losing custody of Corey? He would never have stopped her from seeing their son. He would never have stopped her from returning home. None of it made any sense at all.

He could still remember the disbelief and anger he'd felt when his mother had related tales of Sarah telling her how unhappy she had been in Banff. How she hadn't wanted to hurt him, that he and Corey would be better off without her, which was why she had stopped contacting them. Gradually he'd had to accept she wasn't going to come back so he'd buried his emotions, had placed all his concentration into getting Corey well again.

Pulling his thoughts back to the present he lifted his head and looked back along the lake. Such a beautiful place with the sun shining and the mountain tops, still with a light covering of snow, but he felt desolate as if his soul had been ripped out. If what Sarah was saying was true then his mother had lied to him all those years ago. Had deprived him of his wife and his son of his mom. No, he argued with himself. That couldn't be right, she wouldn't have done that to him, and especially not to Corey. He jumped up, causing the boat to rock.

Sarah looked up as he came down the steps, pale beneath his tan.

"Okay," he said, "you've had your say, now it's my turn."

Sarah nodded.

Jeff sat opposite to her. "Why did you stop phoning home when you were in England? Didn't you think I was waiting every day to hear from you?"

"Yes, I know you were, and I did phone at first as regularly as I could with the time difference and being at the hospital. You know I did, but then when I phoned I kept getting your mother, and she would tell me you were in a meeting or out, but I always left a message for you both, and then she told me you had taken Corey away on holiday for a few weeks and I couldn't contact you as she claimed she had no number. I thought it was strange that you had gone away, and even stranger she had no number, but she was very plausible. Told me it was to distract Corey so he wouldn't miss me so much. I couldn't argue with her from that distance. With no way of contacting you I had to accept what she said."

Jeff listened intently. "Well, we never got any messages and we certainly didn't go away. Oh God, Sarah, surely you had more faith in me than to think I would just walk away from you and take our son with me? Why didn't you phone the hotel, and at least leave a message for me, after mother first spoke to you?"

"Don't you think I thought of that?" She raised her voice matching her tone to his. "Together we were able to stand up to your mother on the occasions we needed to, but on my own, thousands of miles away from you, bombarded with what she was saying and with everything else that had happened, I didn't know what to do. Of course I wanted to phone and speak to you but, at the same time, I was terrified that you would refuse the call, or worse, tell me yourself what your mother was saying and I couldn't have borne to hear those words from you. So I had to accept what she said."

Looking at her through narrowed eyes he asked, "So after my mother had seen you why didn't you ever try to contact us, or at least Corey?"

"I did, but like I said your mother wouldn't allow me any direct contact and said any contact had to be through a Box Number."

"No!!" he shouted so loud she jumped. "We never had anything from you. Nothing...at...all." He emphasized every word.

Raising her own voice she shouted back. "That's not true. I sent letters and cards and presents for Corey, every birthday and Christmas. You must have got them."

"I said nothing, and I mean nothing," Jeff shouted again and jumped up from the seat. "If you are lying, Sarah."

"I'm not...I swear I'm not," she said, lowering her voice.

"Okay, so what about the money?" he asked quietly.

"What money?" she said frowning.

"The money I've been sending you every month since you left? Don't tell me you know nothing about that either."

"No, I don't. I have never had anything from you, and, anyway, why would you send me money?"

"Why, because you were my wife and the mother of my son, and that actually meant something to me." And because I loved you. "So don't tell me you know nothing about it. My mother set the account up and arranged for the money to be sent overseas every month. I know she did that because I've seen the accounts and signed the cheques."

Sarah was angry before but she was furious now. She had bared her soul to him and it seemed he still didn't believe her.

Her eyes blazing she glared at him. "How dare you accuse me of lying? You stand there in your designer clothes thinking that only you know the truth. Look at me, Jeff, these jeans, this t-shirt, shirt and fleece, do you want to know where I got these…charity shops, the whole lot probably cost me less than twenty pounds. I don't have money for fancy clothes, or for any luxuries. If you want the truth, I live in a rented one bedroom flat, not much bigger than the Johnson's unit. I run a small car and work five days a week. By the time I've paid the bills I don't have cash to spare for anything. I'm only here because a small legacy from my grandparents bought my flight and I scrimped and saved the spending money."

"Your grandparents? Oh, this gets better. You never mentioned them," he said sarcastically.

"No I hadn't got to that part in my story," she said, glaring at him. "They only came into my life about eighteen months ago. It was they who initially persuaded me to find out about Corey."

Realising that she was going to have to continue and tell him the rest of her story she calmly started to speak.

"My grandparents had no contact with my mother after they effectively kicked her out and they knew nothing about me. They didn't want me ending up the same way, with a lost child I knew nothing of. My grandmother had been poorly for a number of years but then she became seriously ill. She persuaded my grandfather to find out what happened to my mum and the baby. Seemingly they regretted turning my mum out all those years ago, but had never had the courage to try and find her until my grandmother was ill and they realised that they could die and never know what had happened. They hired an investigator to make enquiries and, to cut a long story short, they found me.

"We managed to build up some kind of relationship, then when I eventually told them about you and Corey they insisted that I found out about you both. They didn't want me to make the same mistake they did. Sadly, about a year ago, my grandmother died and my grandfather only lasted a few more months, so I was on my own again. Most of their savings had gone on rent for the warden controlled flat they lived in, and on carers over the years, but there was a small amount left that I inherited. I used the Internet to search the local newspapers for any scrap of information. When I found an article that mentioned Corey's forthcoming wedding Annie insisted that I come here."

Jeff continued to stare at her. He couldn't take in what she was telling him. He wanted to dismiss all that she'd said, but he couldn't. There was something about the way she was, which told him she was speaking the truth. Truth, what the hell was that in this mess. If what she said was true then he had been living in a world of deception for the past eighteen years. His life, and his son's, had been a lie. He couldn't believe that his mother had blatantly lied, but neither could he ignore the element of doubt that was beginning to bother him. All he needed to do now was to get back to shore and try to piece this jigsaw together. Without another word he went back on deck, pulled up the anchor and started the engine. They drove back to the landing dock in silence.

Sarah ventured up onto the deck. She felt sick but the beauty of the landscape couldn't escape her. Even now, in the cool of late afternoon with the sun starting to sink in the sky, the scene was one of majesty. She felt a need to store this picture in her mind, to remember this short journey back to shore, where this small deck space was shared with the only man she had ever loved. She had tried to hate him over the years, but never could. Now, being with him again, she knew why.

Arriving back at the dock, Jeff secured the boat and then disappeared below. He appeared a few minutes later with the small rucksack, locked the cabin doors, then jumped onto the dock where Sarah was waiting. Without a backward glance, he strode along the boardwalk with Sarah almost running to keep up with him. Once in the car he started the engine and they drove back to town, in a silence that Sarah found unbearable.

She ventured to speak. "Haven't you anything to say?"

"No...not now," he said in a clipped tone. He dropped her off outside the Johnson's. "I'll see you tomorrow," he said before driving off.

No time, no nothing, thought Sarah, as she was left staring after the car in disbelief. Letting herself into the unit she sat on the small sofa, letting the tears she had been holding at bay run down her cheeks. She couldn't believe what had just happened. She had at least expected Jeff to say something, even if it was only that he didn't believe a word she said. But he'd given her nothing, no indication whether he believed her or not. The thought of everything that had been said made her feel physically sick and the intention of going out for a solitary dinner, suddenly held no appeal. Brushing away the tears she made herself a coffee, then found enough bread to make herself a sandwich. Although she put on the small television it couldn't hold her attention. Her mind kept going over and over what they had each disclosed. None of it was what the other had seemingly been led to believe.

Telling him about her past had been painful, but to bear her soul and to effectively have it ignored was unbearable. His mother's part in what had happened had been chilling to hear. How could someone hate her so much that she would destroy her life and that of her own son and grandson? She had taken from her the two things that she had cared for the most. It was wicked.

She lay that night in the double bed and, for the first time in many years, she cried herself to sleep.

While Sarah was in a state of shock at his reaction, Jeff was beyond shocked. All he could think of doing was to get back to his office as quickly as possible. What Sarah told him had rocked his world beyond imagination. He went to the family's main hotel, 'Saunders on Banff' where his Company's head office was. As he walked through reception he called out to Dean who was manning the desk and asked him to get Douglas Conway on the phone on his home number. By the time he had got behind his desk the phone was ringing and he quickly picked this up.

"Hi, Doug. Look, sorry to trouble you at home but I need to see you urgently tomorrow, about one of the company accounts. No I'm fine and the Company is fine, but I have a situation partly personal that I can't discuss on the phone. Yes, eleven is good for me, so I'll see you then."

As he put down the phone Jeff tried to recall all that Sarah had said, but he just couldn't make sense of it. All these years he'd believed she had just walked away from him and Corey. That had taken a long time for him to accept. Now she was telling him that she hadn't. Not only that, but that his own mother had contrived to keep them apart. Everything he'd believed in was disintegrating around him and he had no idea as to where it would end. He needed to go home so he could clear his head. Closing up his desk he headed back through reception. "I'm going home now, Dean, if there are any problems you can get me there. Oh, and I won't be in until quite late tomorrow. I have a meeting in Calgary, so can you leave a note for Jenny and tell her to contact me on my cell phone if she needs to, but I would really appreciate it if she doesn't."

Nodding his understanding Dean wished him a good evening.

"You too," replied Jeff. Walking outside he climbed back into his car and drove away.

One thing Jeff and Sarah shared that night—a bad night's sleep.

Chapter Six

Sarah had been staring at the ceiling for over an hour. The urge to pull the covers over her head and ignore the day was strong, but not one she could follow. Looking at the clock it was almost seven-fifteen and if she wasn't going to be caught out again by Jeff, she needed to be up. Throwing back the covers, she headed for the shower. A quick glance in the mirror told her the wash-in colour was fading fast. Picking up the shampoo she stepped under the shower. Thirty minutes, and three hair washes later she emerged looking more like her normal self. By nine she was beginning to get nervous, so made another cup of coffee. By ten-thirty she was pacing the unit. As the clock told her it was eleven-thirty her nerves were gone and she was angry. If you think I'm wasting my last day waiting for you, Jeffrey Saunders, think again.

Grabbing her fleece and jacket she picked up her purse and headed out. She knew exactly where she was going, and to hang with the cost. Once at the top she headed out to the end and leaned against the rail and looked down on the town site. She could see the Rocky Mountaineer train moving slowly along the track, way down below. She imagined all the tourists on board, some seeing the mountains for the first time. The impressive Banff Springs Hotel stood majestically below. They had once walked through the public rooms pretending they were guests there, but that was a long time ago, and no doubt it had changed. Being here made her realise that she loved this country more than ever. The thought of going back to England broke her heart, especially now she had seen Corey. She loved her son, always had, now having seen him as a young man it was going to be almost impossible to walk away.

She stayed on the mountain lost in thought, absorbing the atmosphere and the scent of the pines, until late afternoon. Taking a last walk along Banff Avenue she called into the supermarket to buy some sandwiches to take to the airport the following day. Once back in her room she finished packing, then took another shower. Seeing no point in getting dressed she slipped on the cotton nightdress she'd left out, then pulled on her fleece and sat on the sofa watching television. There had been no message, no note from Jeff, and all she could make of that was that he didn't believe her. She was tired, emotionally drained, and at that point didn't care. But she knew she would when she got home, but she would have to deal with it then.

* * * *

Jeff made it to Calgary in good time for his meeting. Doug's firm had dealt with the company's accounts for over twenty-five years so if anyone knew what was going on he would. Doug greeted Jeff, and both men sat down.

"Well," said Doug, "I am certainly intrigued by your phone call last night."

"I wish I was just intrigued," replied Jeff, "but what I have to tell you must remain in this room, and between us alone. I know about client confidentiality and I'm not referring to the general company information, but I need to tell you some personal things that I don't want to go beyond this room."

"Okay, Jeff, now you have really got me worried, so you had better tell me what's going on."

"I'd better start at the beginning," said Jeff. "Sarah, Corey's mom, is back."

Doug sat upright in his chair with a start. "You're kidding me, after all these years, and after walking out on you both? When did she come back?"

"Last week. I first saw her at Corey and Laura's wedding. Just a fleeting sight of her but I managed to track her down."

"Does Corey know?"

"No, and I want to keep it that way for now. Anyway, we had a long talk yesterday, Doug, obviously I wanted to know why she didn't come back, and to be honest what she told me has left me shell shocked. She also informed me of some other things that simply cannot be true, but she was so convincing, I need to get to the bottom of it."

Seeing his friend's anxious face, Jeff continued. "You know the account you set up for the payments to Sarah?"

"Yes, but I didn't set it all up. The account in England was set up by your mother. She gave me the details of the account the payments were to go into, which was Mrs S. Saunders, and then she and I sorted the account out at this end together. As you know the payments have been made regularly since then, in fact a payment will have gone out last week."

"Well, Doug, that's the problem. Sarah says she has never had any money at all from me. In fact, from what she's told me, she's been living in near poverty and has never had any money to come back here."

"No, that can't be true," said Doug, becoming increasingly alarmed at where the conversation was headed. "That account is separate to the company accounts and I have overseen it personally, and can vouch for every payment that has gone out."

"I'm not doubting you, Doug, don't think that for a minute. I've seen the account myself and know the payments have been made. I've never had any reason to check the account, or wanted to have anything to do with it, until now. What I need to do is to find out what happened to that money once it left my account, and where it actually ended up. I know it may take some time but it is vitally important that I find this out. If Sarah is telling the truth about the money then I will have little reason to doubt the other things she has told me and, if that's the case, this is going to blow, not only mine, but Corey's world apart. I need to find out the truth before Laura and Corey come back from their honeymoon, Doug. I need you to help me find out the truth, because I'm beginning to suspect that we have all been manipulated by a very clever and cunning woman."

"Who, Sarah?"

"No, my mother. I need someone who can dig deep and get to the truth."

"Okay, Jeff. Look, I'll get someone on to it straight away. It's a bit beyond our remit but I think I know just the person. His firm does work for the government, tracking down hidden accounts belonging to people trying to avoid taxes. So if anyone can find out what has happened he can."

"I really appreciate it, Doug, and I don't care how much it costs. I need to know before the kids come home."

Having left Doug's office, Jeff made his way back to collect his car. He was tired and the thought of the ninety-minute drive back home did little to lift his mood. Making his way through the early afternoon traffic he was soon out on the highway heading back toward Banff. Both he and Corey loved this journey through the farming area and then the foothills before the Rockies wrapped themselves around you, tall and majestic with their tops crowned with snow often even in the summer. Today was no exception, but Jeff couldn't appreciate their beauty, there were too many things racing through his mind. He felt as though his brain was on a roller coaster.

As he drove through the mountains, he saw the Three Sisters in the distance reminding him he was due to visit their Canmore hotel the following day. Making a quick decision and checking the road was clear behind, he moved into the right lane, then further ahead turned off right into Canmore. He would call at 'Saunders in Canmore' now to save coming back out tomorrow. Parking, he noticed the number of cars in the area. Looked as though they were fairly busy. He spoke briefly to Mary on reception before going through to the office.

His manager, Steve, looked up as he walked in. "Sorry to barge in," he said, seeing the surprised look on Steve's face. "There's no problem just a change of plan, Steve. I needed to go to Calgary unexpectedly today so wondered if we could do the monthly meeting now, since I'm out this way, instead of tomorrow."

Realising that he should have phoned ahead to warn him of the change Jeff quickly apologised to Steve for not doing so.

"It's okay, Jeff, nearly everything is ready and I was just about to print off the advance bookings for next few months."

"We seem to be quite busy judging from the parking lot," said Jeff, sitting down in one of the chairs.

"Yes, the idea of afternoon tea in the conservatory has gone down well with the tourists, and has drawn in quite a few people from other hotels. I suspect that they may hijack the idea next summer."

"I have no doubt," said Jeff. "As long as it continues to pay for itself, it can run."

He spent the next hour and a half going over paperwork with Steve, managing to grab a coffee and sandwich before finally climbing back into his car for the last part of the journey home. Glancing at his watch he calculated that he should be back in Banff by about five-thirty. It had been a long day but he also needed to call into 'Saunders on Banff' to check for any problems before he could consider going home, and he couldn't do that until he had seen Sarah. He said he would see her today but hadn't expected to be quite this late, but it couldn't be helped.

Having finally finished at Saunders, he drove the short distance to Sarah's unit but realised it was late. She may be out having dinner. He walked along the pathway and through the outer door. The door to the unit was closed and he knocked sharply.

"Who is it?

"It's me, Sarah, open the door."

He heard the key turn and the door partly opened. She stood in the doorway. The first thing he noticed was that her hair was back to its proper colour. Well, actually if he was honest, it was the second thing he noticed, the first was that she appeared to be ready for bed.

"Can I come in?" he asked.

"I don't think so, Jeff. Can't you say what you want to here?"

"Not really, but if you don't want to talk now then I'll come back in the morning."

"I won't be here. I'm leaving for the airport tomorrow morning," she said warily.

Jeff closed his eyes and ran a hand through his hair in exasperation. With all that was going on it had slipped his mind what Max had said about her only staying for one week. "You can't leave, Sarah, not yet."

"I can't stay, my flight leaves tomorrow."

"Get the flight changed," he argued.

"I can't, it's non-transferable."

"Here, let me have a look at it," he said, holding out his hand.

She turned back into the unit and returned with a folder. Jeff took it from her before she could say anything and took out the airline ticket. "What's the other voucher for?"

"It's my coach transfer from Banff to the Airport."

He looked at it; he knew the company. "I'll sort it out and the airline, leave it with me."

"No, Jeff, I can't stay."

"Can't, or won't?" he asked sharply.

"Can't. If I don't get the flight tomorrow I don't have the money to buy another ticket," she said with a spurt of annoyance.

"If that's all that's worrying you, don't. I'll pay for a new ticket."

"I can't let you do that."

"You're not, I'm offering and anyway I seem to have the upper hand since I have your ticket and you can't go anywhere without it."

Realising her mistake in handing it over, Sarah wasn't going to give him the satisfaction of asking for it back so she just scowled at him.

"I'll pay you back for it, somehow," she said.

"Whatever," said Jeff, knowing full well that he wouldn't take the money. "Now that's sorted I'll go. I'll be back tomorrow about lunchtime and we can talk some more."

"I can't, I have to vacate the unit by ten-thirty as the Johnson's have some other people arriving tomorrow afternoon."

"So, what you are saying is that after tonight you have nowhere to stay?"

"Yes."

He sighed. "Leave that with me as well. Go to bed, Sarah, and don't worry. Everything will sort itself out." With that he turned and walked away.

Sarah locked the door and settled back onto the sofa. Go to bed and don't worry. How was she supposed to do that, and how stupid had she been to hand over her ticket to him? Now she was trapped here until he decided that he had finished with her, and then he would pack her off back to England.

Now she was stuck here, and was eventually going to be beholden to him for getting back home. The thought was not one that pleased her. She needed to leave, not that she wanted to go, but there were too many memories here. Too many things that pulled at her emotions in a way she hadn't expected, and the biggest one of all had just taken her ticket.

Sarah saw her situation going from bad to worse and wondered if it had been worth it for her to come here in the first place. She wanted to go before she encountered Jeff's wife face to face. Knowing she existed was bad enough, but she didn't want to actually see them together again as a couple, she couldn't bear that. This trip had made her realise one thing, Jeff was still the man she fell in love with all those years ago and, much to her horror, the man she still loved. Crawling into bed later, Sarah had little doubt that the next few days were going to be difficult. She would have to do everything possible to keep some distance between herself, Jeff, and his wife.

* * * *

All Jeff wanted to do when he left Sarah was to drive home but he had promised that he would sort things out for her. He drove down to the bus depot and cancelled her airport transfer for the following day. Once back home, he phoned the airline and told them she was unable to travel the next day due to family commitments, leaving his contact details so she didn't go down as an over-stayer. Although she probably still had residency status, but the last thing he wanted was any risk of immigration getting involved, things were complicated enough. At last he was able to change into shorts and a casual top. He debated between painkillers for the headache he had or a whisky; the whisky won. Having poured a large measure he wandered out into the pool area. The water wasn't particularly warm so he turned on the hot tub, peeled off his clothes, and sat naked letting the jets gently pound his body.

His mind drifted back over the events of the day, still hardly believing what he had found out in the last forty-eight hours. What Sarah had told him bore no resemblance to the story his mother had relayed to him, and what about the money he had been paying to her all these years, money she says she never received. What she said about buying her clothes from charity shops had come back to him when he saw her earlier. The thin cotton nightdress that came to just below her knees and the blue fleece wrapped protectively around her body; that wasn't the Sarah he remembered. She wore silk nightdresses, or at least she did until he removed them.

His mouth moved into a smile as he recalled the times he would silently creep up behind her, slipping the straps from her shoulders and allowing the thin material to fall to the floor. He could almost feel the softness of her skin under his hands as he lifted her off her feet, before carrying her to the bed. They would lay together, her slim body fitting perfectly against his, then they would begin the slow and wonderful act of making love until it came to its final climax in an explosion of passion that would leave their bodies trembling. Thoughts of how they used to be tore at his emotions, and he could feel the hardness in his body. God, this is tearing me up. With a swift movement, he pulled himself out of the tub and plunged into the pool. Nothing like a cold shower to bring him back to his senses and remind him that he was a married man. But in reality he knew it would take more than that to get Sarah out of his head.

Chapter Seven

Next morning found Jeff outside Sarah's unit just before ten. He quickly placed her small case in the car and, once she was settled in the passenger seat, started the engine and drove along the road out toward the Hot Springs.

"Where are we going?" asked Sarah.

"To your new lodgings." His voice was tense.

Sarah didn't ask any more and Jeff didn't offer any other information. They turned off the road and into a long drive.

Sarah was looking out of the window when suddenly she recognised the area. "You bought it?" she said, turning toward him.

"Yes. I bought it from the Trustees. It once formed part of my late grandfather's estate. It was meant to be a surprise for Corey's mom, but she never came back," he said bitterly.

He knew the words would hurt. For a moment there was a flicker of pleasure from hurting her the way she'd hurt him. But just as suddenly it was gone, leaving him sorry for the way he said it. How could he hurt her when in reality it was looking as though she hadn't hurt him? They had looked at the plot before she left and talked about how good it would be to have a house built there.

His words cut into Sarah, as he intended. The knowledge that he had bought it, was now living there with his new wife, was unbearable for her.

Then suddenly she realised that he was taking her to his home, a home where his wife would be. There was no way she could go there.

Oh God no. She sat upright. "Stop," she called out.

He looked across at her questioningly. "Why?"

"Are you taking me to your home?"

"Yes." The reply was short and clipped.

She shook her head. "No, I can't go there. What will your wife think if you turn up with me?"

He hesitated for a moment before answering. "My wife isn't home, she's away at present, but don't concern yourself. She won't be worried about your being here. In fact, she knows you will be staying here for a while until things are sorted out."

He knew she would pick up on the emphasis of the word wife, a warning that this home, and him, belonged to another woman. There was no reply to what he had said, just a nod of her head acknowledged she had heard him.

The house was beyond wonderful. Sarah looked along the drive taking in the cedar wood frontage. The drive was set at either side by small paddocks. This could have been my home, our home, where we could have brought our son up together, she thought. Then wondered if Corey had had a pony when he was growing up.

"Did Corey have a pony?" She ventured to ask the question.

"Yes, for a while but then skiing became the big thing and now it's snowboarding."

She had no time to ask more as Jeff had pulled up outside the front entrance and was starting to get out of the car. Sarah took this as her cue to move. She felt dwarfed by the tall house, but at the same time in awe of its beauty. Following Jeff in through the door it was impossible to prevent the sharp intake of breath as she took in the large open entrance hall. The walls were of pine and directly opposite the main door was a staircase, set to the right, which curved up sweeping to the left and leading to another floor.

She looked around noting that the rooms seemed to lead off the entrance hall. The floor appeared to be oak, and to the right of the door was a row of hooks from which hung a couple of jackets. Underneath were a pair of working shoes, which suggested you removed your shoes as you entered.

Jeff was watching her. Was she thinking that this could have been theirs? The thought made him frown. At that moment her eyes met his and he wondered if she'd read his thoughts because immediately her eyes lowered. There was an uncomfortable moment, before he slipped off his shoes and began to walk toward the staircase. "Follow me; I'll take you to your room."

Leaving her shoes by the door Sarah followed him. The top rail was the most beautiful wood she had seen, pale pine she thought, running her hand over the smooth wood. It felt warm under her touch. The side panels were etched glass. No definite pattern, just a soft swirling that started at the bottom then worked its way up. At the top there were large double doors on the left that she presumed led to the master suite. He turned right, and walked purposely along the passageway before opening one of the doors on the left. Then he stood watching as she walked toward him, waiting for Sarah to go ahead into the room.

She stifled the gasp before he heard it. The room was huge; she could fit her whole flat into it. A king-sized bed to the right dominated the room and an open door off to the left that led into a private bathroom. There was a small bench seat in front of the windows and, as Sarah walked across the room, she saw they overlooked gardens at the back of the house. Looking down, there was a large paved patio leading to a lawned area edged by borders but beyond that she could see the snow-capped mountains. This was heaven, she never wanted to leave, but reality hit her as she heard his voice speak from somewhere behind her.

"I'll leave your case here. Come down when you're ready. Bottom of the stairs, turn left and you'll find the lounge."

Turning, she nodded, then watched as he disappeared, closing the door firmly behind him.

Jeff walked quickly along the passage and opened the doors to the master bedroom. He'd heard her gasp as she came in. His face had softened when he saw the childlike expression on her upturned face as she took in the details of his home. A home that should have been theirs. He sighed as he hung up his jacket, wondering if he had done the right thing bringing Sarah here. He hadn't realised the effect it would have on him seeing her here, in this house. He had built this house for her even after he knew she wasn't coming back, but in the hope that she might change her mind. That never happened so he and Corey had lived here, created a new family. Gradually, as his life moved on, it had changed from being a house to becoming a home and he'd added to the land over the years.

He went down to the kitchen and put on some coffee. He really needed to go back to the hotel but wanted to make sure Sarah would be okay before leaving. She appeared just as he was pouring himself a coffee. He saw her walking toward the lounge.

He called out, "I'm in here. Do you want a coffee?"

"Yes, please," she said, walking into the kitchen.

He watched her closely as she took in the kitchen. All the appliances were stainless steel with black worktops and solid pine units. Modern but welcoming. This was just how she had imagined the kitchen would be when they were daydreaming all those years ago. He saw the questioning look she gave him, a look that told him she had noticed.

"Some ideas are too good to let go. Although some things have been updated over the years," he said, handing her a mug of coffee. He wasn't sure why he was explaining, but felt that he needed to.

She walked across the tiled floor to the double doors that led out onto the large paved area. Outside there was an oval table and matching chairs set to one side, and he had no doubt the biggest BBQ Sarah had ever seen. He opened the doors so she could go out.

Jeff watched from the doorway. How many times over the early years had he imagined her standing there, and how many times had he had to face the reality that she wasn't coming back? He could almost feel the pain he'd felt then. Even after this length of time. Even after his life had moved on. "I need to go to the hotels. Will you be okay here on your own?" he said briskly, covering up his thoughts.

"Is anyone likely to come?" she asked, fearful that she may confront his wife.

"No, but if they do just tell them I'll be back later this evening, probably about six. If the phone rings don't answer it. It could be Corey and I don't want him to know anything about this. Well not yet."

"Okay. I guess I'll see you later."

With a nod of his head Jeff was gone.

On her own, Sarah walked to the edge of the patio, looking across the garden to the woods and beyond that to the mountains. She felt at peace for the first time in years, in a home that should have been hers, but now belonged to someone else. Having no wish to go back inside she stayed outside sitting at the table with her coffee letting the warm air wash over her. This was the most wonderful place, and a house here was all that she imagined it would be.

Delightful as it was outside, it wasn't long before curiosity got the better of her, tempting her back inside to explore the downstairs rooms. The lounge was everything she had come to expect in this house. Large and airy. The walls were the same wood as the hall. Floor to ceiling windows looked out over the garden and there was a door that led outside. The pale green drapes were tied back at the windows giving a clear view of the garden. The floor was the same wood as the hall, and large rugs gave a homely feel to the room.

At the far end of the room an open doorway led through to another room. Tempted to know what was there she made her way across the lounge, peeped through the open doorway, and found herself looking into a formal dining room. Beyond that she could just see the sparkle of sunlight on water. She presumed this was an indoor swimming pool, but had no intention of prying further. Returning to the lounge, she gazed at the large fireplace that took centre stage, set on an angle in one of the corners it was imposing. The chimney section, made up of varying stones, reached out and up toward the ceiling. Three large comfy sofas were placed at strategic points around the room. This was a room that spoke of warmth and comfort. Sarah settled on one of the sofas, tucked her legs up, and gradually felt the tension ease out of her body. Before long she had drifted off to sleep. She was still there when Jeff came home.

Jeff let himself in and, noticing the silence, believed Sarah was in her room. He kicked off his shoes in the entrance and walked toward the lounge. Then he saw her, curled up like a child on the sofa, asleep. He stopped in the doorway, moved by the sight of her. She looked so young and vulnerable. It was hard to believe that he had spent all those years trying to hate her, but seeing her now made him realise how futile that had been. Just looking at her pulled at his emotions in a way nothing else could. She was older, but was still beautiful, and underneath he could see the Sarah he'd fallen in love with. He wanted to believe the story she'd told him. Hell, he needed to believe her. It was the only way her leaving would make any sense to him. Now, he could see a light at the end of a long tunnel, but if what she said was true, where did that leave his late mother?

As if sensing his presence she stirred and slowly opened her eyes. It took a moment for her to remember where she was. As he moved into the room she swung her head around, her hair falling loose about her shoulders, then lowered her feet to the floor. She stood quickly, immediately regretting it as she became dizzy. Losing her balance, she reached out for something that wasn't there.

Jeff covered the ground between them in record time and caught her just before she hit the floor.

"Steady on," he said as he gently sat her back down on the sofa.

"Sorry, I just stood up too quickly."

"I know, its okay. I'm guessing you haven't had anything to eat?" he said, stepping back and putting some distance between them.

She shook her head. "No, I fell asleep."

"In that case, I guess we could both do with something to eat. How does steak and salad grab you?"

"That sounds fine, but I need to ask a favour."

"What?" he asked, somewhat cautiously.

"As you know I was supposed to be going home today, well Annie was meeting me from the train tomorrow. I need to let her know what has happened."

"No problem, phone her from here. Use the phone in the den, I'll show you where it is."

She followed him out into the entrance hall, then across to the left where he opened a door which led her into a spacious office. Pointing to the chair behind the desk he suggested she make herself comfortable. When she was seated, he pulled the phone toward her and passed the handset to her. "I'll leave you to talk while I make a start on dinner."

After he had left, Sarah phoned Annie's number and was relieved when her friend answered. Knowing she had arranged to take the day off from work tomorrow to pick her up she would have been upset if she hadn't been able to contact her, and stop her from wasting a day's holiday. She filled her in with what had happened and, as expected Annie being protective of Sarah, warned her to be careful reminding her that if his mother was capable of lying then Sarah couldn't be sure of Jeff's motives. Sarah smiled at her friend's concern but promised that she would take care and would phone again in a few days.

Jeff was selecting ingredients for the salad when Sarah returned to the kitchen. He glanced up. "The steaks are on the grill. I just need to throw a salad together."

"I'll do it," said Sarah, "it's the least I can do. And, thank you for the phone call."

"Okay, if you don't mind doing the salad that would be good. I just need to make a quick call and then we can eat. The salad dressings are in the fridge door," he called as he made his way to the den.

Closing the door he picked up the handset and quickly wrote down the last number called. Tucking the slip of paper into his pocket, he then sat at his desk for a short time, remembering that he was supposed to be making a call. He hated being devious, but he needed to speak to this Annie. He needed to find out just what had happened when his mother had gone to England. He didn't know if he was trying to find a way to prove Sarah wrong, or right? A couple of days ago he would have said, to prove her wrong, but now his gut was telling him she was right. And the knowledge was weighing heavily on him.

Sarah was just finishing the salad when he walked back into the kitchen. She had set the small table in the corner near to the window. Jeff went out to check on the steaks and came back with them on a plate. He poured them each a glass of wine, then they sat and ate in a strangely comfortable silence.

Once the meal was finished, Sarah ventured to ask about Corey's wife and how they had met. "I know I don't know anything about Corey, or his life, but I would love to know something about the person he's fallen in love with?

Jeff felt somewhat guilty at her words. "If you want to know about Corey, just ask. I'll tell you what I can. As for Laura, they first met at junior high school but then Laura's parents moved to Canmore so he didn't see her for a few years. Corey was doing a two year Business and Management course at Calgary University, but would be working in the hotels when he was home. There was a party at Saunders one night and he and Laura met up again there. It was just toward the end of his first year, and that was that. Spent all of their spare time together and couldn't wait to get married. Laura works in Banff, at the hospital as a personal assistant to one of the doctors there."

Sarah listened in silence trying to gain some insight into her son's life, but it left her feeling sad that she had to ask for information about her own son and his wife. She kept this thought to herself so as not to appear ungrateful. But there was one more question she longed to ask, and taking a deep breath, inquired whether Corey had any brothers or sisters. Waiting for Jeff's reply seemed to take forever but eventually he answered her.

"Not as far as I am aware. Unless you—"

"No," she replied quickly,

She made no comment but was conscious of a feeling of relief. That she was the only one to have given him a child was strangely comforting to her. It gave her a connection to him that his wife didn't have. She watched him gather the dishes then stack them in the dishwasher before he disappeared into his den, leaving her to go into the lounge and browse through the various magazines in the rack. She could see family photos around the room, one in particular caught her eye. It was of Corey and Laura with Jeff and the woman she had seen him with at the hotel. The perfect family photo. She quickly moved away trying to ignore the pang of jealousy, concentrating on those with just Jeff and Corey.

It was getting dark by the time Jeff re-appeared. Deciding she'd had enough for one day, said goodnight and climbed the stairs to her room.

She awoke late, surprised to realise that she had actually had an undisturbed night's sleep. Climbing out of bed, she went into the adjoining en-suite and decided to investigate what appeared to be a walk-in shower room at the far end of the bathroom. She ventured into the open entrance that curved to the right before opening up into a large wet room. The controls looked complex, but she wasn't an idiot. She would work them out. This was way more than her simple bathroom at home. Collecting her clothes from the bedroom she left them in the bathroom, walked into the wet room, and enjoyed the most wonderful shower she had ever had.

Standing in the centre, with the large showerhead above her, she let the hot water run down her body. A quick wash of her hair and body she was soon back out in the bathroom and drying herself with the softest of towels. There was a hairdryer on the vanity top which she plugged in and quickly dried her hair before tying it back in a ponytail. Dressing in jeans and a tee shirt before pulling on a pair of sandals she was aware of the late hour. Venturing downstairs, she found the house empty. On the worktop in the kitchen was a note from Jeff saying he had gone into the office, wasn't sure when he would be back, but to make herself at home. Again there was a reminder not to answer the phone.

After coffee and toast, she explored outside. Opening the doors leading from the kitchen onto the patio, she walked across the paving out onto the lawn. It was neat and tidy with a small border running around the edge planted mainly with shrubs, the whole formal garden was enclosed with a brick wall. She walked across the grass, finally reaching a gate leading into a paddock beyond. Drawing back the bolt she pushed the gate open, remembering to close it behind her, then walked across the paddock. Beyond this was another, then another before the forest started.

Sarah knew what could be in the forest so had no intention to venture that far. It was peaceful in the paddock and the views across to the Rockies were out of this world. She sat cross-legged on the ground simply enjoying the peace and tranquillity of the world around her, and that was where Jeff found her.

Having left early to go to the hotel he'd begun to feel guilty about deserting Sarah. He'd needed to put some space between them, which again made him wonder if it had been a good idea to have her stay at the house. It was ironic that with two hotels in Banff he couldn't put her up in either in case one of the long serving members of staff recognised her. And he knew that Tom would recognise her, even after all these years, he'd always had a fondness for her. Even their Canmore hotel could have been a problem, so the only secure solution had seemed to be the house. He didn't want word of her presence getting back to Corey before he'd had a chance to sort out the mess apparently created by his mother.

By lunchtime, Jeff's guilt got the better of him so he headed back home. However, the house was empty but the doors from the kitchen were unlocked. He had to presume that Sarah had gone outside, but he couldn't see her in the garden. He walked into the paddock, but it was also empty. Walking farther it wasn't long before he noticed the small figure sitting in the middle of the far paddock with her back to him. She looked small and vulnerable, he thought. Walking steadily toward her he made little noise and she didn't appear to hear him coming. He watched her for a few moments before eventually speaking.

"I could be a large black bear thinking I have just found lunch." He saw her jump when he spoke and she quickly turned her head around.

"I would have heard a bear."

"That's what you think, they can move very quietly when they want to. Anyway, maybe you should be more worried about snakes in the grass than bears in the woods."

The mention of snakes had Sarah on her feet in an instant looking at the ground around her.

"Are there any around?" she asked anxiously."

"Not usually, but it does pay to keep one's eyes and ears open."

"What are you doing back?"

"I actually felt guilty about you being here on your own, so thought you might like to go out somewhere this afternoon."

To Sarah this was like being offered a bag of gold. To spend an afternoon together would be wonderful. "I'd like that, but you don't have to."

He had started walking back toward the house so Sarah followed.

"I've made the offer so take advantage of it. Where would you like to go?"

"I don't know, there are so many places I remember."

"Well, pick one of your favourites."

Sarah knew all along where she wanted to go but was reluctant to say, it would bring back memories for both of them, but she would love to go there. Taking a deep breath, she asked if they could go to Moraine Lake.

She saw his body stiffen when she mentioned it and thought he was going to refuse, but he just shrugged his shoulders. "Okay, if that's where you want to go, consider it arranged."

Once back at the house, Sarah quickly changed her sandals for sneakers, before picking up her fleece on the way out of the bedroom. Jeff had also changed and was waiting in the lounge. Sarah couldn't fail to notice the casual shirt tucked into the waistband of the denim jeans that fitted closely over his hips. Both complimented by the leather belt fastened with a silver buckle. She felt her pulse race at the sight of him. Years ago she would have kissed him for looking so good, tempted him until he gave in to her. But now, she needed to at least try to give the appearance of being cool and detached. Something that was going to be hard to do.

While Sarah was taking in the sight of Jeff, he was doing the same with her, although perhaps not quite as appreciatively. He couldn't fail to notice the thin t-shirt and cotton shirt thrown on top. The jeans were the same she'd worn previously, and the sneakers on her feet had clearly seen better days, but the clothes only accentuated her slim figure, which was something Jeff was beginning to appreciate the more he was in her company. Something he was going to have to deal with. The clothes she wore certainly seemed to bear out her denial of never having seen the money he had been sending to her.

Going into the kitchen, he lifted two bottles of water out of the fridge and put them in a small backpack together with some packets of trail mix. "Come on," he said, "let's hit the road."

Sarah followed him outside and climbed into the car.

The drive to Moraine Lake was one they had both loved to take. Sarah was feeling both apprehensive and excited at the same time. She was secretly delighted when Jeff turned off the main highway, taking the old 1A back road, which they used to do in the past. This was where they would often see wildlife, she remembered how excited Corey would get if they saw elk or bears. He would point and shout, aminal, aminal and they would laugh at his mispronunciation. The thought brought a wry smile to her lips, those were happy days; days that were gone just like the years of her son growing up that she'd missed. She shook the upsetting thought away, wanting to avoid anything that might spoil this time together.

They drove passed the view point for Castle Mountain. She would have loved to have stopped for a moment, but felt unable to ask. Sadly, today the wildlife was not to be seen and, as they joined the main highway, Sarah was sorry that they hadn't at least seen an elk.

She noted the new road junction at the turning to Lake Louise village but they bypassed that and drove on, heading toward Lake Louise, but then took the left turn to Moraine Lake. Sarah could see the mountains in the valley coming closer and closer. She loved this road and how it wound its way toward the lakeside. Every now and again she would catch a glimpse of the valley through the trees. There were a couple of places to pull off the road to admire the view, but today the tourists were there. She would have to be patient until they got to the end.

As they reached the end of the road Sarah was surprised to see the large car park area, but then realised that everywhere had become more tourist orientated over the years. There was now a modern lodge with shops and restaurant on the site, but as she looked beyond the car park she saw the crystal turquoise waters of the lake opening up before her. Surrounding the lake were forested slopes and the jagged peaks of the Wenkchemma Mountains. She was home.

Jeff heard the sharp intake of breath as she saw the lake for the first time in years, and he felt his heart softening as he realised how much she seemed to have missed all of this. He began to appreciate how hard it must have been for her not to be able to come back to somewhere she clearly loved, if what she'd told him was true. Not for the first time over the last few days did he question his own part in this, for believing too quickly in what his mother had told him. He should have gone with his own instincts, like he did when they first met and he knew there was something special between them. He should have ignored his mother and gone after Sarah once Corey was out of danger.

Having parked the car he hitched the backpack onto his shoulders and they set off to walk toward the lake. At least Jeff walked but Sarah couldn't contain herself and he smiled as she half-walked, half-ran to the beach which was littered along the edge with fallen logs.

She turned and looked back at him, a radiant smile on her face that, unbeknown to her, made his heart flip.

"It doesn't look any different," she said excitedly.

"No, mountains don't change."

She glanced at him. He saw the look and realised how his words might have sounded to her. But there hadn't been any underlying accusation. He didn't want to spoil the mood so smiled to dispel any worry she may have. She smiled back.

"Can we walk to the top of the moraine?"

"Only if you think those sneakers will make it," he replied.

"Of course they will, if not, they will give up trying."

He laughed at that and Sarah laughed with him. Together they set off along the path before starting the climb to the top of the moraine. Ground squirrels ran out from the rocks, and now and again they caught sight of a chipmunk.

By the time she got to the top, Sarah was out of breath, but nothing could spoil this moment of pure joy for her as she stood looking down and out along the lake. It was breath-taking. She started counting the mountain peaks just to make sure the valley still deserved its name of, The Valley of the Ten Peaks, as once depicted on the Canadian twenty dollar bill. She had just finished counting when Jeff joined her at the top.

"You took your time," she said teasingly.

"No," he said, "I paced myself and didn't go dashing off trying to give myself a heart attack."

Sarah laughed and sat down on the wooden seat that had been erected so people could enjoy this spectacular view. He sat next to her and passed her a water bottle. She took this readily not realising how thirsty she was. Jeff opened a pack of trail mix before handing it to her. They sat in the sunlight sharing a snack without needing to make conversation. Just as we used to do years ago, she thought, except then his arm would have been thrown around my shoulders and I would have been nestled against him. She sighed at the thought.

How long they stayed there she didn't really know. They both seemed absorbed in their own thoughts, thoughts they didn't share. The sun was starting to lower in the sky when Jeff suggested they should perhaps make a move to go back down. Reluctantly, Sarah stood, and took a last look at the lake from her favourite spot before following Jeff down to the car. They drove back in a comfortable silence. Before long Sarah's eyes closed and she drifted off to sleep.

Jeff, looking sideways at her, again thought how vulnerable she seemed when she was asleep. He was finding it hard to understand his feelings toward her. At times it felt as though they had never been apart. He had no idea where his feelings were leading him, or the impact this would have on his wife. Sarah slept until the car turned into the drive to the house. Turning her head she smiled and then stretched.

"Hello, sleepyhead," he said.

"Sorry, it must have been the fresh air that made me so tired."

"Well, it doesn't come any fresher," he replied. Having pulled up outside the house he lifted out the rucksack and let Sarah in.

"I hate to drop you off and run, but I need to call into the office for a short time. I won't be long and then we can have dinner when I get back. Don't bother with anything. I'll throw something simple together. Why don't you relax after that climb and enjoy the pool, or the hot tub? I'll switch it on for you."

With that he disappeared off into the conservatory area and she heard the hum of the hot tub as it started up. He walked back into the kitchen where she was waiting. "There are swimsuits in the closet in the pool area. I'm sure you'll be able to find one to fit. We always keep a variety of sizes in for Corey's friends."

Sarah smiled, thanked him, and then he was gone. All that could be heard was the sound of tyres on the drive as he drove away.

Chapter Eight

Jeff drove to the office and, having said he didn't want to be disturbed, picked up the phone and called Annie's number. He hoped the time difference meant that she would be home, it being a weekend. He was just beginning to think she wasn't there when the phone was answered. Having told her who he was he was totally unprepared for the hostile silence that greeted him and then the barrage of angry remarks, about his treatment of Sarah, that poured down the phone line at him. When he did manage to get a word in he assured Annie that he had no intention of hurting Sarah, but had every intention of getting to the bottom of what had happened all those years ago. It may have been the sincerity in his voice but suddenly he found Annie prepared to listen to him.

"Look, I need to tell you what I know about the events of eighteen years ago," he said, "and then I need you to tell me what you know."

If Annie found his request strange when he could ask Sarah she didn't say. After some hesitation, she agreed to give him a chance to try and explain himself. He had no doubt she would then decide what she would, or wouldn't tell him. Having explained in detail all that his mother had told him he then waited for her reply.

There was a long silence before Annie spoke. "Okay, I've heard your version, and, knowing what I know, I can see how the situation, and both of you were manipulated. But, whilst I'm not prepared to break any confidences I have with Sarah I feel that you deserve to be told all that I know."

He listened in silence as she gave him full, and unedited, details of his mother's behaviour. Hearing of Sarah's heartbreak at losing her own mum and then of his mother's visits, and her belief that he no longer wanted her, he felt an anger rising inside that he had never experienced before. Then Annie told him something that Sarah had made no mention of.

He sat upright in his chair, his exclamation of, "No!!" ringing down the line in Annie's ear.

"She didn't tell you?" she said immediately concerned.

"No," he replied quietly.

"I'm sorry, if I'd known I would never have mentioned it."

"It's okay, I'm glad you did. She just hasn't said anything to me yet, but I think she will in her own time, when she's ready. Annie, I'm glad Sarah had a friend like you looking out for her, but I need to ask you to do one thing for me."

"That depends what it is?" was the cautious reply.

"I don't want you to tell Sarah that we have spoken. I promise you that I'll tell her shortly, but there are still some pieces of the puzzle that I have yet to unearth."

Hearing Annie starting to accuse him of not believing her he quickly continued, "No, no, I do believe what Sarah has told me, and what you have told me. I'm just finding it difficult to equate the woman I knew as my mother, with the person who was apparently vindictive enough to create this mess." He hoped his words re-assured her. The last thing he wanted was more misunderstandings between himself and Sarah. But until he knew exactly what had taken place, he didn't want to have this conversation with her.

He sat in his office completely stunned by the revelation Annie had just unwittingly told him. Sarah had lost their child, just days after his mother's last visit to her, but she had yet to tell him that herself. He couldn't begin to imagine how she must have felt and he experienced a hatred toward his mother he thought himself incapable of. He could feel the stinging of tears in his eyes and, although this had happened years ago, he had just found out that his child had died. Holding his hands up to his head he raked his fingers through his hair. Taking several deep breaths to pull himself together he brushed his hand across his eyes wiping away the wetness. He didn't know how he would be able to face Sarah, but knew that he must. For now he would bury the grief he was feeling until she felt able to open up to him. Then they would deal with this, together.

Back at the house, Sarah was enjoying the sheer indulgence of the hot tub. This was something she could get used to, but in reality was something she would probably never enjoy again after this visit. She had managed to find a swimsuit to fit; a royal blue one-piece, which she quite liked. It was something she would probably have bought for herself, if she'd had any spare money.

As she lay in the water, her mind drifted back over the day. The outing with Jeff had been so unexpected. When they were out she'd felt as though they'd never been apart. She'd cautiously watched him from behind her dark glasses, still seeing the firm body that she used to curl into, and she'd longed for the feel of his arm around her shoulders. It had taken all her resolve not to move closer to him as they'd sat on the bench, to move her leg so it pressed against his, just the way she used to tease him into awareness. She smiled at the recollection of how that awareness used to play out, feeling a tremor go through her body at the thought. She let her mind go further. Imagined this was her home, that she was waiting for her husband to come home from work. What would they do? Go out for dinner, stay in, make love? The thought pulled her sharply back to the present. What was she thinking? But she could dream, couldn't she?

Glancing at the poolside clock, she realised she had soaked for so long she was in danger of looking like a prune. Reluctantly, she pulled herself out of the hot tub and walked to the edge of the pool. With one swift movement she dove in, gasping as the cool water hit her. She swam lazily up and down the pool until she had managed to exorcise all her earlier thoughts.

Walking up the steps and out onto the side, she undid the tie, shaking her hair out around her shoulders. Standing on the side, silhouetted against the light, she raised her arms, lifting her hair up, before twisting it to get some of the water out. It was at this moment Jeff walked in.

She wasn't sure if she heard his sharp intake of breath, or whether she just sensed his presence. But when she turned and saw him her face broke into a smile, as her stomach began doing somersaults.

She looked at him, but he made no move, nor did he say anything. She felt it. It was there between them. It had always been there. The pull that had first drawn them together. The air was tense. Then she saw the desire in his eyes. The smile disappeared from her face as she remembered her own thoughts of earlier. She felt as though she was caught in a trap, exposed to something she didn't quite understand. Unable to move she stared intensely at him, had she done something wrong? Her first thought was to run but that would have been immature, so she walked as steadily as she could toward him.

"I'd better get dried," she said as she moved past him.

Her arm brushed against his and his hand shot out holding her back. Turning toward him their eyes met, neither said anything, they didn't need to. She could see clearly that he wanted her, and she could only hope that he couldn't read the same desire in her eyes. He dropped his hand and she moved quickly away, walking as calmly as she could toward the pool door that led directly into the hall. Once out of sight, she ran up the stairs to her room.

Shaking with emotion and cold from the wet swimsuit, she quickly stripped this off. Dropping the swimsuit on the bathroom floor she walked into the shower. Standing under the water as the heat warmed her body, her mind was in turmoil over what had just happened. She shouldn't feel like this, he was no longer hers he belonged to someone else. Another woman now shared his life and his bed. She had no place there anymore. If she kept telling herself this for long enough she might just begin to believe it. But could she forget the feelings that were now racing through her body. And what of him, what of the look on his face. Had she imagined that he felt the same?

When Sarah disappeared upstairs Jeff went into his den, poured a large whisky, downing it in one go, and then poured another. He couldn't get the sight of her part naked body out of his head. It brought it all back, the way they used to be together. Their wedding night, the night she had given him everything. The life they had shared and the child they created. They'd had everything, then it was gone. But what now? Could they have it again? He realised that he had reached a turning point and, if he'd got this wrong, he didn't know how he could put it right. Nor did he know what the implications were going to be for him and his wife. All he knew was that he couldn't stop what was about to happen and the consequences would have to be faced later. Placing the untouched whisky on the desk he walked out into the hall, climbed the stairs, and headed toward Sarah's room. Without knocking he turned the handle and went in, hearing the sound of the shower as he did. Walking into the bathroom he stripped off his clothes before walking through into the wet room.

He inhaled sharply when he saw her. She stood in the middle of the room with her back to him. He took in her naked body, the slim legs and hips, feeling his own body re-act to the sight of her. He moved toward her.

* * * *

Sarah had heard the slight noise behind her and knew he was there. If she was honest she had wished him to come to her. His hands reached forward and came to rest on her hips, drawing her gently back against his body. Her body trembled in his hold. The hardness of him pressed into her back as his hands moved slowly across the flat of her stomach then upwards to cup a breast in each palm. They stood together without saying anything. She shivered as his thumbs moved slowly and seductively across her nipples, teasing them until they stood hard and erect. Her body arched in sheer pleasure. She was transported back to when they were together, remembered how it used to be.

He groaned her name. "Sarah."

Lost in the moment, she took the initiative and turned in his arms. Running her hands up his body and over his chest she thrilled in the pleasure this gave her. She had dreamed of doing this so many times over the years, but the dreams had always ended in tears. This time it was no dream. Moving her arms around his neck she drew his head down, bringing his lips to hers. The kiss that began gently and exploring of each other deepened into a passion that took her breath away.

Jeff cupped his hands under her buttocks, lifted her off her feet and moved a few steps until she was rested against the wall, then she felt the hardness of him entering inside her. No foreplay, none was needed, neither of them could wait. She clung to him, legs wrapped around his body as he supported them both and took them to the heights of ecstasy. Sarah called out his name, arching her body so that she could devour every part of him, her arms clasped tightly around his neck. He held her close as they came down from the dizzy heights of passion. His lips kissing her face and crying her name, holding each other as if they would never let go, until they were both spent.

Sarah brushed his hair back from his face as he lowered his mouth and kissed her.

"Don't cry, Sarah, please, and please don't regret what just happened," he whispered, seeing the tears running down her cheeks.

"I'll never regret what just happened. And I'm not crying because I regret anything. I don't really know why I'm crying because at this moment I'm happier than I've been since I left you. Not that I really left you, but you know what I mean." Her words were rushed and garbled.

He smiled at her. "You know you often did talk too much at the wrong time, but I do know what you mean, Sarah. And I don't regret what has just happened, but whilst I would be happy to stay here and don't want to be the one to spoil this moment, it might be good if you could free your legs, as we are in imminent danger of falling down," he said huskily.

She giggled nervously and unwrapped her legs as he carefully withdrew and lowered her to the floor. They stood looking at each other. Sarah had known this was inevitable since she saw the look in his eyes earlier. She pushed thoughts of his dark haired wife away. He had been her husband once and, despite all that had happened, she couldn't deny that she still loved him. She wanted to enjoy being with him and forget about any repercussions.

"Well," he said, tucking a strand of wet hair behind her ear, "what do you suggest we do now?"

"I don't know," she replied, looking at him from under her lashes.

"We'll have to think of something then," he said with a laugh before sweeping her off her feet and carrying her through the bathroom, pausing only to collect a large towel.

Once in the bedroom, he threw back the covers and placed her on the bed, before cocooning her in the towel. What had happened just now was something he'd been fighting for days, but seeing her in the pool, he knew the battle was lost. Being with her again had been explosive and told him only one thing, his feelings for her were still as strong as ever. He could argue with himself, say it was wrong, totally out of character, but he wanted to explore what was happening, and didn't want to think of the consequences. Her laughter brought his thoughts back to the present.

"I can't move."

"I know, that's the idea."

With that, he lay next to her on the bed then leaning over, started to shower her face with kisses. Gradually releasing the towel a bit at a time, he kissed each released portion of her body until he reached the flat of her stomach. He looked at her lying naked and exposed to him and knew this risk had been the right one. God, I want her. He needed and wanted to be inside her again, it had been far too long since he'd enjoyed her body. His own responded to his need. His hands slowly moved over her stomach until he reached the silky softness at the base before moving gently between her legs, easing them apart, allowing him to lower his head so his tongue could feel the softness and wetness of her femininity.

As his tongue flicked across her clitoris he thought she was going to explode. Her body jerked in his hands.

"Please, Jeff," her voice so soft he barely heard it. She wanted him inside her again; the thought was enough to drive him insane. The urgency of wanting him had her body arching up to him in anticipation of what was to come. He was lost, no longer able to contain his emotions.

Raising his head he looked into her eyes. The green of her eyes had turned pale as passion flooded through her body. He moved on top of her, keeping his weight on his elbows. Then pushed gently forward, slipping in without any effort. He moved slowly, savouring every moment of possessing her, until he suddenly turned, manoeuvring her so he was on his back and she was above him.

She looked at him in surprise. "Sit up, Sarah," he whispered, knowing this would make their lovemaking more intense.

She moved her position until she was straddled comfortably above him, then smiled. She liked this position, he remembered that. Remembered how she said it made her feel in control, but for him it made their lovemaking more intense. He watched her as he remembered, her eyes flirtatiously lowered as she bent forward to kiss his chest.

His hands took hold of hers and he pushed her back so she was sitting upright.

"Don't look at me like that, you don't have the upper hand, Sarah," he teased. "I still have control of things." He moved his hips upwards, pushing deeper inside her.

As he did he remembered the times in the past when they'd done this, when they'd been younger and possibly a bit more agile. But he wanted this; he wanted her and everything they used to do before she left. Life had given them another chance to be together, for how long though, he didn't know. But he was prepared to take what he could, what they had now, for as long as possible. He might be damned in hell, but it would be worth every moment.

She gasped, biting down on her bottom lip as he moved further into her and that small gesture only served to heighten his desire. He thrust deeper and deeper while she pushed down on him, the soft moans showing clearly her delight in what was happening. Then just as he knew the tide would be rising inside her, he deftly turned them so she was underneath him again. He caught her lips with his own as their bodies rose and fell together. Their cries mingled as one as they again reached the dizzy heights of passion before crashing down. He couldn't speak, he was beyond capable thought, so they lay holding each other until the trembling in their bodies ceased.

They lay together in the bed holding each other and talking, not of serious things, just silly talk, remembering things they used to do, and things they said. Eventually as the room darkened, they had to move and Jeff was the first to do so. He stood at the side of the bed, then leaned over and dropped a kiss on her nose.

"I think you should finish your shower, while I go and shower as well."

With a boldness coming from their lovemaking, she coyly suggested they could do it together.

He laughed. "No, I don't think that would be a good idea. I'll see you downstairs. I don't know about you but for some reason I'm ravenous." With that he was gone leaving Sarah to enjoy a solitary shower and to push thoughts of a dark haired woman to the back of her mind.

They shared a light supper washed down with a glass of wine. The talk was light banter, neither wanting to mention what had happened years ago, or try and rationalise what had just happened upstairs, but neither could deny the attraction pulling them together. Jeff finally announced he was going to turn in, then kissed her lightly on the top of her head before heading upstairs. Sarah had thought they would have gone up together and was disappointed he had left, but had no intention of letting him see that it upset her, so deliberately stayed up for another half an hour before going to her room.

Lying in the large bed thinking of the last time she had been there she wished she could fall asleep. Then the door opened and footsteps were treading softly across the room. She smiled. He climbed into the bed and pulled her body back into his.

"I thought you would never come to bed," he said.

"When you left I thought you wanted to sleep alone. In your own room."

"No. I just didn't want to presume that you wanted me here. Didn't want to be waiting when you came up."

"So you thought you would just creep up on me, in my bed."

"Perhaps. But you can kick me out if you would prefer to sleep alone. There's no pressure, Sarah. I'm taking nothing for granted."

Sarah laughed and turned round into his arms as his mouth descended on hers.

The next morning, Sarah lay thinking of how he had woken her in the night, how they had taken pleasure in each other's bodies again. He made her feel like a wanton hussy. She couldn't get enough of him, she had ached for this for eighteen years and intended to savour every moment, no matter what the consequences were. She couldn't help but think of all the years they had missed, times they could have been making love, making more babies. No, she quickly pushed the thoughts away. Some were too painful to remember.

He stirred beside her and she turned to kiss his upturned face. A mistake she later realised when they had again made love before laying back exhausted on the bed. Jeff was the first to move leaving her with a kiss to go back to his own room. By the time Sarah got downstairs he was busy making scrambled eggs with ham. They ate a late breakfast but she couldn't ignore the smouldering looks passing between them, which had her breathing heavily. By the time they had finished she was squirming in her seat.

Walking back with fresh coffee, Jeff could hardly believe the events of the last twenty-four hours. He was behaving in a totally irrational way, and had crossed a line without having any idea of where he was going. When he'd seen her yesterday by the pool, every longing he'd had over the past eighteen years had flooded through his body. She was still his Sarah, still the young girl he'd fallen in love with, and married. But she wasn't the person he was led to believe had walked away from him all those years ago. He knew that now. Every part of his body told him she hadn't. They'd lost everything, all the hopes and dreams they'd shared were lost. She was here now, but for how long. As he sat down and looked across the table at Sarah, he knew one thing; they couldn't stay in the house.

"I think we had better go out somewhere otherwise we are likely to see very little of the day," he said, smiling to make the suggestion more appealing.

"Sounds good to me," said Sarah, but just at that moment the phone rang.

"Can you leave it?" she asked, not wanting to break the mood.

Jeff looked at the caller number and shook his head. "Sorry, I can't," and picked up the handset.

"Hi, just a minute. I can't talk at present; let me go into the den."

Sarah frowned. He smiled, leaned forward, and kissed her forehead. He mouthed won't be long and walked off toward his office talking softly into the phone.

Sarah sat in the kitchen feeling suddenly sad. Was it his wife on the phone, and that's why he couldn't talk? She tried to feel guilty about their lovemaking the night before, and this morning, but couldn't. Jeff had been her husband too and she still loved him and was prepared to take any crumbs that were on offer, on any terms, for as long as she was here. She didn't want to dwell on his infidelity to his wife. This was a brief interlude that would soon end.

In his den, Jeff listened to all that Doug was telling him and made notes of the conversation. "So you are saying that this account trail ends in a lawyer's office in Vancouver?"

"That's right, Jeff, but it's a large, well known law firm and I can't see anyone being involved in anything that wasn't legitimate."

"Well, we'll have to see what they say when I start asking questions. Thanks for the info, Doug. Yes, I know I'll get the bill but I think it will be money well spent."

"Has Sarah gone back to England?" asked Doug.

"Err..no, she's still here."

"Is that why you couldn't speak at first, is she at the house?"

"Yes."

"Is that wise?" asked his friend.

"I don't know, Doug, at this point in time I don't think I know anything anymore."

"Okay, but you take care, and don't let the situation get out of hand. I know it's outside my remit but I would really appreciate knowing the outcome of things, if you feel able to share the information."

"I'll bear it in mind and once again thanks, Doug."

Jeff placed the information in the drawer of his desk and locked this away. He couldn't do anything about it now as it was Sunday, but tomorrow he would put matters in motion to, hopefully, sort out the final part of this mess.

Sarah was still sitting in the kitchen when he walked in and one look at her face told him that she was worried.

"That was your wife, wasn't it?" The words came out in a rush.

"No, but it related to a matter that will concern my wife, eventually," he answered carefully, not wanting to cause her any more worry. That Sarah was going to have to meet his wife before long was becoming clear to Jeff and he didn't know how that meeting was going to work out.

"Come on, Sarah, let's go and enjoy this beautiful day." He knew he was going to have to go away for a couple of days, but had no intention of spoiling the day by telling her that yet. Nor did he want to break the connection that was between them.

They drove away from Banff and out into Kananaskis country, an area they had both visited often in the past. Jeff pulled into the parking lot of a local Provincial Park and they walked along one of the trails. Sarah ever conscious of the possibility of wildlife kept talking loudly much to Jeff's amusement. He wasn't concerned, he had pepper spray if necessary, but he doubted whether they would need it. Bears were likely to be well into the trees away from public areas, although one could never be certain. They stopped in a clearing with a picnic table and enjoyed a makeshift lunch before venturing further.

Neither of them had spoken again about the past events that had torn their family life apart. Their conversations were spent in getting to know each other again. Sarah was happy and content to walk hand in hand along the track, or to sit looking at a spectacular view with Jeff's arm thrown casually around her shoulders. The way it used to be. She was still not certain Jeff believed everything she had told him about his mother, but if his actions and what was happening between them was any indication, he no longer believed she had just walked away. And for now that knowledge was enough for her.

Later, as they were driving back, Jeff broached the subject he had avoided all day. "Sarah, I need to go away for a couple of days, but I should only be away for the one night."

"Is this because of the call this morning?"

"Yes, I'm afraid so, and I can't put the trip off, nor can I do it in one day."

"It's okay, I'll be fine. I realise that you have other commitments."

He took his hand off the wheel, reached across and took hold of hers, raising it to his lips. "I'll be back before you know it." Jeff took a risk on the way back to have dinner in a small restaurant on the outskirts of Canmore. For both of them it was a perfect end to a day they had spent like an ordinary couple, neither wanting to acknowledge their time together would be short lived.

Waking the next morning, Sarah stretched out her hand but the other side of the bed was empty. She sat up and jumped out of bed. Surely he hadn't gone without saying anything. Grabbing a robe from the chair she ran down the stairs straight into his arms as he came out of the kitchen.

"Whoa...where's the fire?"

"I thought you left."

"Not without saying goodbye." He dropped a kiss on her nose. "I just needed to make a couple of calls and then I was going to bring coffee up to you."

"Well since I'm up we can have it together, now, down here."

"I'm sorry, much as I would love to I really don't have time. I need to leave for the airport shortly. I've managed to get a flight at midday, but it will take me about ninety minutes to get to Calgary and to park, and you know what checking in is like."

"Okay," she said, "I understand."

He kissed the top of her head and was gone, taking the stairs two at a time.

Throwing a change of clothes into a holdall he collected the other incidentals he would need for an overnight stay. He wished he could do the trip in a day as he hated the thought of leaving Sarah on her own overnight, but it was impossible. Then he had a thought. Dashing back downstairs, he went down into the basement area. He spent very little time down here; it had been more a hang out place for Corey and his pals. The vast space with its large sitting area, complete with oversized television and two additional bedrooms both with their own en-suite was perfect for the youngsters.

One area had been set aside for storage and that was where Jeff headed. He opened up a large cabinet and took out a number of albums. This would keep Sarah happy while he was away. He climbed back up the stairs and closed the door behind him with his foot. Walking into the lounge he saw Sarah outside in the garden. He put the albums down on the long coffee table. Picking up a slip of paper he wrote a message on it then placed it on top of the albums.

Dashing back upstairs he quickly showered, changed into a suit, then picked up his holdall and walked back downstairs. Sarah was in the kitchen washing her coffee cup.

"Use the dishwasher," he said.

"Sorry, force of habit, not used to such luxury."

Jeff felt a pang of guilt that she had not been able to enjoy the everyday things that he and Corey took for granted. Walking up behind her, he pushed her hair to one side before kissing the nape of her neck.

"I'm going to miss you, and my bed is going to be empty tonight."

Turning in his arms her hands went around his neck. "I'll miss you too."

He brought his mouth down on hers, his hands wandering down her back to her buttocks. He pulled her against his body. "You see what you do to me? What you've always done to me?"

She felt the hardness of him against her and pressed herself closer. "Are you sure you have to go right now?"

He moved his hands back to her waist and with a supreme effort held her at arms' length. "Oh yes, I most definitely need to go now."

She looked at him and her heart flipped. He was handsome in his dark grey suit with a white shirt and pale grey tie. The perfect businessman.

"Right," he said, "I'm going. Are you sure you'll be okay?"

"Yes, I'm sure."

She walked to the door with him.

"If the phone rings..."

"Yes, I know, don't answer it, let it go to messages, unless the message is from you and then I can pick up."

"Good girl. I know it sounds a bit cloak and dagger but if the kids phone home..."

"I know, it could get awkward."

Gazing down at her upturned face, he felt guilty. She looked so trustingly at him. If only she knew where he was going the look could be so different. Pulling her toward him he kissed her long and hard on the lips. "There's something in the lounge that might help you pass the time," and with that he quickly turned and walked to the car.

Sarah stood in the open doorway watching until the car disappeared out of sight.

Chapter Nine

She turned and walked back into the house, locking the door behind her. Her curiosity aroused by his last comment, she went straight into the lounge and immediately saw the books on the table. The note was short, simply saying that they wouldn't keep her warm that night, but would help the time to pass. Picking up the books she saw they were photo albums, and each one was marked for a five yearly period. Opening the earliest album she curled up on one of the large sofas. Each album portrayed a period of Corey growing up and, as she started looking through the earliest album, she saw pictures of Corey and Jeff together. They gave her an insight into her son's life as he grew from the toddler she had known into the wonderful young man he now was.

Sarah couldn't stop the tears running down her cheeks. Corey riding his first pony and then his first day at school. His school photos over the years and birthdays and Christmases. His graduation from High School and then his University years. Pictures of him skiing with his dad and then with Laura. All of these events she had had no part of, but by leaving the albums for her to see Jeff had given her the greatest gift he possibly could, even though it broke her heart to see them. The one thing she did realise was there were no photos of them as a family, and the books only started at a time after she had left.

There were also no photos of Jeff's wife. The albums were simply marked, 'Corey,' so presumably that was the reason why he'd left them. Jeff wouldn't have given them to her if there were photos of his wife, it would have been too cruel.

It was dark by the time Sarah finally put the books down. Emotionally exhausted, she realised she had eaten virtually nothing since Jeff left. She wandered into the kitchen, thankful that the lights came on automatically at dusk. Having eaten she went to her room, pausing to look at the doors leading to the master bedroom before carrying on to her own room. She didn't want to see what was beyond the double doors, to see the room or bed he shared with his wife. If she didn't see what was in there she could pretend his wife didn't exist. Unable to face the shower room without him, she settled instead for a soak in the large bath. Coming back downstairs she heard the phone. Waiting until it went to messages she heard his voice.

Picking up the receiver she couldn't believe how hearing his voice affected her. Jeff then asked if she had enjoyed the surprise he had left for her. Sarah wanted to say so much to him about the photos but ended up babbling a few words in between tears.

"Hey, they were supposed to make you happy, not sad."

"No, I'm not sad, well yes I am, seeing all that I have missed. I knew I'd lost those years, but it was easier to push everything to the back of my mind and not think of it when I wasn't here."

"I guess so," he replied solemnly. "Look I just wanted to say that I was missing you but I'd better go as I have a busy day tomorrow before my flight. I'll see you later tomorrow night."

They ended the call with a simple, "bye," neither saying anything that gave a clue as to their feelings about one another. After the call, Sarah wandered about the house not able to settle before deciding to go to bed. All she kept thinking was the sooner she was asleep, the sooner it would be tomorrow and he would be back.

Leaving Sarah had been hard for Jeff, and the drive to the airport had seemed to take forever. He got caught up in the Calgary traffic, then construction works, and only just got to the airport in time for check in. His flight to Vancouver was on time and the short flight enabled him to try and relax. As he looked out of the small window, seeing the land below, he recalled his telephone conversation with Martin Bradshaw's P.A. earlier that morning and his annoyance that he wasn't going to be in that day. He did pressure her into arranging an appointment with him for the following morning. He had hoped to see him today so he could get an early flight back the following morning, but it now looked as though he was going to have to catch a late afternoon flight instead.

He liked Vancouver airport. It was vibrant and full of western culture, but today he barely noticed these things as he'd hurried through arrivals, before taking a cab to the downtown hotel where he was staying. Once in his room he had phoned Doug and managed to get some more information about Martin Bradshaw. From what Doug said the guy seemed honest and dependable. Jeff still couldn't see how he could have a connection with his late mother.

He ate a solitary dinner in the hotel, took an early shower, then lay on the bed flicking from channel to channel on the television before giving up and phoning Sarah, which left him feeling frustrated. With a sigh he threw back the covers and climbed underneath the sheet. He missed Sarah. The bed felt big and lonely.

He woke early the next morning, and after a quick shower dressed in his suit, intending to portray exactly what he was, a no-nonsense businessman. After a light breakfast in the hotel, the Concierge called a cab to take him to the offices of Martin Bradshaw, whom he hoped was going to finally give closure to the nightmare he was suddenly caught up in.

The offices were in the centre of downtown Vancouver situated in a large glass fronted building. He was met by the P.A. he had spoken to the day before and took the opportunity of apologising if he had seemed rude when they spoke. She led him along the corridor to Martin Bradshaw's office. After knocking, she opened the door, and stood aside so he could enter.

As the door closed behind him, Jeff found himself looking at the man who had risen from his desk, and was now walking across the room with his hand outstretched.

"Martin Bradshaw, Mr Saunders. How can I help you?"

Jeff shook his hand and they both walked to the desk. Sitting in front of this man, who appeared to be in his early sixties, Jeff was now trying to read his expression.

"That's what I'm here to find out, Mr Bradshaw," he said.

Meeting the younger man's steady gaze he asked, "What is it you want to know, and perhaps we can be a little less formal and dispense with the mister?"

"Certainly," said Jeff, "if it's going to get me the answers I want."

Martin sat back in his seat and looked at the young man before him waiting for him to speak again. He'd wondered over the years exactly when, and if, this day would come, but what Jeff told him depended on whether he was able to tell him everything. His client's instructions were quite clear and precise to him, even though she was no longer alive. While he may not agree with her instructions, he had no alternative but to follow them to the letter.

He listened to what Jeff was telling him about Corey's mother turning up, about the story she had told him, and of the fact that although he had been paying money to her regularly, she had never received any of that money. He went on to describe that his accountants had investigators track the account the money had been paid into, and how that trail had traced the money to an account originally in the joint names of his mother and Martin. Then, after her death, in his name alone. During the telling of this Martin sat listening intently not saying anything.

"What I want to know," said Jeff firmly, "is why this money was redirected into another account and not paid to Corey's mother, and what your involvement is with my mother and this account?"

Martin sat forward in his chair, linked his hands together, and began to speak.

"I was approached approximately eighteen years ago by your mother to act on her behalf in the handling of this account. You are right, the account was originally in our joint names but your mother left specific instructions regarding the transferring of the account into my sole name in the event of her death, and into the name of one of my partners, should I die before I was able to fulfil your mother's instructions fully." He paused, allowing the younger man to digest this information, before continuing.

"My instructions are to maintain the account until your son reaches the age of thirty years, provided no enquiries have been made about the account prior to that happening. On his thirtieth birthday the bulk of the account was to be transferred into his name and sent to him with instructions that it was a legacy from his grandmother and, for as long as the moneys were paid into the account after that event, I was to make further annual payments to him. If the moneys stopped, then after a period of six months, the account was to be closed and the balance of the moneys sent to him as a final payment."

Jeff was stunned by this revelation. "Do you know where the moneys came from?" he asked.

"Yes, they were transferred in from a holding account in the name of Mrs S. Saunders, who I took to be Mrs Sylvia Saunders."

Shaking his head in disbelief, Jeff asked the obvious question. "I am assuming that you didn't know those moneys originated from me, and were intended for my son's mother, Mrs Sarah Saunders?"

Martin sat upright in his chair. "No, I did not. Not until now. Your mother was an upstanding member of the business community, and I had met her in the past with your late father. I had no reason to suppose at the time that there was anything underhand, or wrong with the arrangement. Which clearly is what you are suggesting. I believed, until a few moments ago, that the moneys were hers, transferred from her own holding account."

"Mother was a very persuasive person when she wanted to be. Have you never had cause to question the arrangement regarding this account?" queried Jeff.

Shaking his head, Martin replied very precisely, and slowly, "Not with regard to the account."

"What do you mean?" asked Jeff sitting forward in his seat, and suddenly alert to something else he possibly didn't know about. "Is there more to this than just the account?"

"I can't really say. Even though your mother has died I am still bound by client confidentiality, and to the terms of the specific agreement between us."

Jeff was puzzled by this reply and began to wonder just how devious his mother had been. "Are you saying you cannot tell me everything about your relationship with my late mother?"

"Not necessarily," said Martin, hesitating slightly before he spoke. "I can only give you further information if you ask for it."

Jeff was even more puzzled. "You mean what you can or cannot tell me depends on what I ask you?"

A quick nod of the head confirmed this was the case.

"Can you at least give me a clue as to what I may, or may not already know, that will release this further information?"

Martin thought for a moment. Watching the young man trying to come to terms with what he'd just discovered he wanted to help him. He really wanted to tell this young man everything and, after what Jeff had already told him he knew he deserved to know the full story.

Pushing the boundaries of his instructions he said, "Look, Jeff, tell me everything that Corey's mom told you, and I mean everything, word for word and see where we go from there. From what you have already said when your wife left she deserted you and your young son and has ignored you both for years." Having emphasised the latter words, Martin waited.

Jeff shook his head. "So what you're saying is that any questions must be based on what I know, and what Sarah has already told me?" he asked as Martin again nodded.

Jeff tried to think of what else Sarah had said that would have some meaning. He went over their conversations in his head remembering the heated discussions in the first couple of days. He recalled shouting at her about not contacting Corey and remembered her saying she had, and that she had sent presents over the years. Was that the clue Martin had given him when he said ignoring them for years but according to Sarah, she hadn't. He looked at Martin and spoke slowly and clearly,

"The only other significant thing I can think of is that Sarah says she didn't ignore Corey and wrote to him regularly, but I know for a fact that he never received anything from her. Did my mother have something to do with this as well? Is that what you want to hear me say, or do I have to go over every conversation I have had with her?"

An incline of his head confirmed this was what he needed to hear and Martin felt a weight lift from his shoulders. The account had never bothered him over the years. There was no reason for it to, until now, but the other things that he had been holding had caused him concern. He had taken this up with Sylvia on more than one of her visits, but she had become extremely annoyed and reminded him of his contract with her, and that the things he was holding would cause extreme pain for a lot of people if they became public knowledge.

Her instructions regarding the account were clear if Jeff or anyone else made enquiries about it, but with regard to the other matters, they were to remain unknown unless specific reference was made to them. Then and only then was the letter from Sylvia to her son to be handed over which would explain everything. Martin figured that the fact that Jeff was aware that Corey's mother had been in contact with him over the years was sufficient for him to discharge this last instruction.

He looked at Jeff who was waiting expectantly for him to speak. He leaned forward and opened the top drawer of his desk and withdrew an envelope, handing it to him. He'd taken it from the vaults that morning in the hope that he would be able to hand it over, and now he was thankful for his forethought. "This hopefully might explain things."

Jeff looked at the envelope, his name on the front clearly in his mother's handwriting.

Martin stood up. "I'll leave you while you read it. I'll send in some coffee."

Jeff sat looking at the envelope not opening it until after the coffee had been brought in. Having taken a quick drink he slowly opened the envelope and pulled out the sheets of paper, recognising again his mother's handwriting. He started to read, pausing every now and again trying to comprehend and take in what she was saying.

She started by admitting that if he was reading this then he was aware of what she had done.

Darling

I hope that you can forgive me, I am sorry for the hurt I have caused you, but it was necessary to do these things to protect both you and Corey, and also the family name. I accept that perhaps I may have been wrong in telling Sarah what I did, and for going to England armed with signed divorce papers saying that you had sent them over. Believe me when I say I'm sorry for duping you into signing them, but it was the only thing I could think of at the time. When I found out her family were criminals, I couldn't let that be known, and I did what was necessary to protect my family, and particularly Corey. I couldn't let it become common knowledge that his mother was from a criminal background. Once I had done that there was no going back.

I was never in favour of your marriage, as you well know. She wasn't the type of girl for you, and I certainly wasn't in favour of you sending money to her. I offered to set up the accounts so I could divert the money back into an account for Corey to have later. I wanted Sarah to simply disappear, but I found her more difficult to deal with than I thought she would be. She insisted on maintaining some contact with Corey, and fearing that she may try and contact you or him in the future, I insisted that anything be sent to a Box number. Then it was easy for me to have things re-directed and stored away. What was the point of Corey receiving anything from her, from someone he would not remember? It would only upset him, better that he got nothing.

Jeff broke off from reading; he couldn't believe that his mother had been so cruel, although he was always aware of her fixation on the importance of the family name. But how she considered what she had done to be a necessary course of action was beyond him. He returned to the letter.

But, now you know what I did, and I only hope that you will forgive me. Move on with your life, forget her, she wasn't good enough for you.

Forgive me,

Your loving mother.

Jeff was stunned. Everything Sarah had told him was true and he didn't know how he was going to be able to face her or ask for her forgiveness. What a bloody mess, he thought, and how on earth was he going to explain all of this to Corey, because he would have to know.

Martin ventured back into his office, and seeing the young man with his head in his hands he felt guilty at his part in the whole affair.

Jeff, hearing the door close, turned to face Martin.

"What about the contents of this box number? Mother's letter says they were re-directed. Do you know where?"

"Yes, they were re-directed to me here and I have been keeping them in the strong rooms. I can have them brought up for you but it may take a while. Could I suggest that we re-convene after lunch, say about two, and deal with the outstanding matters?"

Jeff nodded and stood up. "I'll see you then."

He left the offices in a daze and walked down Robson Street toward Canada Place, stopping only to collect a coffee on the way. He needed some fresh air, and to clear his head before meeting up again with Martin. One thing was for certain, he wasn't going to be able to catch his flight home today. He needed to contact the airline and re-arrange his flight for the next morning.

Normally he would have enjoyed sitting and looking out across Burrard Inlet but today everything seemed to be surreal. The floatplanes took off and landed, the crews prepared the cruise ships ready to take on another batch of passengers, but none of this penetrated his thoughts. Taking his mother's letter out of his pocket he started to read it again, as if trying to convince himself it didn't say what it did. His mind was taking him back to the darkest time in his life; a place he had locked away years ago. A time he had tried to forget.

* * * *

When his mother had returned from England he'd expected Sarah to be with her. She'd given no indication she was returning alone. He'd been sleeping at the hospital at Corey's bedside and the doctors had just told him the next forty-eight hours would be critical. He had hoped that hearing his mommy's voice would be enough to pull their little boy through. When his mother had walked into the hospital room he had looked expectantly behind her for Sarah, but there was nobody there. He could remember looking at his mother who had just shaken her head. Even now he could remember the pain those words, "She wouldn't come." had inflicted on him. The feeling of utter helplessness for a situation he had no means of knowing how to control. He recalled how his mother had put her arms around him, telling him everything would be alright.

Needing to be on his own he'd left her at the hospital with Corey, while he returned home to shower and change. Walking into their apartment all he could see was Sarah everywhere, and he was so angry over the decision she had made. Her things were on the dresser top in the bedroom, just as she had left them, a rage he had never known before had risen inside him and he'd raised his arm and swiped everything off the top so they smashed onto the floor. After that he'd laid on their bed and, despite his twenty-five years, had cried like a baby until he had no tears left. At that point, he vowed never to let another person close enough to hurt him or Corey again. But now realisation washed over him. She hadn't hurt them, and she'd been hurting too. Alone, thousands of miles away from them, with no one, no one apart from Annie.

Pulling his mind back to the present he saw people walking about and thought it ironic that life went on as normal, even though his own seemed to be falling about his ears. He was angry with himself for accepting what his mother had told him all those years ago. Why didn't I have more faith in Sarah? They had been a strong team together, but alone his vulnerability must have become apparent to his mother. Juggling work with a toddler had been difficult but when Corey fell ill he had been so scared, and the only person there to help had been his mother. Now it was apparent she had clearly taken full advantage of the situation.

Persuading him to let her go to England to bring Sarah home must have been a triumph for her. She must have plotted all that she had done before she'd even left, without any thought of the consequences for Corey growing up without a mom, or for him believing his wife had deserted them both. His frustration and fear for Corey, and the now remembered whispered comments about Sarah's absence, had turned his love into anger then eventually hatred. No, hatred was the wrong word, he thought, for the moment he saw her again, he knew he had never stopped loving her, something that had been very difficult to come to terms with. How could he hate her when he clearly still loved her? He'd asked himself that question many times in the early days since their meeting and couldn't make any sense of it. Now it was different, he knew that she hadn't been to blame. Neither of us were, he told himself, we were pawns in a game played out by someone with no consideration whatsoever for anyone but herself, and the family name.

Now, knowing everything, he was angry. He should have realised that Sarah would never have left them. He'd been so gullible. Was his mother returning home, without saying Sarah wasn't with her, her warped way of turning him against Sarah? Letting him believe she was coming back, then watching as he crumbled before her eyes when he realised she wasn't. Allowing her to then manipulate matters to her own end.

It was strange now knowing what had happened, he could recall the way he'd been persuaded by his mother. Once Corey was on the mend he had wanted to go to England to see Sarah. His mother had been very sympathetic telling him there was no way of knowing where Sarah would be. Told him she had been planning on moving on, and maybe even going abroad. Then saying she hadn't wanted to hurt him any more by telling him that earlier. And all of the time she knew exactly where Sarah was.

He couldn't bear to think how Sarah must have felt when his mother turned up and then later presented her with papers for divorce. Telling her that she couldn't go back to her husband and child must have ripped her apart. No wonder she miscarried their baby.

Sitting in the sunshine with his head in his hands he attracted some concerned looks from passers-by.

Eventually pulling himself together, he looked at his watch. Time to go. Standing, he started to walk back toward the city centre, disposing of the coffee cup as he went.

Five minutes to two saw him heading into the reception area of Martin's offices. His P.A. was waiting and led him through to one of the conference rooms.

The room was light and airy, the large glass windows taking in a view toward the Harbour Tower, but Jeff's attention was drawn to the two large suitcases placed on top of the desk. There were keys next to them and, once he was on his own, Jeff opened the first case and then the second. They were full of what appeared to be cards, letters, and parcels all addressed to Corey. Looking at the date on them they went back to a time after Sarah had left, and none of them had been opened. He slumped down onto the chair as tears rolled down his face. How must Sarah have felt sending all of this and getting nothing back in reply, and how cruel was his mother to deprive Corey of his own mother's love?

He didn't know how long he sat there just staring at the contents of the cases before he heard the door open and Martin ask if he could come in. He nodded and quickly brushed the back of his hand across his face. If Martin saw the gesture he didn't comment. "Did you know what was in these?" Jeff didn't know why he asked the question, it had no relevance.

"No, but I had my suspicions."

"They were for my son, from his mother."

"I'm sorry," said Martin. "If I could have done anything about this sooner I would, but my instructions from your mother were very clear, even to the extent that if you hadn't mentioned that Sarah had told you she had written, I would not have been able to give you the letter or the contents of the cases."

"God, my mother was evil," said Jeff, bitterly.

Placing a hand on the young man's shoulder, Martin said, "No, I don't think so, just deluded into thinking that the action she was taking was right, and doing everything in her power to protect what was hers."

"Trouble was, it wasn't hers," replied Jeff angrily. "Corey belonged to Sarah and to me, and all those years ago Sarah and I belonged together. It was not my mother's right, or anyone else's, to tear my family apart."

Jeff was angry, but although he would have loved to have taken his anger out on the man standing in front of him, he knew he couldn't. His hands had been tied professionally, just as his mother had intended.

Standing up he looked at the older man. "Thank you, Martin, for what you have told me and for this," he waved his hand at the cases on the desk. "I need to take these with me. There is someone they belong to, and he's waited a long time for them."

Martin nodded his head. "I understand."

"I only hope that he does. What about the account and the moneys?" enquired Jeff.

"Well, since the moneys are technically yours, if your accountants can send me a copy of the investigators findings that should be sufficient for me to release the moneys to you."

"Fine, I'll get onto that when I get back. I've already put a stop on the moneys being paid out so there shouldn't be any more coming into the account."

He carefully put the few unopened packages he'd taken out back in the cases and locked both with the keys. Dropping the keys into his pocket he turned to Martin and held out his hand. "Thank you again."

"I'm only carrying out my client's instructions, Jeff, but sometimes they end up leaving a nasty taste in the mouth. Let me get reception to call you a cab."

Sitting in the cab on the way back to his hotel, Jeff realised he would have to phone Sarah to let her know he wouldn't be back today as planned, and he wasn't looking forward to that. In fact, he wasn't looking forward to his meeting with Sarah at all.

Chapter Ten

Sarah was eagerly looking forward to Jeff's return. Having roamed around the house and garden most of the day, not able to settle, she decided to surprise him with a home cooked meal. Although her culinary skills were not the best and the appliances unknown to her, she was sure she could manage a simple roast with vegetables.

The chicken she had discovered in the freezer was now defrosting. She peeled and prepared vegetables to roast in the oven later. A bottle of wine was in the fridge for them to share and for dessert, well she knew what she was hoping dessert would be, but there was plenty of frozen yoghurt and fresh fruit if they really needed it.

Wanting to look her best, she showered, washed her hair, then laid out the only skirt she had with her on the bed, thinking it would go well with her silky top with thin straps, and a pair of low sandals. She wished she had a nice dress to wear but she hadn't planned on any of this happening. Hadn't thought she would want to dress up for someone. She was just coming out of the bathroom when she heard the phone ringing. Although she ran quickly down the stairs, it was too late. By the time she reached it, the ringing had stopped. She listened to the message. Just a short message to say he had been delayed and wouldn't be able to get back tonight. Hoped she was okay and would see her tomorrow.

It wasn't just the brief message that caused her concern but the tone of his voice. She knew immediately something was wrong, and could only assume it had something to do with his wife. Was he with her now? Was she annoyed that she was still staying in their home, had she said she had to go? Or even worse, did she know they had slept together? Was that why he sounded so distant? Sarah was devastated. She had been longing for him to return. She wanted this stolen time together to last as long as possible. The sensible Sarah told her she was a fool, but the Sarah of eighteen years ago wanted to hold onto what she had found.

Wandering into the kitchen she looked at the ingredients for the meal she'd planned. The vegetables were bagged and placed into the fridge with the defrosted chicken. Suddenly, she wasn't hungry, just sad. Curling up on one of the sofas in the lounge, tears rolled down her cheeks as she hugged one of the large cushions.

It was dark outside when she was able to pull herself together sufficient to lock the doors and then climb the stairs to her room. She wished he had come home. Not only because she missed him, but the wind was getting very strong. The rain, which had started some time earlier, had turned to hail and was lashing against the windows. She was scared. Climbing into bed, she pulled the covers over her head to block out the noise and tried to sleep.

* * * *

Jeff hated leaving a message on the machine, but in a way he was relieved that Sarah hadn't picked up. He didn't feel that he could talk to her at present, he was too emotional. But he was also angry, not just with his mother, but with himself for being so gullible all those years ago. Also, he was angry with Sarah for having so little faith in him and believing what his mother said. But then they'd both been guilty of that, believing his mother. He, easily persuaded because of his worry over Corey, and Sarah, because of her grief. Both of them caught up in a situation they couldn't control, which made them vulnerable to the lies. And, because of his mother's lies three lives had been ripped apart and he wasn't sure what, if anything, he could salvage out of the present situation.

He wasn't sure how Sarah would react to what he had discovered. Nor, what her reaction would be when finally meeting his wife. But that was something that had to be done, and sooner rather than later. They had both been carried away over the last few days savouring each other's bodies as they used to years ago, but things had changed and were about to change even more.

Looking at the suitcases in his room he was tempted to open them now, but he needed to get something to eat. Picking up his jacket he ventured out, making his way to the hotel restaurant. He didn't feel like eating but he'd had nothing since breakfast. He ate a solitary meal oblivious to the admiring looks he attracted from the female diners.

Having eaten he returned to his room. Closing the door, he stripped off and pulled on the hotel bathrobe. Sitting on the floor with his back against the bed, he opened the first of the cases. As he had seen earlier it contained parcels and what appeared to be cards and little else. The second case seemed to contain the same but underneath everything there was a large brown envelope. Opening this, he pulled out the contents and, to his absolute horror, saw the divorce papers Sarah had referred to. There was his name citing for divorce from Sarah. Just looking at it made him feel sick. He read through the pages, which were mainly standard legal clauses, and the reason for divorce was given as separation for one year. There was a claim by him for full custody of Corey on the grounds that Sarah had deserted them. He couldn't believe it and there, at the foot of the page, was his own signature. Looking closely at it he knew it was his signature, just as his mother had said in her letter to him. Not only that, it had been witnessed by a member of staff, someone he realised Sarah would have known. No wonder his mother had been so convincing, Sarah would have had no reason to doubt that he had signed the papers.

With the papers was an envelope from England addressed to him and he recognised Sarah's writing. Before opening it he raided the mini bar and poured himself a large whisky. He had a feeling he was going to need it. Sitting back down he picked up the envelope, turned it over, then cursed when he realised that it had already been opened. He took out the single sheet of paper inside and began to read what Sarah had written to him, all those years ago. When he had finished he knew why his mother had hidden all of these things, and why he had never seen this letter from Sarah. No matter how many times his mother apologised for what she had done, and she had done that in her letter to him, he would never forgive her. But his biggest problem would be trying to explain all of this to Corey.

Sarah had never wanted to leave them, she wanted to come home. The letter to him was begging him to let her come back, if only for Corey's sake and saying how much she missed and loved them both. How his mother could have been so callous he would never understand. He was only glad she wasn't here to answer for what she'd done. Very carefully he folded the paper and put it back in the envelope, before getting up and placing it in the inside pocket of his jacket. The other items he put back in the cases and then locked them both, ready for the journey home tomorrow. He felt an emotional wreck. Walking into the bathroom, he threw off the bathrobe and jumped in the shower.

He hoped the water would wash away some of the pain he felt, but he was wrong, so he tried to drown some of it with the remainder of the whisky before falling into bed.

The next morning, he was awake before the early alarm call came through. He'd slept badly. Dressing quickly, he ordered a cab to the airport. Grabbing a coffee and sandwich he waited for the flight to be called. Why is it, he thought, when you want time to go slowly it speeds by at a ridiculous rate, but if you want to get somewhere quickly it drags its feet? Under any other circumstances he would have been impatient to get home, but this time he was dreading seeing Sarah, and had no idea what he was going to say to her. He'd played this wrong. Should have told her the truth instead of avoiding the issue. What a bloody mess, he uttered.

The flight landed early in Calgary. He waited impatiently with the trolley for the baggage to come through. Finally he was through security and pushing the trolley toward his parked car. He loaded the cases in the back with his holdall, paid the fees, and was finally out and heading toward the highway and home. It was evident that there had been a storm in the night, not only from the branches lying about, but from the reports on the radio. Damn, he had never thought about a storm. He should have told Sarah about the storm shutters. If he hadn't been so pre-occupied the night before he would normally have watched the weather channel and seen what was going to happen. God, he hoped she was alright.

As he turned into the drive, he was relieved to see there was no apparent damage to the house or gardens, so perhaps they had missed the worst of it, he hoped so.

Leaving the bags just inside the door he walked through the hallway toward the kitchen and the lounge. It was very quiet and there was no sign of

Sarah, for the moment he was thankful. He wanted to delay their meeting for as long as possible.

Going into his den he called Doug and put him in the picture as to what had happened in Vancouver, asking him to send copies of the investigator's findings to the lawyers so they could deal with the account closure, and also instructed him to have the monies from that account placed into an account in Sarah's name. He was undecided as to whether to tell Doug about his mother keeping all the packages meant for Corey but decided he deserved to know the truth. After they'd spoken he was glad he had told him. It would make things easier in the future him knowing the whole story.

Having finished the call and, after checking things were okay at the hotels, he made his way back into the kitchen. Dropping his jacket on one of the chairs he switched on the coffee machine before opening the doors to the patio and going outside. The air felt so fresh. He loved to smell it like this after a storm, as though everything bad had been washed away. He only wished this mess was capable of being washed away as easily. Going back into the kitchen he poured himself a mug of coffee then made his way back outside. He stood looking out across the garden and paddocks to the mountains. He had bought this land for him and Sarah and the house had been designed with her in mind, although he may not have fully realised it at the time. He never tired of the view; winter or summer the mountains were spectacular and they brought their own peace to him. He sighed; right now he needed that peace.

* * * *

Sarah stirred in her sleep and gradually opened her eyes. She'd been awake for most of the night listening to the storm outside. She'd been scared the wind or hailstones were going to smash the windows but eventually, in the early hours, the storm had eased. Even then she had found it difficult to sleep, worrying about Jeff's message. Propping herself up on one elbow she looked at the clock on the bedside. It said eleven-fifteen. No, she thought, it can't be that late. Throwing back the covers she jumped out of bed and ran toward the window.

Pulling back the drapes the sunlight flooded into the room. Peering outside, the brightness of the day told her it was that late. About to turn away, she saw Jeff standing outside looking out toward the mountains. Running back across the room she pulled on a bathrobe then ran as quickly as she could down the stairs. She reached the doors leading to the patio before coming to a halt, suddenly wary, remembering his tone last evening. He still had his back to her but then he turned slowly around.

She knew straight away that something was wrong. He looked different, his face was strained and the smile didn't quite make it to his eyes. She just wanted to run to him, have him hold her close, but the look on his face told her this was the last thing he wanted.

Neither of them spoke, until Sarah broke the silence. "Something's wrong, isn't it?"

Jeff nodded. "Yes, we need to talk."

This is it, she thought. He's going to tell me I have to go because his wife is coming back or, suddenly remembering the cases she had seen in the hall as she ran through, perhaps she's already back. Oh God, no.

"It's your wife, isn't it, she's back?"

"Yes," he said quietly, "my wife's in the house and I think it's time you met her."

"No," said Sarah, with a sob. "I can't. I won't." Then she turned and ran as fast as she could through the hall back up the stairs into the sanctuary of her bedroom, slamming the door behind her.

* * * *

Jeff watched her retreating back. He'd wanted nothing more than to take her in his arms, but he couldn't do that. It was time for Sarah to know the truth and finally meet his wife. He knew he had to follow. This needed to end. Needed to end now.

With a sigh he walked through the kitchen, pausing only to put his coffee mug on the table, then walked slowly up the stairs toward Sarah's room. Reaching the closed door he hesitated for a second, then took a deep breath and walked in.

She was sitting on the window seat, her knees drawn up under her chin and her arms wrapped defensively around them. She looked up as he opened the door. Had it not been for the seriousness of the situation he would have laughed at the defiant expression, but in reality his heart broke at the sight of the tears running down her face.

He walked across the room toward her. "Sarah, I'm sorry, but there are some things that need to be sorted, and this is one of them. I should have told you the truth about my wife long before now, and before things got complicated between us."

"So I'm a complication?"

"No, I didn't mean it like that."

"Well, whatever you meant, I'm not going to meet her. I don't care what you, or she says, it's not happening. I'm leaving."

With that she jumped up from the seat and ran past him heading toward the bathroom. He caught her before she disappeared inside. Holding onto her wrist he pulled her gently back and turned her to face him.

"Sarah, you can't run away, there's nowhere to run to. Now please, just trust me?"

"Why should I?" she demanded.

He longed to say, because I love you, but knew he couldn't, well not yet. "Because I'm asking you to."

She tried to pull away from him but he held her firmly.

Moving his hands to her shoulders he turned her around so she was looking at their reflections in the long mirror on the wall. She kept her eyes down but he whispered in her ear, "Look at me, Sarah, please."

She raised her eyes until they met his.

He spoke quietly, "Sarah, I want you to meet my wife."

She turned her head toward the door dreading what she would see but the door was closed. She looked back at his reflection and saw the serious and worried look on his face as he watched her.

"Where is she then?" she said defiantly.

"I'm looking at her," Jeff replied warily, his eyes never leaving hers.

Slowly he saw the realisation of what he had said dawning on her. Her eyes widened as the colour left her face and she became deathly white.

"Don't you pass out on me, Mrs Saunders," he said as he felt her body slump against his.

Calling her Mrs Saunders sent shivers down her spine but eventually she managed to find her voice. "You mean, I'm your wife?"

"Yes, we're still married, we have never been divorced." He waited for her reply.

"I don't understand, the divorce papers, and you kept referring to your wife."

"No, you mentioned my wife, asking if she was at home. Which of course she wasn't, as you were with me at the time. Everything you asked, or I said about my wife was correct, although I admit it was misleading. You thought we were divorced and, until I had sorted out this whole bloody mess, I didn't want to tell you different. When we slept together, I knew I should have come clean, and for that I'm sorry."

"But the woman I saw you with, the day before Corey's wedding."

This time Jeff was puzzled and frowned. "What woman, and where?"

"Small, dark haired, she came into the hotel lobby, and you put your arm around her."

Jeff thought back, and then smiled. "That's Laura's mom, Julie. We'd been finishing up some last minute preparations for the wedding. You thought she was my wife?"

"Yes."

"Oh, Sarah, sweetheart, you have been going down the wrong road. I thought you simply assumed I had re-married. If I'd known you had seen me with Julie, I would have told you the truth sooner. Anyway what were you doing at the hotel?"

"I'd been watching Corey from the coffee area. You almost bumped into me as you came in."

"Oh my God, Sarah, I had no idea."

"No, I know you didn't, but just because she wasn't... sorry, isn't your wife doesn't explain the divorce papers that you signed."

"No," said Jeff looking back at her reflection, "it doesn't, and those papers are part of a very long story that I need to tell you. I don't know how you are going to feel about anything once you hear what I have to say."

They were still married. She was still his wife, her world had just been turned upside down. Or had it just righted itself? Gathering her emotions, that felt as though they had been blasted into a million pieces, she looked back at him. "You can tell me what you want later, Mr Saunders. All that matters to me now is that we are here together, and I need to know whether the last week has meant the same to you as it has to me." She turned slowly around into his arms and anxiously waited for his reply.

"Actions always speak louder than words," he said huskily, as he swiftly lifted her off her feet and walked toward the door. Opening it with one hand he carried her along the passageway.

"Where are we going?"

"To the master bedroom, where else would I take my wife?"

Sarah flung her arms round his neck, kissing him long and hard.

"Let's reach the bed first, Sarah," he said as he quickly turned the handle and kicked the door open.

Sarah didn't take in anything about the room, her senses focussed solely on the pleasure his hands were bringing to her. The nightdress and robe were dispensed within seconds, followed by Jeff's clothes. Then they paused, stood looking at each other, taking in every detail of each other's body. She flirted with him, her eyes teasing, teeth gently nibbling on her bottom lip, until Jeff could wait no longer and pulled her toward the bed. The passion with which they made love was overwhelming.

They lay spent on the bed locked in each other's arms. For Sarah this was her destiny. Jeff had always been her soul mate, the only man she had ever loved. But what of him? Surely there had been others over the years? The jealous thought came suddenly to her. Made her breath catch.

"Have there been many women since I left?"

He leaned over her and looked into her eyes. "How can you ask me that after what has just happened between us?"

"I know, but I just need to know if there was anyone special."

"If it will keep you quiet, then the answer is no, there has never been anyone else, nor would there have been. If I had wanted anyone else I would have sought a divorce, but that was never on my agenda."

She smiled. "I'm glad."

"Okay, so what about you. You thought you were divorced, so there must have been other men?"

"No, none. I never wanted anyone else but you. Why do you think I gave in so easily to you when we first made love last week? I couldn't have stopped you if I had wanted to. I have always loved you, Jeff, even when I tried to hate you. Just because we were apart made no difference."

"I hate the idea that you hated me..."

"I said I only tried, but apparently not successfully," she interrupted, teasingly.

"Okay, Mrs Saunders, you can quit teasing now. I think it's time we tried out the shower in this room." With that, he pulled her to her feet and held her naked body against his. Looking down at her face he put his hand under her chin tilting it upwards. "Just for the record. I love you too, and always have. Even when I tried not to."

Bending his head, he pressed his lips on hers and gently parted them, moving his tongue inside her mouth. She quivered with anticipation. With one hand he lifted her off her feet and carried her through into the wet room. Her legs wrapped around him, as he slowly and tenderly proceeded to take them both on a journey of delight.

Later, as they sat on the patio sharing an early dinner, he decided that what he had to tell her could wait another day. He felt a coward for putting it off, but he was tired and didn't think he could cope with another emotional upheaval until he had had a decent night's sleep. Although that might be wishful thinking. They spent the evening curled up on the sofa while Sarah told him about the dinner she had planned for the previous evening, and then about the storm and how she'd been scared. He listened to her chatter, thinking how normal this felt. It was only the prick to his conscience, as he kept the conversation away from his trip, that told him otherwise.

Chasing Sarah off to the master bedroom saying he would only be a few minutes, Jeff carried the cases down to the basement and left them in the family room. That task done, he climbed the stairs and for the first time he felt a thrill as he opened the doors to the master bedroom. Sarah waiting for him in the king sized bed, a look of anticipation on her face, was something he had never thought to see. His clothes were gone in seconds and she laughed nervously as he jumped into the bed next to her. Noting the lack of a nightdress and the mischievous grin on her face he gathered her to him. The worries of tomorrow pushed firmly out of his thoughts.

Chapter Eleven

After breakfast, Jeff filled two mugs of coffee for them, but instead of sitting down Sarah watched as he walked toward the door. It was another typical early summer day, blue sky and sunshine.

He paused and looked at her. "I think what I need to tell you may be better told outside in the fresh air."

Breakfast had been somewhat strained. Now she could see the worried look in Jeff's eyes and was scared of what he was going to tell her. They had spent an idyllic time together over the last week or so, away from the real world.

Since finding out they were still married she had let her imagination run away with her, picturing them living here, together, as it always should have been. This was all she wanted, but now wasn't sure if that was what he wanted, despite his declaration of love. His eyes and his body were telling her one thing, that he wanted and desired her, and his lovemaking proved that over and over again. But for how long, she wondered, is this just a recapturing of the youth they lost, or something deeper and lasting? His preoccupation, plus the fact that he was up and dressed by the time she had woken, all gave her cause to worry. She had lost everything once, and now worried that what he was about to say would blow her imaginary world apart.

Setting the mugs down, Jeff pulled the seats round so they were facing each other. Resting his elbows on his knees started to speak.

"You need to know what I have found out, Sarah. There's no right or wrong way of telling you this so I'm just going to tell it as it happened, or at least as I have found out it happened."

He began by explaining how he had been sending money to her over the years, and finding out she hadn't received this he had had the account investigated.

Sarah listened in awe as he went on to tell her about his trip to Vancouver, why he went, and what he had found out. Then how his mother had manipulated their lives for some devious reason of her own.

"I can't believe how gullible I was, Sarah, to believe everything she told me at the time as to why you wouldn't come back. I knew nothing about your family until you told me. All I was told was that you didn't want to be tied down with a husband and baby, and wanted to enjoy your life while you were young. That going back had made you realise all you were missing."

"Why would you think that, Jeff? How could you believe that I would just walk out and abandon you both?" The bewilderment was clearly heard in her voice.

"I don't know. I honestly don't know. It was a very difficult time and all I can say in my defence is that I was missing my wife, our young son was dangerously ill and asking for his mommy, and I was scared out of my mind that we were going to lose him. When my mother told me you wouldn't come back I was devastated. But our son needed me and I was determined that I wasn't going to lose Corey as well, so I concentrated all of my waking hours on him. Once the danger was over I told myself that I would never let anyone hurt him again. I was angry, Sarah, angry with you for not coming home, for abandoning Corey when he was so ill."

"But I didn't know."

"I know now you didn't, but at the time I didn't know that. I was young and, yes, my pride was hurt that my wife had left me, so I buried all the feelings that I had and spent my time caring for Corey. Everything I have done over the years has been for him. To give him the stable life I wanted him to have. Although I realise now that I shouldn't have let my mother have such an influence on his life, and that worries me because he will have to be told what I have found out."

"Do you have to tell him, Jeff? Can't you leave things just as they are?"

"No, I can't. I've found out too much and a lot of it affects him, and you."

"Forget about me, I just want Corey to be happy."

"I know you do, so do I, but he grew up thinking that his mom didn't want to live with us, didn't love us, and he needs to know that his mom didn't desert him. He needs to know the truth, that she had always loved him and never stopped thinking of him. Which brings me to the suitcases you probably saw in the hall."

He then went on to tell her how they had been kept at the lawyer's office in Vancouver, and that he had brought them back with him. "You need to see them, Sarah." Taking her hand he led her down into the family room. She watched in silence as he lifted the keys from his pocket then knelt on the floor and opened both cases. Raising the lids he turned to her.

"I think you'll recognise these?" he said standing up.

Sarah cried out. The sight of the cards and parcels that she had lovingly wrapped over the years lying in the cases unopened was too much. She knelt down picking up a small package and stroked it tenderly. "Why?"

She turned to look up at him, her eyes brimming with tears that started to slowly run down her cheeks. Jeff moved quickly to take her in his arms but she held up her hand, shaking her head. He stood still, saddened at the rejection.

"I am so sorry, Sarah, I had no idea, and if you hadn't told me that you had been in contact with Corey this way, I would never have known they existed."

"What do you mean?" she asked quietly.

Hearing of his mother's instructions about the cases Sarah couldn't believe the extent of the hatred this woman must have felt toward her.

"There's something else I need to show you."

Jeff moved toward the cabinet against the side wall, opened one of the drawers and pulled out the divorce papers. He handed them to Sarah.

"I think you might have seen these before."

Sarah looked at the papers and the signatures. "You kept them all these years and did nothing with them?"

"No, Sarah, I didn't keep them. I'd never seen them until a few days ago. They were in one of the cases with everything else. I never signed them, well apparently I did, but not intentionally. Mother was always putting various papers in front of me to sign relating to the business and it would seem that's what she did with these, making sure I never saw what I was actually signing. Any member of staff would then simply witness my signature without question. Mother was clever though, she had them witnessed by someone whose name you would recognise, thus making the document seem genuine."

Sarah was stunned by the extent of her late mother-in-law's scheming and her head was spinning. "She must have planned this before she even left for England?" She used my trip to tear our family apart. It felt like something out of a nightmare, but the frightening thing was, it was real.

He nodded. "I'm finding some of the things she has done unbelievable, but you never expect your own mother to hurt you. She's supposed to look after you and protect you. There is something else I want you to see," he said, pulling the letter from his mother out of the drawer. He handed the envelope to her.

"It's addressed to you," she queried.

"I know, but I need and want you to read it so that you understand that none of this was my doing. I'll be upstairs when you've finished. There's no rush, so just take your time."

He waited outside for Sarah to come and join him but she didn't. Eventually he went back into the house and ventured down to the family room. She was sitting where he had left her. The letter he had given to her was lying open on the floor and she was gently picking up parcels from the cases, then carefully putting them in some sort of order on the floor. He didn't feel able to intrude so quietly went back upstairs and headed for his den.

It was dark when he finally made his way into the kitchen and discovered Sarah methodically preparing a salad. Taking her actions as a cue, he fired up the barbeque and put some chicken on to cook. They sat in virtual silence as they ate and afterwards Sarah took her coffee upstairs. Watching her go up the staircase he was sad to see her turn and go to her old room. Lying in the large bed on his own later he acknowledged to himself how scared he was of losing her again. He had no wish to put any pressure on her. The last thing he wanted to do was ruin what they had recently found together. His mother had torn his family apart once and he was determined that she wouldn't do it again. He intended to fight to keep his family, and only hoped that patience would be the key to holding them together.

Over the next few days they fell into a routine of Jeff going to the hotel while Sarah spent her time walking in the garden and putting the contents of the cases into a yearly order. Each year's parcels and cards were tied together with some ribbon she had found until they were all in order. Very carefully she placed them back in the cases. It wasn't for her to open them, they belonged to Corey. Perhaps someday he might open them and see how much she had missed and loved him.

She had cried so much as she carried out this task she felt an emotional wreck. All she wanted to do each night was to sleep, but even that evaded her. All she could think when she closed her eyes was how the little money she had managed to save had been spent on carefully chosen presents for Corey. How she had imagined his little face when he opened them, saw they were from his mommy. But he had never got the chance to do that. These thoughts, and the words in Sylvia's letter to Jeff, kept playing over and over again in her head until eventually she would fall into an exhausted sleep in the early hours. By the time she got up Jeff had already left for work so the only time they saw each other was in the evening. Dinner had become an automatic affair neither saying anything of real meaning. Just small talk about how each other's day had been, then Sarah would go to her room and sit in silence, trying to work everything out in her head.

By the end of the week the atmosphere in the house was strained, and Jeff felt as though he was walking on eggshells. He was afraid to say anything to Sarah relating to his mother in case she decided to leave, so he took the only course of action he could and tried to keep out of her way as much as possible. Having put in long hours at the hotel all week he desperately needed a weekend break, but this meant being at home all day, and he wasn't sure how Sarah would feel about this.

On the Friday evening, just as Sarah was about to go upstairs, he broached the subject. "I'm not working this weekend; so I'll be at home. If that's okay with you?"

She nodded. "That's fine," but her eyes barely met his.

Waking early on the Saturday morning, Sarah lay in bed staring at the ceiling. She had finally given up trying to work out why Sylvia had done what she had. For the first time, since Jeff had told her the whole story, she was able to see how all of this would have affected him. She tried to imagine how he must have felt; struggling to look after a sick child, and then being told his wife didn't want him or their son. She'd had her own kind of hell but so had he, and he'd coped with it and raised their son. She knew he'd been keeping his distance over the past week, for which she was grateful. She had needed time to come to terms with all she'd been told. It wasn't something that could be brushed aside, while they got on with life. And what of their relationship, did they have one? Did he want one, or was this the end? Remembering his words the previous evening, asking if she was okay with him staying in his own home, she felt guilty that he even had to ask the question.

She decided today was the day she needed to pull herself together. She had grieved enough for the lost years of her son, and her husband. If she continued down this path she could lose what they had found, and she had come to one conclusion; she wasn't going to let the events of the past ruin what could be a future. If that happened then Sylvia had won, and Sarah was determined not to let her win again. This was her family, she was unable to do it before, but now she was prepared to fight for it. She needed to put this right. Today was going to be the start of a new beginning; whatever and wherever that might be, and her fighting spirit was ready to take charge.

Throwing back the covers she walked across the room and sat on the window seat looking out across to the mountains. Lowering her eyes to the garden she saw Jeff sitting at the table, his head rested in his hands. Her heart went out to him. He looked so lonely. How could she not have seen what this was doing to him? Running to the bathroom she quickly showered. Pulling on shorts and a top she made her way downstairs, walking slowly down the stairs thinking of how she could start to put things right.

He was still outside but standing on the lawn looking across to the woods. She walked toward him feeling the grass under her bare feet. She spoke his name softy. He slowly turned around, noticing the pain in his eyes her heart ached for him.

"I'm sorry, Jeff. I just needed time to try and work things out in my head. I've had so many years of believing one thing, and then to be told it was all a lie it was too much to cope with. I didn't mean to shut you out, but it was something I had to do on my own, in my own way."

He nodded. "I understand, Sarah. I've had a hard enough time coming to terms with it so I can't begin to imagine what it's been like for you. Have you managed to make some sense of it all?"

"Not really, apart from the fact that your mother must have really hated me."

"I don't think she hated you, Sarah. I think she simply couldn't let go of what she thought was hers, and was prepared to do anything in her power to protect her family. I suspect she would have done exactly the same with anyone else I'd married, if they didn't meet her expectations. But that wasn't her decision to make. It's strange how a situation makes you remember things, but I can recall my dad once saying to me not to let my mother have too much control over my life. I didn't really think much of it at the time, but now I know what he meant. Then, of course, after my dad died, although we were co-owners, I was pretty much reliant on her until I was able to take over the day-to-day running of the hotels.

"So I guess, when we married, she saw her control slipping away. I can't forgive her for what she did, and I don't expect you to either. All we can do is try and move forward, but what worries me is how Corey is going to understand it. He was very close to his grandmother and I realise now that I allowed her to have far too big an influence on him over the years. But that's a problem that will have to be faced another day, after he and Laura are back from honeymoon. What is important now, Sarah, is where does this leave us?"

Looking at his worried face as he waited for her reply, Sarah knew that she wanted to be nowhere else but here, with him. She hoped he felt the same. Taking a deep breath she replied, "It leaves us wherever you want us to be."

"You know what I want. I thought I'd made it clear. You're my wife, you always have been, and I want you in my life, in my home, and in my bed. I've spent a lot of years trying to hate you for what I thought you had done, but the moment I saw you I knew that my feelings hadn't changed and that I had never really stopped loving you."

His gaze never left her face as he waited for her response, then when she smiled she saw the tension leave his body. They both moved toward each other and he held her in his arms, telling her he would never let her go again. For Sarah this was the dream that for years she had felt was beyond her reach.

Later nestled in his arms on one of the loungers, she knew that there was still one thing between them that she needed to tell him. "Jeff."

"Mmmm," he replied, not opening his eyes.

"There's something else I need to tell you, one part of my story that I left out because it was too painful to talk about."

His eyes slowly opened, he knew what she was going to say but waited for her to tell him.

"A few days after your mother had been to see me for the last time, when she got me to sign the papers, I was ill. Well, not really ill, and it was another reason why I didn't feel able to contact you as I felt I had let you down." She sat up and stared ahead. "I lost our baby. I had been so wrapped up in worrying about my mum that I hadn't realised I was pregnant. The doctor told me I was about four months but he couldn't tell me what had caused the miscarriage. It could have been the worry and stress, but I felt as though I had failed you. Not only had I left you and Corey but I had probably endangered the life of our baby, and it had died."

Jeff said nothing but sat up and put his arms around her. "I know, my darling, and I wish that I had known at the time so I could have been with you."

Sarah didn't understand what he was saying. "No, you didn't know."

"No, I didn't know at the time, but I found out recently," he said quietly, realising that he was going to have to own up to the phone conversation with Annie.

"How, from whom?"

"From Annie, and before you ask how I managed to speak to Annie, I have a confession to make."

Sarah listened in silence as he told her of how he got Annie's number and then spoke to her and that Annie had read the riot act to him for what he had done. Despite the serious conversation that made her giggle, it was typical of Annie to defend her.

"I'm sorry, but Annie let it slip, she thought you had already told me but I persuaded her to keep our conversation from you as I needed to find out first of all what had really happened. I told her that you would tell me about the baby in your own time when you were ready; and you have. I like Annie and I'm glad that she was there for you. I'm so sorry, my darling, that you had to go through a miscarriage on your own. If I had known I would have done everything I could to have been with you. You must know that?"

"Yes, I do now, but back then it was all such a nightmare."

"Well that nightmare has ended and this is a new beginning for us. However, there is one other thing that was with the cases, and that was a letter from you to me."

Sarah remembered the letter well. She had poured her heart out to him, begging him to let her come home. Then she had waited hopefully, for days, then weeks and finally months, but had never received any reply.

"I'm afraid mother had opened it and I only saw it for the first time when I was in Vancouver. If I had seen that letter, my darling, I would have been on the first flight I could get to bring you back home. Nothing to do with your family would have stopped me from loving you, or bringing you home."

She nodded slowly. "I know that now, but I don't want to dwell on the past any more, it's too painful thinking of all that we have missed out on. I want to look forward to the future."

Settling back in his arms she was content to stay there forever, but that wasn't to be as the first splashes of rain started to fall causing them to make a dash indoors.

Watching the rain running down the windows Sarah couldn't believe that she was going to stay here. Jeff had disappeared into his den to make a couple of calls, so she wandered into the lounge. Looking around the room, she wanting to pinch herself. This was now her home. Well as mistress of the house she supposed that she should think about feeding her husband. Just thinking that gave her a thrill. By the time Jeff came through, dinner was well under way, a beef roast with lots of vegetables. Opening the fridge he pulled out a bottle of champagne and, lifting down two flute glasses, he carefully popped the cork. Then they shared a toast to their future.

After a relaxed dinner, they sat and talked properly, talked openly and without any secrets left between them. Later, as they climbed the staircase, Sarah made to go to her old room but he caught her wrist.

"Whoa, where are you going?"

She smiled seductively at him. "To get my night things."

"That would be a complete waste of time, Mrs Saunders." And with that he caught her hand and pulled her along the passageway, pausing only to open the door to the master bedroom. A few seconds was all it took to dispose of clothes before they both lay naked in each other's arms. She stretched her arms up around his neck and pulled him down until his lips met hers.

His mouth moved slowly over hers, while his tongue parted her lips and moved seductively around her own. His lips left hers, tracing their way down to her breasts, caressing them before his teeth nibbled gently on her nipples bringing them to a peak of arousal. All the time his hands roamed freely over her stomach feeling the softness of her skin, before moving between her legs and gently parting them. His palm pressed on her pubic bone while his fingers slipped between her legs. He could feel how aroused she was. Slipping a finger inside, she was so ready for him, and he gently moved his finger, gliding through the wetness of her arousal.

Not wanting him to have all the fun, she moved her hands down and took hold of him, gently closing her hands around the length of his hardness then started moving her hands slowly up and down, bringing him close to surrender. He was about to lose control and asked, no, begged her to stop, until reluctantly she gave in to him. Being so close, his own exploration of her body had ceased.

"Sarah, my darling, I'm sorry, I can't wait."

Moving over her, his weight was taken on one elbow as he lifted her and eased inside. Holding himself above her he pushed gently at first then, feeling her mounting arousal, pushed deeper and deeper inside until she burst around him taking him with her as they both fell apart, with Sarah crying out his name as the convulsions tore through her body.

Lying contentedly in his arms she was brought back to the present by Jeff brushing her hair away from her face.

"Well, my little wanton wife, I hope that this is the way things are going to be from now on."

"Only if you want them to be," she replied mischievously.

"Oh, I certainly do, and I would be very happy to have a repeat performance. But, reluctantly, I think we both need some well deserved sleep because I have had very little of that this past week, and neither I suspect have you."

Nodding, she snuggled down in his arms.

Next morning, Sarah awoke to find herself still wrapped in Jeff's arms. The events of the previous day came flooding back. She watched his face as he slept and thought how peaceful he looked. The strained lines that she had seen on his face over the past week had gone, wiped away by the open conversations they had shared. She felt so happy, but there was one thing she had to do, and that was to phone Annie and tell her what had happened. Her mind started whirling with thoughts. She would also need to ask Annie if she would give notice on her flat, and sell her car for her. There was no doubt in her mind that Annie would do this. Just as she was certain she would pack up her few belongings and send them out to her. Not returning to England meant she wouldn't see Annie again, well not for some time, and that made her sad. But Annie would be happy for her. Only Annie knew the tears she had shed over the years and the pain she'd felt at being away from the people she loved.

Jeff stirred, and she waited, watching his face until his eyes slowly opened. When he saw her, his face broke into a smile.

"So I didn't dream yesterday then?"

"If you did then so did I," she said, freeing her arms and putting them up to his face. "I do love you, Mr Saunders."

"Just as well," he replied, "otherwise we would have a real problem, especially in view of what I have in mind."

Feeling his arms move round her body she gave herself up willingly, hardly able to contain her longing for what was to come.

After a leisurely breakfast, which was closer to lunch, they again took a drive out into Kananaskis country. Having no desire to do anything energetic they simply drove along some of the side roads playing at being tourists, and looking out for wildlife. Stopping off for dinner in a small town restaurant, Jeff wished he could take Sarah into the smarter restaurants in Banff or Canmore, but they would have to keep a low profile until after he had been able to speak to Corey. As he looked at Sarah's happy face he realised that it didn't really matter where they were as long as they were together. Later that night they made love slowly and gently, before falling into an exhausted sleep.

Chapter Twelve

If anyone at the hotels noticed anything different with him from that Monday nobody made any comment. And if they had he would have fielded any remarks. He was too happy to have his mood ruined.

By the middle of the week, things were running smoothly enough for them to do without him for a few days. Having made the decision he called into Mountain View and told Tom he was going to the Lodge for a few days. At least this meant he was within calling back distance if there were any problems, and it would give him and Sarah a break away from the house. Driving home, he stopped off to pick up some provisions, enough to keep them going for a couple of days.

Sarah was surprised but not disappointed to see him back early. While she loved the house not being able to get out and about was beginning to frustrate her.

"You're early?"

"Yes, I made an executive decision this afternoon," he said as he released her. "We need to have a break, away from the house. So I thought we could risk going to the lodge for a few days, and anyway, it's about time you saw your second home."

"The lodge, second home?" queried Sarah.

"Yes, it's a lodge, or rather a town house I bought when Corey was in his early teens, and somewhere we could spend some quality father and son time without interruption. Corey was into skiing by then so it seemed a perfect choice. Hiking in the summer and skiing in the winter. It's out near Radium Hot Springs, so being only ninety minutes away I can get back quickly if there are problems at work."

"That sounds wonderful, when are we leaving?"

"First thing in the morning, if that's okay?" The sparkle in her eyes gave him the answer before she spoke.

"Perfect," she replied excitedly. "Do you want me to go pack my case?"

"No, but you can pack our case. No reason why we can't share a case like a normal couple if that's okay with you?"

The reference to them as a couple sent a tingle down her spine. "Sounds perfect to me."

"Good. I'll go and get one from the basement," he called, disappearing down the stairs, "and then you can get started."

Waiting patiently for him, she could hardly contain her excitement. They were going away together. Spending a few days away from the house, just like a normal couple. The thought gave her goose bumps. But she was conscious there were practical things to do when they got back. Things she'd been putting off, like phoning Annie. She'd put it off because she was scared something would go wrong, but they'd slipped effortlessly back into being a couple again,

She woke up early, excited for the day to start, and feeling more like a teenager than a grown up woman. Jeff was still asleep so she slipped quietly out of bed and tiptoed across to the window seat. Drawing back the drapes enough to see the view she sat watching as the sun rose and began to shine on the mountains. Every now and again she would look back toward the bed, willing Jeff to wake up, but still he slept on. Eventually, she couldn't wait any longer and quickly moved to the bed. Taking hold of the covers she was about to pull them, when her wrist was caught in a firm grip and she was pulled onto the bed.

"Good morning, Mrs Saunders," said a lazy voice, "I hope you weren't thinking of doing something drastic to get me out of bed?"

Sarah loved it when he teased her and called her Mrs Saunders. She started to laugh, in fact, she was so happy that she couldn't stop laughing as Jeff pulled her fully onto the bed so she lay on top of him.

He lay looking at her, a bemused look on his face. "Care to share the joke?"

"There isn't one. I'm just so happy."

"Okay, let's keep this happy mood going." With that he swiftly turned so she rolled off him and onto the empty side of the bed.

Waiting for him to lean across to her, she was surprised when he threw the covers back and leaped out of bed. As he looked back she knew he would see in her eyes what she had been expecting to happen.

"Not now, Mrs Saunders, lots to do and places to go."

Propping herself up she watched as he walked to the bathroom, taking in the full length of his tanned, naked body.

"If you've finished taking in the sights you can always join me in the shower."

Sarah didn't need asking twice. Jumping off the bed, she ran after him, laughing, shedding her nightdress as she did. He caught her in his arms and carried her into the wet room, turning on the shower.

Later than planned, they loaded the car but before driving to the highway Jeff said, "There's something I want to show you."

"What is it?"

"Wait and see."

Driving into Banff, he drove along Muskrat Street, turned into Deer Street then back along Antelope Lane before turning and coming out on Banff Avenue.

"We're going back the way we came," said Sarah, puzzled.

"Yes, I know, but I want you to see this before we leave. You've seen the old Mountain View hotel but I want you to see this one."

Pulling into the right he stopped the car in front of what appeared to be a fairly new hotel, which was constructed of wood and glass. Sarah looked at the sign 'Saunders on Banff.' She didn't know what to say as her gaze came to rest on the glass windows and doors that were etched with figures of the animals that roamed the countryside. The larger animals, bear, elk and moose were depicted on the glass entrance doors and the smaller animals, wolf, beaver and ground squirrels on the windows. She remembered how they had talked years ago about somehow showing off the wildlife in the hotel, to bring home to tourists the diversity of the wildlife in the area, but she never imagined how beautiful it would look in reality.

"Oh, Jeff, this is wonderful."

"I know, my wife had the idea years ago and I thought it was too good not to make it a reality. I'm only sorry that we can't get out, but you will be able to see it properly soon, I promise. I just wanted you to see it today. To show you what I had built up for our family, and our son."

Checking the traffic, he pulled away from the curb. He didn't want to stay any longer in case any of the staff recognised the car. Although they could see out nobody was able to clearly see in through the darkened windows, which was why he had risked pulling over.

"When did you buy it?"

"About eight years ago. It was the old Highway Inn, but it was in such a bad state it was easier to knock it down and build a new hotel in its place. Mother wasn't keen at the time until I pointed out that Mountain View will eventually have to be replaced and building a new hotel would keep the name of Saunders on Banff Avenue until that could be rebuilt. Then, when it is rebuilt, Corey will run that after Tom has retired. Eventually, she recognised the common sense of it so we built Saunders on Banff. We also have a sister hotel in Canmore which is run by a very competent manager called Steve Barrett. Sometimes Corey would go over there, although he was more eager to do that before he was married, as Laura's family moved to Canmore a few years ago. Now, I suspect he will want to stay in Banff since their apartment is here."

"Not the apartment we used to have?" asked Sarah.

"Yes, the same, although it's been modernised over the years. Corey doesn't remember much about living there as we moved in with my mother and then I built the present house."

"I'm glad he's living there. I was so happy in the apartment. It was our first home together." Her voice threatened to break as she remembered the fun times they had before Corey was born, and even better times after.

"Hey, no sadness. We're looking to the future, and that future starts right here and now," he said, squeezing her hand.

They chatted while covering the miles between Banff and Radium. But she couldn't forget the new hotel, nor how hard he must have worked while, at the same time, bringing up their son. If only. No, she told herself, there would be no recriminations. Pulling her thoughts back to the present she concentrated on the views. She had been to Radium many times before and could remember some of the scenery. She loved the way the road passed alongside the public hot springs before narrowing between the rock walls of the canyon, then passing on through the Park entrance before going down to the town site itself. As they came into the centre she was amazed at how little the town appeared to have changed. Oh, there were new properties on the ridge but the structure of the town site looked the same to her.

"It doesn't look any different," she said. "Well, apart from some new housing."

"No, very little changes in the town site. But there have been a lot of changes outside the town. New holiday complexes but they have to adhere to strict rules in the National Parks."

They turned at the junction, turning left before travelling along a minor road toward a development of town houses. Judging by the weathered wood they had been here for some time. She couldn't see the front as the road ran at the back of the properties. Jeff pulled up outside an end town house, pressed a control inside the car and the garage opened. Driving the car straight in he stopped and switched off the engine.

"Well, here we are. It's easier to take everything in from the garage, plus it doesn't pay to leave the car out in view of the bears roaming around."

Sarah decided to ignore the reference to bears and climbed out of the passenger seat then started to lift some of the boxes out of the back, while Jeff unlocked and opened the door leading from the garage into the house. Turning back to the car he took the boxes from her.

"Here, let me do that. You go in and explore."

Sarah didn't need telling twice. She handed the box to him, went through the door and ran up the stairs. At the top she opened the door and found herself in a large room with a kitchen area at one end and a dining table at the other. The floors and walls throughout were of wood. Walking into the dining area she noticed the windows overlooked the valley and, at the side, was a door that led out onto a deck complete with table, chairs and a barbeque. Leading from the room was a staircase that took her up to the next level, and another large room. This was clearly the lounge area with large picture windows, again overlooking the valley, and with a slate fireplace against one wall. As with the lower level, the floor was wood but with two large rugs covering part of the floor. Two huge cosy sofas were set near to the fireplace with a television nearby, and a third sofa was positioned where you could see the view from the window. There was a door in the corner opening out onto another deck. The far end of the room was fitted with units containing books and DVD's, plenty to while away the winter evenings she thought. At that end of the room was another staircase and Sarah found this led up to a third floor containing two large bedrooms, each with its own en-suite.

One bedroom was clearly the master and, as she walked inside, saw it looked out across the valley toward the mountains. She could clearly see the ski runs where Jeff and Corey would have spent many an hour over the years. How she wished she could have shared those years with them. There were also double doors leading out onto a small deck, where Sarah could imagine them sitting and watching the sun set over the mountains. She was so engrossed in looking at the view that she didn't hear Jeff enter the room.

"Does this meet with your approval, darling?"

Turning, she looked at him. "As long as I'm with you everything has my approval, but yes, it's wonderful. I'm so glad that you brought me here. This view is breath-taking." She turned back to look out of the window.

"Good," he said coming up behind her and, slipping his arms around her waist, gently dropped a kiss on the top of her head. They stood there for some time, their bodies relaxed, enjoying being together and away from the recent problems.

Sometime later, when they had put away the provisions and made up the bed, Jeff took her for a walk around the small complex. The units were occupied by tourists and none of the actual owners were on site, which was why he had taken the risk of coming here. Although he could have passed Sarah off as a friend, anyone with a scrap of common sense would see they were more than that.

As they walked, he explained to Sarah how the complex had grown over the years and now housed about two hundred and fifty units in total, the majority of which were bought as letting investments. "That was never an option for me. I bought the property as a second home for me and Corey. It was our escape from everyday life, and gave us quality time together."

"I'm glad that you were able to do things together. So often in England I would see children just roaming about the streets, and I used to wonder where their parents were. I would have spent all my spare time with my children, teaching them about life, and well...you know, just doing things together as a family."

Hearing the wistful note in her voice, he pulled her close. "Well, you can catch up on all of that when Corey and Laura get back. But for now, enough of melancholy. We're here to enjoy ourselves and to relax."

It was late in the afternoon when they walked back to the house and started to put together the makings of dinner. The cooker was modern, as opposed to the rustic old feel of the rest of the kitchen, and had a separate griddle at the side. Sarah made a simple green salad and put a couple of potatoes in the oven to bake. She left Jeff in charge of the steaks and went upstairs to the lounge. Selecting a book from the shelves she curled up on one of the sofas.

She was still there when Jeff came up, but not reading. The book had fallen from her hand and was lying on the floor and she was fast asleep. Jeff hated to wake her but knew that he must. Crouching down in front of the sofa he brushed the hair back from her face, leaned forward, and kissed her on the cheek. She didn't stir, so he leaned forward again but her head moved and the kiss landed on her lips.

She opened her eyes and smiled. "Hi."

"Hi, to you. Dinner is ready if you feel you can stir yourself."

"Of course I can, I'm starving."

He held out his hand and pulled her to her feet holding her close for a second. "Come on, wife, you're not the only one who's starving, and I don't just mean for food."

She followed him down to the dining area where they sat enjoying their dinner while watching the sun set behind the mountains. After dinner, they took coffee up to the lounge and Jeff turned on the gas fire.

"I'd forgotten how chilly it can get in the mountains at night," said Sarah.

Jeff smiled as he sat next to her on the sofa, then pulled her into his arms. He made no attempt to kiss her, but just held her close. He still couldn't believe all that had happened over the last few weeks. That Sarah was back here with him and they were together again was like a dream, but he was still scared that it could all turn out to be a dream. He knew the problem he was going to face with Corey, although he didn't think Sarah had any idea of the impact this revelation was going to have on him. For now all he wanted was to push those thoughts out of his mind; and concentrate on the here and now. Holding her made it all real.

Eventually, they had to move. Standing, he turned off the fire and, stretching out his hand, helped her to her feet. With their arms wrapped around each other they climbed the staircase to the bedroom.

Sarah was surprised at how warm the room was but then noticed the gas fire. Jeff must have put it on earlier. She was touched by his thoughtfulness. They didn't bother to put a light on since the moonlight was enough and more romantic, plus there was the additional light from the fire. Jeff pulled his shirt out of the jeans but before he could do anything else Sarah moved toward him and started to undo the buttons. Slipping this off, she then proceeded to undo his belt and then his pants. She'd done this many times in the past, but she'd been a lot younger. Now, although she felt she belonged with Jeff, there was part of her that was a stranger to the life she now found herself in. It was as if she was feeling her way through. Trying to find the Sarah that was.

Jeff made no attempt to stop her and stood watching while she completed her task and he was completely naked.

"Well thank you, Sarah. I guess I'll get into bed now."

Sarah put her hands on her hips and pouted. "Well if you want to, you can, or…"

With a laugh he reached forward and very quickly stripped off her clothes then led her to the bed. They made love slowly before falling into a contented sleep. He woke her in the night, kissing her until she responded, before taking her again with a passion that only two people in love could share.

Waking early next morning, Sarah lay content in his arms until he stirred before turning and kissing her on the nose.

"What do you feel like doing today?" he asked.

"I don't know. I'm happy just to lie here and look at the view through the window."

"Well I'm happy to lie here and look at the view next to me."

Sarah turned to look at him and saw his eyes looking down. Following his gaze, she noticed that the sheet had slipped exposing a soft pink breast. She moved to pull the sheet back up but he stopped her. Lowering his head he started to kiss the exposed part while his hands roamed over her naked body. Beneath the sheet his hands found the soft silky part of her before moving between her legs and gently inside her. She gasped when he entered her and looked at him wide eyed. His mouth moved to hers and he rolled over on top of her. His hand withdrew and the hardness of him slowly entered. No words were needed. Her body arched up to his while his hands slipped under her buttocks, pulling her upwards to him. He moved slowly at first and then with an urgency that took them both to the heights of delight.

Much later they shared a breakfast of ham and eggs before wandering down to the commercial part of the complex. There were various shops and Jeff headed in the direction of one of the mountain clothing shops.

"We need to get you some decent walking shoes and also a warmer jacket," he said as they entered the store.

Sarah longed to say that it was more under-clothing that she needed, but there didn't seem to be any of that type of shop. Following Jeff into the store she saw him picking up various jackets and marvelled again at the way they had become a couple so easily. Holding up a mid-blue waterproof jacket he called her over. Sarah slipped it on over her fleece and found it fit perfectly. Before she knew what was happening they were leaving the store with the jacket, a body warmer, a pair of jeans, shorts, walking boots, some new sneakers and a blue checked shirt. Jeff carried the parcels in one hand while the other was thrown casually round her shoulders. They stopped at one of the smaller stores and bought ice creams, then made their way back to the lodge.

After a quick lunch Jeff drove them along the road beyond the complex until they came to a small ranch.

"You can still remember how to ride, I hope?"

"I guess I'm about to find out," replied Sarah.

An elderly man was waiting with two horses saddled and ready for them. Jeff mounted the taller of the two while Sarah hoped she could mount the smaller bay without difficulty. Fortunately, she just managed it and looked at Jeff in triumph.

"That's my girl. I wasn't going to make it easy for you."

He led the way out across the meadow, then through a gate that took them onto a track, explaining to her that he and Corey had often ridden this way in the past. For the next couple of hours they happily walked and trotted along the tracks enjoying both the sun and peace of the countryside.

Sarah hadn't ridden since leaving Banff, but it was like riding a bike, you just didn't forget. The feel of the horse as it moved beneath her, its feet surefooted on the rough track, was peaceful. Memories flooded back, of times they would steal away for a few hours and ride around the lakes. She was still wary of the possibility of meeting a bear but knew that Jeff would be prepared for that eventuality. They rode side by side in comfortable silence, broken only by the sound of the horse's hooves, and the occasional creak of leather.

Having returned the horses they drove back to the lodge.

"I thought we could go out and have an early dinner, if that's okay with you?" he said as they climbed the stairs to the kitchen.

"That's fine, but I think I need to shower before I do anything. I love horses but they do leave a lingering smell on you."

"Sounds like a good idea. I might join you but it will just be for a shower if we want an early dinner before the tourists turn out to eat."

They laughed as they shared the shower cubicle, after the wet rooms at home it seemed so small. They washed each other's bodies and Sarah could see Jeff was having a tough time in keeping to his word of this being only a shower. She turned away from him, tilting her head back under the shower, letting the water run through her hair. She knew this looked provocative and was taking the greatest delight in teasing him. She could feel him standing behind her and how hard he was. Enjoying this power over him she raised both hands to her head and started to wash her hair. When she finished, she leaned forward to let the water rinse it clean. She felt the smack on her buttock.

"You are a minx," he said, "but you have failed. A shower I said and a shower I meant." With that he opened the door and, wrapping a towel around his hips, walked out into the bedroom.

Sarah threw back her head and laughed. "Coward," she shouted after him. She dressed quickly, then dried her hair before putting on the new shirt and jeans they'd bought that morning.

Jeff took in the new clothes as they walked round to the complex. She looked good in the shirt and suddenly realised she would need to buy a whole new wardrobe of clothes now since she wasn't going back to England. They went into a small Italian restaurant. The meal was good although the service a bit slow, which didn't go unnoticed by Jeff who suddenly turned into the hotel owner explaining,

"The trouble with places like this is that they are a bit out of the way and have to rely on students looking for summer jobs. In reality, the kids just want to get away from mom and dad and enjoy themselves. That means the standard of service tends to slip but it's the best they can do, and the friendliness of the youngsters often makes up for the lack of other things. In Banff and Canmore, we're fortunate that we're able to employ full time staff for most of the year then take on just a few students in the summer."

Smiling, she listened to the practical explanation before reminding him how they first met. "I recall you taking on staff who walk in off the street."

Seeing the mischievous look on her face he replied, "Yes, I know you do but that was the best thing I ever did, the worst thing I did was to listen to my mother."

"Stop," said Sarah, putting her hands over her ears. "It's a problem free zone while we are here, and the word mother is definitely banned."

Jeff held up both hands in surrender. "Sorry, slip of the tongue,"

After paying the check they walked hand in hand back to the lodge. While Sarah put on some coffee Jeff disappeared down into the garage, coming back with a square box that he carried upstairs to the lounge.

When the coffee was ready Sarah followed him up and put the mugs down on the small table. Jeff had already opened the box which she saw contained photograph albums, the ones he had left out for her to see while he was away.

"I know you've looked at the albums but I thought we could go through them together and I could explain who some of the other people are, and what was happening at each event."

"That would be wonderful."

"However, before we look at them, there is another album that I thought we should look at together. I haven't opened it in years and I think perhaps now is the right time."

Sarah was intrigued at his words and sat on the floor next to him, her back resting against the sofa. Jeff pulled an album out of the box and placed it in her hands. She knew what it was straight away. It was Corey's baby album, the one they had started together. Opening it carefully she saw the photographs of herself while she was pregnant, looking like a beached whale. Then the three of them just after Corey had been born and the pages continued on showing Corey at various stages of growth, then his first birthday. They looked at the pages passing through his second and third birthdays, and then the photos of the three of them stopped, the last one being the photo Jeff had taken at the airport just before Sarah's flight had left. Corey's life from then on was in the other books.

For Sarah this was such a poignant reminder of what they had had together as a family, and what they had lost. There was nothing she could do to stop the tears from running down her face as she recalled the happy times they had shared. Seeing her tears Jeff put his arm around her shoulders and pulled her toward him, before gently kissing the side of her head. Wiping her eyes with the back of her hand she put the album down then picked up the next one. Turning to look at him she asked him to describe the pictures to her.

They sat happily going through the rest of the albums with Jeff explaining as much as he could about who people were and what was happening at each event, but when they had finished Sarah couldn't help but pick up the first album again. As she looked at the pictures she remembered so much about when they were taken and kept telling Jeff so many things that even he couldn't remember.

"How can you recall it all?" he asked.

"It's all the memories I had of our time together, so they were precious to me. The only thing I had was a photo of Corey taken at his birthday before I left, the one I kept in my wallet."

He pulled her toward him again and held her close.

"We'll make a new album from now on, a proper family album." He dropped a kiss on her nose and stood.

Holding out his hand he pulled her to her feet, then turned off the fire and lights, before leading her up the stairs to the bedroom.

Chapter Thirteen

If she had thought there would be no repercussions from the riding, she was wrong. Turning over in bed the next morning, muscles she didn't know she had, ached. Hearing her groans Jeff laughed, knowingly exactly what the problem was.

"Come on, I know just the thing we need."

Sarah groaned as he leapt out of bed and pulled the covers back from her. He disappeared into the shower and was out again before she was able to join him.

"I'll make breakfast," he called as he bounded down the stairs. Sitting in the kitchen some time later with her hands wrapped round a mug of coffee Sarah watched as he cleared away the plates, before going back upstairs. Rinsing her mug in the sink she slowly followed, wincing as she climbed the stairs. By the time she reached the lounge he was on his way back from the bedroom having changed into a pair of cropped cargos and a cotton top.

"I thought we could go to the Hot Springs. It will be good for your aches and pains," he said mischievously.

Sarah remembered the Hot Springs, it had been one of her favourite places to visit, and was thrilled at the prospect of going back.

"I don't have a swimsuit."

"Yes, you have. I brought the blue one for you from home, but we really need to get you some of your own, and we also need to do some serious clothes shopping. Much as I prefer you without clothes, they are going to be a necessity," he said grinning at her.

She laughed. "I am so glad that you brought that subject up. Not me being without clothes," she said with a giggle. "But the part about serious shopping. I have very little that is suitable for this climate."

"I realise that. Shopping is not one of my favourite pastimes, but on this occasion I think I shall enjoy it immensely. Now, go and put on that delectable swimsuit, which I'm sure has such special memories for us both."

Trying to ignore the aches she climbed the stairs as quickly as she could. The blue swimsuit was laid out on the bed. Stripping off her clothes she slipped this on, then pulled a tee shirt and her new shorts over the swimsuit, before gingerly going back downstairs.

It didn't take long to drive to the Hot Springs and after collecting towels they disappeared into their respective changing rooms. When Sarah came outside, Jeff was already soaking up the sun in the water. She walked down the steps, then across the pool and sat alongside him. Grateful for her sunglasses she closed her eyes before tilting her head back and letting the heat of the sun soak into her body.

Jeff opened his eyes and turned to look at her. With her hair tied in a ponytail she looked like the teenager who had stolen his heart. He moved his hand underneath the water until it found hers and they sat side-by-side in perfect contentment, lost in their own thoughts. Spending the last few minutes in the hot pool they reluctantly walked out and went to get changed.

Collecting her towel from her locker Sarah went into a changing cubicle and peeled off her swimsuit. Towelling herself dry she went to put on her undies and immediately realised her mistake. "Oh, no," she murmured, in her haste to leave she'd forgotten to pick up her bra and briefs. Having no option she pulled on her shorts and top. Pushing the sunglasses onto her face she went outside to find Jeff.

He was sitting at one of the outside table with two glasses of cold juice in front of him. She was conscious of her breasts moving under her t-shirt. Could he tell? Sitting opposite to him she took the glass he handed to her and saw the corners of his mouth twitch. He knew, and she could feel her cheeks burning.

Driving back to the lodge he kept glancing across at her, leaving her in no doubt as to what was to happen. As soon as the car stopped Sarah jumped out of the passenger door, moving quickly she was through the door and up the stairs before he could reach her.

"It's no use running away, Sarah, you know I'll outrun you."

"No, don't, Jeff, let me get dressed."

"Why? I thought you were giving me an invitation."

"No, I wasn't, I forgot my underwear."

"Oh, I know you did, and very provocative you look too, darling."

By this time Sarah had reached the lounge but was out of breath and collapsed on one of the sofas with a fit of giggles. He flopped down beside her and very deftly turned her so she was sitting across his knee. She could feel him pressing into her and the giggles left her immediately. Looking into his eyes she could see the desire, which was a reflection of her own.

Bringing his head down he kissed her passionately.

Some considerable time later they lay wrapped in each other's arms.

"God, Sarah, I can't get enough of you. I just want to be inside you and make love to you every minute of the day."

"I know. I feel the same, it's like being a rampant teenager again."

At that comment he burst out laughing, "I think you've nailed it in one, Mrs Saunders. Although, perhaps we could just say that we are making up for lost time."

Two more days were spent at the lodge walking, riding and making love. It was as though they were re-capturing their youth again, trying to turn the clock back. It was hard for Sarah to pack up and leave the place that had become so special to her. Eventually, they were ready to leave. As Jeff climbed behind the wheel, he looked across at Sarah and saw her sad face.

"Don't worry, we'll be back."

She turned her head and smiled. "I hope so."

They didn't rush to get back and it was early evening before they finally pulled up in front of the house. Sarah still couldn't believe this was home; it looked so beautiful in the late sunlight. Jumping out she went to help Jeff lift the things out of the trunk. He carried the boxes and small case to the door then put them down at the side. Unlocking the door he turned to Sarah and before she knew what was happening she was lifted into his arms. Holding her close he walked through the open door before gently setting her down in the hall.

Looking down at her he said, "Welcome home, Mrs Saunders."

Sarah knew it was a special moment between them, one that told her she truly belonged here. Tapping her on the backside he broke the mood. "Now go and put some coffee on for your tired husband."

Making a mock courtesy she quipped back, "Whatever you say, sir," before disappearing in the direction of the kitchen.

After a light supper, they sat watching the sun finally disappear. Jeff was glad they'd had this short time together to reconnect and become a couple again. He had a feeling that the next week could prove a little difficult. He'd put off mentioning Corey and Laura's return to Sarah, but knew he would have to tell her soon since he was supposed to be picking them up from the airport in a few days. Tomorrow would be soon enough, he thought, not wishing to spoil the evening.

Having made the conscious decision, he settled down on the sofa to enjoy the rest of the evening, with Sarah snuggled in his arms.

Next morning, they both woke late but, with no real plans, pulled on shorts and tops and wandered downstairs. "How about a swim before we eat?" suggested Jeff, going through into the pool to check the water. Following him, Sarah waited while he checked the temperature.

"The waters quite warm," he said, walking back toward her.

"Sounds like a good idea to me. I'll go and get a swimsuit."

"You don't need one, come on in."

She heard a splash and turned back to see his clothes on the side and his head surfacing the water.

Grinning, he swam toward her. "Come on, Sarah, it'll waken you up." Then he grabbed both of her ankles and pulled her in. She landed with a great splash and felt his hands lift her up. Looking down at his laughing face she pushed the hair back out of her eyes.

"You horror, look at me. I'm soaking."

"Doesn't matter," he said, removing his hands and swimming away, "just enjoy it."

Trying to swim even in shorts and a top was difficult so Sarah had no option but to take them off, but she did keep on her bra and briefs, telling herself they were just like a bikini.

They swam lazily up and down the pool. Sarah was conscious every time he came close to her that underneath the water Jeff was as naked as the day he was born. She didn't trust herself, and trusted him even less, so kept her distance, but he kept closing in on her. Finally, she managed to swim near to the steps and began to walk out, but he had climbed out of the pool and was moving determinedly toward her. Thankfully, she noticed he had wrapped a towel around his waist so she was spared the sight of his manhood, which had a very dizzying effect on her. Reaching the top of the steps she called back over her shoulder that she was going for a shower.

"That sounds like a great idea," said his voice a lot closer than she thought.

Turning partly she saw him just behind her, with a look on his face that meant only one thing. Laughing, she ran into the hall and was half way up the stairs before he caught her and lifted her off her feet. Her arms went around his neck as his lips claimed hers.

So engrossed were they in each other that they both failed to hear the front door open, and it was only when a questioning voice called out, "Dad!!" that they froze.

Sarah, partly hidden from view by Jeff's body, pressed her face into his chest. While Jeff, trying to control himself, called back in a somewhat shaky voice,

"Corey. Just a minute, son."

Carefully placing Sarah on her feet he whispered, "Turn around and walk straight into the bedroom. Leave this to me."

He caught sight of her face before she turned and cursed himself for not having told her the kids were returning. She was deathly white and her eyes were like saucers in her face. He could see her shaking as she quickly ran into the bedroom. Taking a deep breath, then fixing a smile on his face he turned around to face his son, who was standing in the hall looking very amused, with his new wife just behind him trying not to laugh. Despite his forty-three years Jeff could feel his face going red. To be caught like this was bad enough, but when it was your own son it was unthinkable.

"You old dog, dad. So this is what you get up to when I go away."

Walking toward them Jeff was thankful for the towel although it left little to the imagination. Responding as casually as he could to his son's remark, "Very funny, just give me a minute while I put something on." With that he disappeared back into the pool area and quickly pulled on his discarded clothes.

Feeling more in control, he walked back into the kitchen where the kids were already helping themselves to coffee, although judging by the sudden silence when he walked in, they quite clearly had been having a good laugh at his expense. Grasping his son in a bear hug and then his new daughter-in-law he started to ask the obvious question. "What's happened? Why are you back early?"

"There was a warning of a big storm coming in and hitting the Islands, so it was advised that those tourists due to leave shortly left early so as to avoid getting caught up in it. Anyway, we managed to get on an early flight then rented a car at the airport and here we are. We thought we'd surprise you and I guess we did," said Corey with a big grin.

"Yes, well there's life in the old dog yet, son," he said, not daring to look at Laura's face.

* * * *

Laura stood at the side watching the interplay with amusement. In all the time she'd known Corey she had never seen his dad with another woman, so this one must be special.

"So, do we get to meet your guest, Jeff?" she enquired.

"Err... I don't think so. I think the lady will be somewhat embarrassed at the moment."

Watching his face as he spoke Laura noticed a tenseness in his jaw, which made her wonder if there was something wrong. Corey did the same thing when he was worried, and he and his Dad were so alike, so perhaps there was something more going on here.

What had intrigued Laura most was the interaction between Jeff and this mystery woman, even for the short time she had seen them it was clear to her that there was a connection between them. She was intrigued. They chatted for a short time before Laura, becoming aware of her father-in-law's edginess, suggested they should go as they had lots of unpacking to do. Also, she had no doubt that Jeff's guest was feeling neglected hidden away upstairs. Hugging his son and kissing Laura, Jeff stood on the doorstep and waved as they drove away.

Locking the door behind him, too late now, he mused, as he turned and walked quickly across the hall, taking the stairs two at a time, before throwing open the bedroom door, dreading the state he would find Sarah in. Glancing quickly around the room she was easy to spot, huddled up on the window seat. Still in her wet undies, the white face staring at him confirmed his worst fears. Striding across the room he reached down pulling her up into his arms.

He held her close. "I am so sorry that happened, darling."

She didn't say anything but he could feel her shaking in his arms and her body was cold. Without hesitating, he picked her up and walked into the shower, ignoring the fact they were both partially clothed, and turned on the hot shower. As sobs racked through her body, he held her close until eventually she relaxed against him.

Turning the shower off, he kept hold of her hand and led her through into the bathroom. Pulling a towel from the rail he wrapped it around her before starting to rub her body. By now the sobs had turned to tears, tears that were running slowly down her cheeks. Gently he wiped them away.

"I'm so sorry. I had no idea they would turn up here today."

Shaking her head, she replied, "It's not your fault. I'm sorry for getting in such a state. It was the shock of hearing his voice and knowing he was standing there watching us. During the last few weeks, I've imagined over and over again my first face-to-face meeting with him I certainly didn't think it would be like that. Not that it was face to face, but for him to see us like that, for the first time. It was just too much."

"I know. It's not the way I would have liked it to be either. But it's happened and we'll just have to deal with it."

She looked at him and, for the first time took in his wet state. "Look, you're soaking wet, let me finish off drying myself and you do the same then we can go downstairs and you can tell me exactly what happened."

"Okay, as long as you are sure you're alright."

She nodded. "I will be." Taking the towel from him she quickly took off her wet clothes and finished drying herself.

Later, sitting in the lounge, she watched Jeff as he poured two large whiskies then handed one to her, insisting she drink it, before sitting next to her on the sofa.

"I was waiting until after dinner tonight to tell you that the kids were coming back in a couple of days. I didn't want you worrying any longer than necessary about it, but I hadn't reckoned on them coming back early. Anyway, rather than phoning and asking me to pick them up they decided to surprise me, so they rented a car at the airport and the rest you know."

"But why have they come back early, there's nothing wrong is there?"

Shaking his head, Jeff sat forward holding his glass between both hands, then explained about the incoming storm and the early flight home.

"What did they say about finding us together?"

"Oh I think they thought it a huge joke finding the 'old man,' as Corey called me, in a somewhat compromising situation, but apart from asking if they were going to meet you they didn't mention anything else. Although I did notice Laura giving me odd looks and I suspect that she is trying to work it all out. She's pretty shrewd our daughter-in-law, and can spot a mystery if there is one."

"I couldn't believe it when I heard his voice. It shocked me and just threw me into a spin. The last thing I wanted was for him to see me like that, or to see me at all, before he knows what has been happening. I just don't know how he's going to feel about me after all these years."

Jeff nodded. "I know, and I'll have to sit him down and tell him everything. I thought I had a few days grace, but I'm going to have to do it sooner rather than later. In a way it could be a blessing in disguise as I'm sick of having to keep you hidden away here in the house. I want everyone to know that my wife is back at my side, but first of all I have to tell our son. And that's not going to be easy. We'll give him a day to sort himself out and then I'll get him over and tell him all that his grandmother has done."

"Don't be too harsh when you tell him. I hate the thought of him being hurt."

"It will be difficult not to hurt him in view of the strong bond there was between him and my mother, but I'll go as easy as I can. Although I can't see any way of explaining this being easy."

The following morning, Jeff went into the hotel and was happy to put off the inevitable call by dealing with a couple of problems. But eventually he couldn't delay any longer so phoned Corey, arranging for him to call at the house the following afternoon, telling him that he needed to have a word with him on his own. Much as he loved his daughter-in-law, this was a conversation that had to be between him and Corey.

Arriving home, he found Sarah busy in the garden tidying up some of the plants. Flashing a smile at him, she came across, reached up, and kissed him. He held her for a moment and then told her that Corey was coming the following afternoon.

"I'm going to sit him down and tell him everything. Then perhaps you two can meet."

By the following afternoon, Sarah's nerves were in shreds and she had no doubt that Jeff's were as well. They had decided she would stay in the bedroom while Jeff spoke to Corey and they would take things from there. Hearing his car on the driveway Sarah took her book and ran up the stairs closing the bedroom door behind her.

Jeff was waiting in the lounge as Corey let himself in. "Through here, son," he called.

"Hi, dad."

Looking at the younger version of himself walking through the doorway he hated the thought that he was about to cause him pain and upset. Standing up he said, "Coffee?"

"Yeah, great. On your own?" he said with a hint of mischief.

He didn't reply, but just gave his son a look that said, enough.

Giving himself some time while he poured the coffees he then took a deep breath and walked back into the lounge. Handing a mug to Corey he sat down again. He saw the grin on Corey's face slip, and knew he could tell this was no ordinary conversation.

"Have I done something wrong," Corey asked, "or messed up at the hotel?"

"No, you haven't. I just need to talk to you about something. Something that I've found out recently that affects both of us."

Sitting opposite to his dad Corey looked worried. "You're not ill, dad, are you?"

"No, I'm not ill, it's nothing like that, but it is serious. Look, son, I don't really know where to start with all of this and I only hope you can understand what I've got to tell you." Taking a deep breath he went on. "You know your mom left us when you were very young?"

"Yes, she didn't want to live here, or with us anymore."

The words came out bitterly and made Jeff wince. "Well, no, that's not strictly true, but it's what I was led to believe at the time, and something I continued to believe, until a few weeks ago."

Taking a gulp of coffee he started explaining to Corey about his mom coming back, what his grandmother had done and about the money he had been sending to her over the years, that his mom had never received. Then he proceeded to tell him how the money had been traced back to an account in Canada, and his meeting with the lawyers in Vancouver. He stopped short of telling him at present about the suitcases the lawyers had been holding, and also that his mom was here in the house and they were back together. That information could wait for another time.

He finished speaking and looked at his son, who had sat in complete silence while he was talking, the shock on his face clear to see. He waited for him to say something, and when he did, it was words he had never expected to hear.

"No, I don't believe you. Grandma would never do anything like that. It's her; she's told you all these lies. Grandma told me she didn't love us and didn't want to stay with us, and she wouldn't lie, not to me."

Sighing, Jeff tried to reason with him. "Corey, I know what she said, she told me that too, and it's been very hard for me to accept what she did, but the proof is there for us all to see. She kept your mom away from us all those years ago, for reasons best known to herself."

He could see Corey was angry, his face was turning bright red. He wasn't prepared to listen to what he was being told, and made this clear in no uncertain terms. Jeff had never seen him like this before, and hadn't heard language like it since Corey had been a teenager and pushing the boundaries. Half of what he was saying was going over Jeff's head, but some of it penetrated and he was able to register.

"No, I will never believe it, and I don't want anything to do with her. Grandma said she was bad, and I believe her." By now he'd raised his voice and was shouting at Jeff. "I'm not staying here listening to you say these things these… these lies about her," he yelled as he jumped up and stalked out of the lounge.

Jeff caught up with him in the hall. "Corey, for goodness sake, don't walk away like this, at least stay and talk it through with me."

His attempt to grab hold of his son's arm failed as he shook him off.

"Fuck you, dad, if you believe her, but I've nothing else to say, not until you take back all these lies," he called over his shoulder.

Jeff followed him as he half-ran and half-walked to his car, opened the door, jumped in and then drove off, scattering dust as he roared away.

Stunned by his son's outburst and the language, Jeff closed the door and turned back into the hall. Looking up the stairs he saw Sarah standing in the doorway to the bedroom with a stricken look on her face. He knew she couldn't have failed to hear what Corey said and his heart went out to her, but at this moment he couldn't speak to anyone. He'd never rowed with Corey like this before, and the hatred in his voice had shaken him. They'd had father and son disagreements over the years, but never a full-blown row like this, and for him to use the f... word at him had shocked him beyond belief. For the second time in his life he had a situation he didn't know how to handle.

Although he had no wish to speak to anyone he knew he needed to make a call to Laura. Picking up the phone he waited for her to answer and quickly told her that Corey was probably on his way home; that he was in a state as they'd had one hell of a row, and he just wanted her to be forewarned. If she wanted to ask more she didn't, for which he was grateful, but before ending the call he told her to get Corey to tell her everything he had been told.

Sarah had tried to concentrate on the book, but the raised voices made it impossible. Listening from the doorway, she was stunned by the way Corey was speaking to his dad. She knew the conversation was going to be difficult, but this was way beyond anything she, or even Jeff, would have expected. Watching Jeff close the door and then meeting his eyes she could see the devastation in his face. When he didn't come up fear ripped through her. Was he blaming her for what had just happened? Was their new found happiness about to be torn apart by the one person they both loved? Undecided as to what to do, she hesitated, paced the bedroom until she could stay there no longer. She found him outside staring out across the valley.

"I guess you heard most of that?" he said without turning around.

"Yes, hard not to."

She sat on one of the chairs nearby and waited for him to speak again. When he didn't she ventured to ask what was going to happen now.

"I honestly don't know. All we can do is give him time to think it all through and hope that he comes to his senses."

Although knowing it would break her heart, she heard herself saying that if it would help she would go back to England.

He turned to face her and said quietly but firmly, "That's not an option, so don't even think about it."

Although they prepared dinner that night they both ended up pushing the food around their plates. The day that had looked to bring an end to their problems, had only served to create more.

Chapter Fourteen

What his dad had told him was unacceptable. He was halfway back to town before he had cooled down enough to properly concentrate on his driving. He drove straight back to the apartment and let himself in.

Laura was doing laundry and heard the click of the key in the lock. Bracing herself, she walked through into the hall. She couldn't pretend that nothing was wrong, his face gave it away.

"Corey, what's wrong?"

"I've had one hell of a bust up, with dad," he said, throwing his keys down.

"I know, he phoned to say you had and you were on your way home." She saw no reason not to let him know his dad was concerned.

"Did he tell you what it was about?"

"No, but he said I should ask you."

"Oh, I'll tell you alright, all about the lies he's been saying about my grandma, lies that she has told him."

"Who has told him, and what lies?" asked Laura puzzled, trying to make sense of his words.

"Oh yeah, that's the good bit, my so-called mom."

Mention of his mom stopped Laura from asking any further questions. "Look, darling, just tell me everything your dad said. I'm sure we can make sense of it and try and work it out." Taking hold of his hand she led him into the lounge and sat him down.

Laura sat quietly, saying nothing, until he had finally told her the whole story.

"Well," he asked, "what do you think about all the lies?"

Sensing that he wasn't going to listen to any reasonable arguments at present she shrugged her shoulders. "I don't know, but it's not like your dad to tell you something so serious if he hasn't checked it out."

"So you're saying you believe him?"

"I don't know, Corey, but what I do know is we should both sleep on it and see what sense it makes in the morning."

She had known Corey on and off since Junior High and had never seen him so angry and distraught before. He was her husband and she wanted to protect him from anything that would hurt him, but she suspected that there was a lot of truth in what his dad had told him. She just needed to find a way of getting him to see that.

Leaving him in the lounge, she finished what she was doing and then suggested they go out for dinner, but he wasn't in the mood to go out, so they ordered in.

Lying in bed a few hours later she figured that she had managed to turn his mind to other matters. It's amazing what a sexy nightdress, plus a new wife with her mind set on seduction can do to her new husband, she thought. Moving her hand across his bare chest she raised her head then kissed his throat before gently nibbling his ear.

Laughing, he pulled her on top of him. "You want more, Mrs Saunders?"

"Perhaps...after all, we are still on our honeymoon." She smiled, rolling to the side and pulling him on top of her.

He teased her neck with his mouth and then moved down to her small breasts. As she strained under him he gently eased himself inside and began the slow journey that would bring them both to the point of ecstasy.

Nestled in his arms later, Laura wondered if this was how Jeff felt with Corey's mom, for she was pretty sure that the woman they had seen him with at the house was her. It all added up. Jeff had never been with anyone else all the time she had known the family, although several women had tried and failed, but there was a togetherness about the way they were that she had noticed, and found odd at the time, but not now.

How would she feel if she lost Corey for eighteen years because of the plotting of someone else? She didn't want to think about it, but it could so easily have happened. Perhaps it was time for her to say something to someone, but not Corey...not while he was in his present frame of mind.

Waking the next morning she waited until Corey had left for work before phoning Jeff. The way the phone was quickly answered told her that he had been waiting for a call but she could hear the disappointment in his voice when he realised it wasn't Corey.

"Sorry, Jeff, it's me. Corey's gone off to work but I wanted to let you know that he's told me everything."

Listening to Jeff's response she then replied, "No, he's still adamant that his grandma wouldn't do such a thing and I think it's going to be a few days before he starts to think clearly about it. You know how stubborn he can be at times. Look, Jeff, I would really like to have a talk with you, about something related to what's happened, but I'd prefer it if Corey didn't find out. I don't want him to think I'm going behind his back, or taking sides, and at the moment that's exactly what he will think. Can I come over tomorrow during my lunch break?" Having agreed to the arrangement, she hung up.

Some homecoming, she thought as she tried to concentrate on unpacking. She had so looked forward to them being together in their own home for the first time. The decision not to live together before the wedding had been hers, and this was to be the start of their new life. Not that everything had waited until we were married, she thought with a smile. Hopefully, this drama would resolve itself quickly.

Hearing the phone, Sarah waited until Jeff put the phone down, then looked questioningly at him. He shook his head.

"Laura, just keeping me updated but at least he's told her everything."

"What's going to happen now?"

"I don't know. I guess we give him a few days to work it out in his head. As Laura said, he's stubborn and I know he gets some of that from me, but he probably gets a lot more from my mother. Anyway, Laura is coming out tomorrow, says she has something she needs to talk to me about, so we may find out more then."

Walking toward her, he put his arm round her shoulders and kissed her on the top of the head. "Don't worry, he'll work it out. Our son does have some common sense, somewhere."

Sighing, Sarah walked with him out to the garden. Leaving him to read his paper she continued to take her frustration and worry out on the few weeds she could find.

Jeff arrived home from work just before lunchtime the following day. He knew what time Laura would get there and wanted to make something for them to eat, but was pleased to see that Sarah had already thought of that. There was salad with a selection of cold meats and bread set out in the kitchen. She had her back to him when he walked in. Walking up behind her he moved her hair to one side and kissed the back of her neck.

"Hi, sweetheart, you've been busy."

"Thought I'd make myself useful, and it took my mind off things for a while."

"Try not to worry, Sarah. Things will sort themselves out," he replied, turning her round and smiling down at her.

She smiled back, but noticed that his smile didn't quite reach his eyes. Hearing a car on the drive, Sarah turned back and picked up the plate of sandwiches she had made for herself.

"Where are you going?" queried Jeff.

"I thought it best if I took these upstairs with a book while you and Laura have your chat."

He was about to speak but she held up her hand, "No, Jeff, it's better this way. Please? It would be wrong for me to be here."

"Okay. You're right of course." She quickly disappeared, picking up a glass of juice on her way. She was right, he couldn't let Laura see her, that would only complicate matters.

By the time Laura got inside, Jeff was on his own in the kitchen. Giving his daughter-in-law a hug he asked how she was and if she had heard from Corey at all that morning.

"I'm fine, and no, I haven't."

Leading her to the small table they both sat. Laura took the opportunity to quickly look around while Jeff's back was to her, but couldn't see anyone else. Maybe she's left, she thought, but didn't really think that she had. Making small talk about the honeymoon until they had finished eating Laura took the offered mug of coffee from Jeff then told him that she felt she needed to tell him something that had a bearing on what was happening.

"I've wanted to say something for a long time but after the accident there didn't seem any point."

Jeff was intrigued, but the reference to the accident told him it was something to do with his late mother. "Any point in what?"

"Corey says you told him his grandmother had effectively split you and Corey's mum up. Oh, I know it was a lot more complicated than that but put simply that's what you told him she had done?"

Jeff nodded. "Yes, by manipulating a situation and lying."

Laura heard the hurt in his voice and that gave her the courage to say what she needed to. "She tried to do the same to me and Corey."

Jeff sat upright and she could see the shock on his face. Tears welled up in her eyes. Suddenly she was scared of what she was about to say. Had she misjudged this? But then he leaned across the table and gently held her hand in his.

"Laura, I had no idea. I'm so sorry. Look, you can tell me anything, after what I have found out recently, nothing is a surprise anymore. But what on earth would my mother have against you? When did this happen?"

"Not long after Corey and I first got together as a couple, during the summer break. At first I just ignored it, but she said some really horrid things to me at times. Told me I was no good for Corey, that I would hold him back. That he was only using me for what he could get, and that he would eventually leave me. I would leave messages for him but somehow he never got them, and eventually I just felt it wasn't worth it, so I broke up with him. I know it seemed like the coward's way out but I was young and I didn't need the hassle, but I had reckoned without Corey. He bombarded me with gifts, flowers; phone calls and would turn up outside my parents' house and just sit there in his car.

My folks didn't know what to make of it and eventually my mom got the truth out of me, and she was so mad, told me I was a fool if I let someone dictate to me who I could and couldn't see. She said that if I wanted to go out with Corey I should do so, and nobody had the right to stop us and that she and my dad were one hundred percent behind me, whatever I decided. Knowing that my mom and dad were there, and that they knew what was happening, gave me the courage to make the decision to get back with Corey."

She paused and took a sip of coffee. "Even then it wasn't easy as his grandmother still made life very uncomfortable for me when she could, and there were many times when my mom wanted to say something because she would find me crying, but I didn't want to cause any bother. Also, I knew that the bond between Corey and his grandmother was very strong and I didn't want put it to the test and risk losing him. I was so in love with him by then, I couldn't bear the thought of us splitting up. So I put up with it. Then the accident happened and, while I was sorry she died, I don't know if I would be Corey's wife if she had still been alive."

Having finished speaking, Laura waited for Jeff's reaction.

"Laura, if I'd had any idea what was going on I would have stopped it. I don't know how, but I would. I've made mistakes over the years. The biggest one, it would seem, was letting my mother have so much control over our lives, and to get so close to Corey. I'm sorry that you had to go through all of that but I'm glad that you stuck with him, otherwise we might not be sitting here today. You and Corey are meant to be together, you complement each other, he's stubborn and hot headed at times but you have a calming influence on him, and the fact that you are madly in love with each other does help," he said, attempting to lighten the atmosphere.

"I'm glad you think that, but my main concern now is Corey. If I tell him about this I don't know how he'll react, but if I don't tell him he won't believe what you've told him."

Jeff remained silent for a while, staring at Laura's anxious face "I would really like to ask a big favour of you. Would you keep this to yourself for a bit longer? I think Corey needs to work through what I've told him and make a decision about his mom, and his grandmother, on his own, without any influence. I know it's a huge favour, Laura, but I think it will be for the best for everybody. I'm not saying that he doesn't need to know, because he does, but just not yet. "

Laura breathed a sigh of relief. She'd half expected him to say this, in fact, she was hoping he would. "That's fine, of course I will. I would rather not mention it at present for the reasons you said."

"You have a wise head, daughter-in-law," said Jeff with a smile. "I'm only sorry that all of this has spoilt your homecoming."

"It's not what I'd expected, but I hope it's sorted out soon."

"So do I, and I promise to make it up to you both when it is."

Laura stood and gathered her things together. "I need to get back to work. Thanks for listening."

"I'll always listen, Laura. You're family now, so have a direct line to my listening ear."

She laughed and kissed him on the cheek.

Driving back to town she was sorry Jeff had been on his own, but was sure that he wasn't alone in the house. A huge weight had been lifted by telling Jeff what had happened with his mother. She had kept this secret for years and had felt guilty about not telling Corey. Perhaps when the time came to tell him it would help him understand, and accept that his father was telling him the truth.

Jeff hoped his decision had been the right one. Although it had caused him a twinge of guilt. It would have been easy to ask Laura to let Corey know what had happened, but he wanted his son to work it out for himself. He needed him to want his mom back in his life because he wanted her there. He needed to believe she hadn't walked out and left him all those years ago. He was pulled back from his thoughts by Sarah joining him in the kitchen.

"How did it go?"

"The revelations just keep coming," he said, turning to look at her.

"What do you mean?"

"Laura has just told me some things that happened a few years ago with my mother."

The look on his face and the tone of his voice told her exactly what he was going to say. "She did it to her, didn't she?"

He nodded. "Yes, but we have a very persistent son, and there wasn't an ocean between them, so they were able to work things out."

Handing her a drink he took her by the hand and they went outside where he told her all that Laura had said.

The next few days passed in a pattern of work and home for Jeff. The one consolation in the whole situation was the knowledge that Sarah was waiting for him at the end of each day. He heard nothing from Corey at all, although he did get the occasional short call from Laura, but all she could tell him was that nothing had changed.

As the first week turned into the second, Jeff was beginning to lose patience. He asked Tom to arrange for Corey to come to Saunders on Banff for a meeting, thinking that dealing with work matters might get some dialogue going between them. He waited for Corey to arrive but the clock ticked passed the appointed time. Asking reception to call Mountain View and find out if Corey had been delayed, he was furious when he got the message back to say that he had gone out, but nobody was quite sure where. Okay, son, he thought, if that's the way you want to play it, do so on your own.

Picking up the phone he made some calls and then phoned Tom to check whether he could cope with both hotels for a while as he was going out of town for a couple of weeks. Puzzled, Tom said that everything was under control and there was no problem. Having been told by his staff that Corey hadn't turned up for the meeting he knew there was something wrong. He had worked for the family for nearly twenty-five years; working his way up to becoming Manager, and this sort of thing just didn't happen. That there was something wrong, troubled him, but he kept his thoughts to himself, just assured Jeff that all would be well while he was away.

"I'll be on my cell phone if you really need me, but I hope you won't, and I don't want anyone else to know that."

"Understood," said Tom, realising that the, anyone, meant Corey, and that told him this was serious.

Before leaving for home, Jeff telephoned Laura at work, told her what had happened and that he was going away for a couple of weeks to give himself time to cool off, and Corey time to come to his senses. Before ending the call he asked Laura if he could drop some suitcases off at their apartment before he left, telling her that they contained items belonging to Corey that were relevant to the present problem.

"If you can get him to look at them, Laura, I think it will help explain a lot to him."

"Okay, if you think it will help I'll do what I can to persuade him. If you want, just use the spare key and let yourself in after we've left for work. If you leave them in the guest bedroom. I'll try and get Corey to look in them."

Arriving home earlier than usual he found Sarah in the swimming pool. Shedding his clothes upstairs he joined her, and for the first time since the kids had returned, he felt at ease, probably because he had taken the decision for them to go away. Oh, they'd been to Radium for a couple of days, but this was a real break and far enough away for them to forget what was going on. It would mean being away from home for Canada Day but he figured that it was a small sacrifice to pay. There would be more Canada Days, and hopefully the next one he would be able to share openly with Sarah. Swimming across to her he lifted her off her feet and kissed her long and hard on the mouth.

His actions caused a feeling of relief. There had been a tension between them, an awkwardness that had not been there since the early days of their meeting and Sarah hated it. It wasn't just the awkwardness, but they hadn't made love in over a week. She was still scared he was going to have to choose between her and Corey, despite what he said. She wanted her family back together. But if Jeff had to make a decision between them, she couldn't let him turn his back on their son. She would go; the last thing she wanted was to come between them.

Resting her hand against his face she saw how tense he was. "Is everything alright?"

"No, and yes."

She laughed at his reply. "How can it be both?"

"Well, the no is because Corey stood me up at a pre-arranged meeting I was supposed to have with him, and the yes is because I've decided we need a break from it all. And I mean a proper break, not a few days at the lodge, so we're going away for a couple of weeks."

"Why did he stand you up?" asked Sarah, failing to register the latter part of his words.

"Because he's being bloody minded, and obstinate."

His final words suddenly registered with her "Wait...going away? Where, and why now?"

"Why now? Because if I stay I'll either do or say something that I will regret, and as to where, well not too far away but somewhere I had always promised to take you but we never did manage it. Vancouver Island. I've made the reservations so all we need to do is pack and take off tomorrow when we're ready."

Throwing her arms round his neck, she hugged him. "I do love you and I'm so sorry for all the trouble I seem to have caused."

"The trouble wasn't caused by you. And if you say sorry once more I'll give you the biggest ducking you have ever had," he said playfully."

Later, after changing and enjoying a lazy meal, he told her that he had one thing to do in the morning before they left, and that was to take the two suitcases to Corey and Laura's. He explained about the conversation he'd had with Laura, and that all they could do now was hope Corey would look inside and see what had been kept from him over the years. "Hopefully, the sight of the contents will make him realise how much his grandmother had lied, and how much his mom had loved him."

Sarah had hoped he would make love to her that night, but was disappointed, although he did hold her until she fell asleep. And they had two whole weeks to look forward to.

Chapter Fifteen

The bags were packed and Sarah was waiting for Jeff to come back from Laura's. Hearing the car on the drive, she ran and opened the door. He pulled up and came toward her smiling.

"Did you drop them off okay?" she asked, before he had time to speak.

"Yes, no problem. I left them just where Laura asked me to."

"You seem to have taken a long time. I thought something must have happened."

"No, I just needed to make one more call in Banff before I left, and that's done now. So we can put the bags in the car and go."

Eager to get away before anything stopped them, the car was quickly packed and within a short time they were driving away. Sarah had no idea how they were getting to Vancouver Island, or how long it would take. Jeff hadn't said anything more and, whilst she had dropped a few hints about the trip, he had just told her to be patient.

As they sped along the highway, her patience was running out. "Are we flying?" She saw the grin and then he turned his head slightly.

"What's wrong, Sarah. Getting impatient?"

"In a word, yes. Please, Jeff, give me some clue. Like, can I settle down for a long drive, or are we heading for the airport?"

"No, not the airport. I thought we could play at being tourists again and drive to Vancouver, then take the ferry across to the Island. We can take our time and go via the Okanagan Valley, stay there for a few nights, and maybe take in some of the Wineries and stock up on the wine cellar."

"Oh, Jeff, that sounds wonderful." The giddy smile told him he'd done the right thing in taking them away.

"Come on, Sarah, settle down for a long drive, let's have some music, and preferably not smoochy country and western."

They spent three idyllic nights in the Okanagan Valley area where they, or rather Sarah, enjoyed sampling the wines with Jeff bemoaning the fact that he wasn't able to as he had to drive. Something he told her they would remedy as soon as they got back. "You need your own car, darling, and we'll have to sort out about getting you a Canadian driving licence."

Although able to drive on her British license, Sarah regretted never taking her Canadian driving test before she left for England but realised that it was now time. The plans for the future seemed unreal, and she kept wanting to pinch herself. Only one thing marred her excitement, they hadn't made love yet. But she hoped this time away would resolve that.

Driving into Vancouver was wonderful. They had been here once before just after they were married, but before Corey was born. She had loved the vibrancy of the city and its cleanliness, and was sorry they were not staying over, but Jeff was eager to catch the afternoon ferry from Horseshoe Bay to Nanaimo. She felt the thrill as they lined up with the other cars, then stood alongside the car watching as the ferry came into dock.

The lines of vehicles started to move so they jumped back into the car and followed the others onto the ferry. Leaving the car deck, Jeff steered them in the direction of the upper deck where they sat watching the sun's rays glistening on the water, while the Gulf Islands passed by. After what seemed too short a time they were heading back down to the car deck and getting ready for docking.

Coming out of the port they turned right and drove along the highway. Sarah's head was turning from side to side, not wanting to miss anything. Before long they turned off the highway into the town of Parksville, then took the road to the beach resorts. Turning to look at Jeff she noticed how tired he looked but he caught her eye and grinned.

"Nearly there."

She nodded, almost too excited to speak. She felt like a schoolgirl on her first trip away from home. Turning into one of the resorts, they stopped at the reception while Jeff picked up the keys. Climbing back into the car he drove down through the resort until they came almost to the beach. There was a small parking area for the units on the beach level, and checking the number on the key he pulled into the allotted space.

Climbing out of the driver's seat he stretched his arms above his head. Taking her hand they walked to their unit and she waited patiently while he opened the door. Then she was swept off her feet and carried inside before being unceremoniously dropped on the sofa.

"Sorry, that's all I can manage at present."

She laughed before jumping to her feet. Then with a surge of energy, brought about by pure excitement, she moved quickly through the unit checking out the kitchen and lounge, before running up the stairs to discover two bedrooms, both with their own en-suite.

"Perfect," she shouted down to him.

"Good, because I don't plan on finding an alternative."

Joining him back in the lounge they stood looking out across the beach to the sea, which could just be seen in the distance, as the tide was well and truly out. The units were set in a bay and Sarah could see other resorts along the beachfront. People were on the beach, some with children playing in the sand, and others just walking along holding hands.

"Come on," she said, tugging his hand, "let's get the car unpacked and I'll see about something to eat."

Having unpacked what provisions they had brought, she decided on a simple pasta dish. Something quick and easy. Jeff had collapsed on the sofa after unpacking, and she watched as his eyes slowly closed. The even rise and fall of his chest told her he was asleep. She had set the small table at the dining end of the lounge, and made a simple green salad. All she needed to do was serve the pasta. Shaking him gently, before pressing her lips to his, she stirred him enough for his eyes to open. She saw the glint and immediately straightened up. Much as she wanted him, now was not the time.

"Dinner's ready."

"I think I'd rather go straight to dessert," he said, grinning at her.

"Well you can't, not yet anyway."

"Okay, I'll go and wash up, won't be a minute."

She turned to go back into the kitchen but he caught her around the waist and swung her to him. His lips captured hers before his tongue gently teased inside her mouth.

Pulling himself away, he turned and began climbing the stairs, calling back over his shoulder, "Remind me where I was later."

Calming her racing pulse, she laughed as she placed the meal on the table. If his actions told her anything, it was that the long wait for him to make love to her was almost over.

Despite being tired they managed a short walk on the beach before the tide came fully in, and then sat looking out through the open windows as the waves gently rolled over the beach. This was heaven and she didn't want to break the spell by talking. Eventually, Jeff said he was ready to go up, then proceeded to lock the doors and windows. Sarah turned off the lights and, placing her hand in his, they climbed the stairs to the bedrooms.

She had chosen the slightly larger room for them and the sight of the bed brought shivers to her spine. Disappearing into the bathroom for a shower, she heard Jeff using the bathroom in the other bedroom. There was a feeling of disappointment. She had hoped he would join her. When she walked back into the bedroom there was a package on the bed. Opening it she lifted out a beautiful silk nightdress in the palest shade of pink. Quickly removing the towel wrapped around her, she slipped the nightdress over her head, feeling the silky material slide down and then cling to her body. Looking at her reflection in the mirror it was hard to believe that the person she saw was herself.

Sensing she was no longer alone, she looked round to find Jeff leaning against the doorframe watching her.

"I knew you'd look beautiful in it, but I just didn't realise how beautiful. It's a shame it's not going to be on for very long."

Straightening up, he walked slowly toward her, dropping the towel from around his waist onto the floor. Reaching out, he placed his hands on her shoulders then very smoothly moved the thin straps until they slipped from her shoulders allowing the nightdress to fall about her feet. Lifting her up, he moved to the bed and laid her down. Then he began, what she would later describe to herself, as the most exquisite devouring of her body she had ever known.

There wasn't a part of her that he didn't touch with either his hands or his mouth, teasing her body until she cried out for him to stop. When she reached that plateau he would kiss her lips, then start over again until her body shook with desire for him. Then, before he took the ultimate prize, he guided her hand down, and urged her to place him inside. "You do this, darling, you decide when this is to happen."

Feeling him hard in her hand she hesitated for a fraction. They had been like this so many times before, but now the intensity of it frightened her. He lifted her chin, gazing intently into her eyes. Her body convulsed at the passion she saw, and the moment of hesitation was gone. Her hand guided him into her most private part, and she gave herself up to the sheer joy and ecstasy of the moment. They reached heights of passion that night that neither of them had known before and the fall back down to earth was all the greater for the wonder they had shared.

She was still naked in his arms when she awoke the next morning. He was already awake and watching her. She blushed, remembering what they had done, and he laughed gently as if reading her thoughts. If there had been any remote thought she was going to be allowed out of bed, she was proved wrong. Hands began to caress her body, while he quietly pointed out they were on holiday and could spend the whole day in bed if they wanted. Surrendering to him she was only too happy to agree. Finally they surfaced, enjoyed a lazy brunch, then spent the rest of the day wandering along the beach, holding hands and talking, whilst trying to avoid the tiny crabs as they scuttled across the sand.

Jeff had reserved a table for dinner in one of the restaurants in town, so Sarah dressed in the skirt and top she had intended to wear the night he hadn't returned from Vancouver. Before they left Jeff sat her down.

"Darling, there is something that isn't right about our present situation."

Looking at his serious face, Sarah wondered what he was going to say next. He took a small box out of his pocket and raised the top. Inside she saw her engagement ring, and nestled next to it was her wedding ring. No it couldn't be, she thought. That had been taken from her in England years ago.

Puzzled, she looked at him. "That can't be my wedding ring?"

"No, darling, it's not. I'm afraid even I wouldn't be able to trace that after all this time, but it's an identical ring from the same shop, to the exact design and inscription that we chose together all those years ago. The engagement ring as you know is the real thing, since you left it behind."

She nodded, not quite sure what to say. "It was a hard thing to do at the time, but I didn't want to risk taking it with me and, as it turned out, I was glad I did leave it. I would have hated to have lost it as well as my wedding ring."

"I know, but now you have a replacement, and that is what's not right yet. Because these rings belong on your finger, and not in the box."

Removing the rings, he took her left hand in his, but before he could do anything with them she took the wedding ring from him, tilting it to look at the inscription inside the band. It was the same. Their names with a heart between them and the date of their marriage. Handing it back to him, she watched as he gently slid the wedding ring onto her fourth finger. Once in place he pressed his lips to it. Then he placed her engagement ring next to it and held up her hand to inspect them.

"Now, everything is right," he said, smiling.

Sarah turned her hand so she could see the rings and knew what he meant. She was his wife once again, wearing his rings for all the world to see. This moment meant everything to her.

Standing up he drew her to her feet and kissed her softly on the lips. "Come on, darling, let's go and face the world together."

They spent the next two weeks as though they were on a second honeymoon. He took her to the most wonderful places. They went whale watching from Campbell River, and strolled through ancient forests. He took her to Long Beach where the beach stretched as far as the eye could see. Then they wandered hand in hand along the shore, which was littered with washed up logs, before having lunch at the Wickanninish Inn and watched as the breakers rolled in over the rocky outcrops.

Canada Day was spent on their own but they watched families sharing picnics on the beach. She knew how special this day was, and asked if he wanted to phone Corey, but he shook his head. "No. It's hard not to but perhaps this might make him realise just how serious the situation is." She smiled and squeezed his arm, understanding how hard this was for him.

They wandered down to see the fireworks that night, before walking back in the dark, their arms wrapped around each other. Their evenings were spent enjoying wonderful dinners, then strolls along the shore, before tasting the joy of lovemaking.

By the time they were boarding the ferry to return to the mainland, they were happy and relaxed in a way they had never thought possible.

The sunny days had left a golden tan on Sarah's skin and, in Jeff's eyes, she had never looked more beautiful. As the ferry docked they waited for the cars to disembark and then followed them out onto the highway. Sarah watched the skyline of Vancouver getting closer and was surprised when Jeff drove into the downtown area.

Eventually, he stopped outside one of the large hotels on the waterfront near Canada Place. Switching off the engine, he turned to her. "You didn't think we were going straight home, did you?" he said, smiling broadly.

"I don't know, you keep surprising me."

"Good, that's what I intend to do."

Climbing out of the car he handed the keys to the waiting porter and Sarah found her door being opened for her. The cases were left to be brought in later and the car taken to the parkade area. They walked across the tiled floor to the reception desk. Giving their details Jeff took the keys, and taking Sarah's hand, led her to the lifts. Unlocking the door to their suite he allowed her to walk in first.

She was amazed by the size of the room, and the picture windows that looked out over Canada Place, the waterfront, and Burrard Inlet. She could hear Jeff laughing as she darted from the sitting area into the bedroom, unable to disguise her cries of delight with what she found.

"I gather this meets with your approval?" he called out.

She came rushing back into the room and flung herself into his arms. "It's wonderful. Oh, my goodness," she said, "I feel like a teenager on her first holiday away from home. Sorry, I really should act my age."

"And what age is that, Sarah? Because to me, you are the still the young girl I married."

The words were spoken lightly, but this kind of hotel suite was not unusual to him. But her joy at it made him reflect on how she'd had to pinch and scrape over the years. He vowed that she would never have to do that again. Would never have to go without what he and Corey had taken for granted. Watching as she went back into the bedroom he strolled over and lounged against the doorway. He couldn't help but smile when he saw her kick off her shoes and test out the bed, then waited to see what she was intending to do next. But she didn't move, just lay on her side looking at him with the most seductive smile on her face he had ever seen.

Being fully aware that their luggage would appear any moment, he just wagged a finger at her, and with a chuckle said, "Later, minx."

She stuck out her bottom lip in an exaggerated pout. Fortunately, there was a knock at the door, announcing the arrival of their luggage, so he was forced to abandon any retaliation.

They were only staying a couple of nights so Sarah simply pulled out a pair of semi smart pants together with a suitable top, then quickly changed while Jeff was in the bathroom.

They went for a stroll along Canada Place before returning to the hotel for dinner. Later, as they waited for the elevator up to their room, she wondered if the, later, he had promised was about to happen.

Over the years on her own she'd never wanted to be involved in a relationship. Never wanted to feel that pain of loss again. She had thought of herself as being reserved but now, when they were together, he made her feel like a testosterone powered teenager again, craving his touch, unable to get enough of him. This was how she used to feel when they were younger, when they would make love whenever and wherever they wanted. There wasn't a room in their old apartment that hadn't been tested out. And what about the hotel, said a voice in her head as she remembered the secret encounters in empty rooms. She wondered if the staff knew the boss and his wife were having a quickie. The thought made her want to giggle but she suppressed the urge since they weren't alone in the elevator.

Closing the door to their suite and putting on the security latch, Jeff turned around to find his wife standing in front of him. Tilting his head slightly to one side he waited to see what she was intending, because the look in her eye told him something was about to happen. He didn't have long to wait before his jacket was quickly disposed of. Then her hands moved to his shirt and started to slowly undo the buttons. She looked directly into his eyes as the shirt was pushed off and allowed to drop to the floor. Holding her gaze he folded his arms across his now bare chest, offering no assistance or resistance; he was quite enjoying this turn of events.

Moving to his trousers, she slid the zip down in record time and before long his trousers were on the floor. He made no move to touch her but held her eyes with his own. Very slowly she unfastened the buttons on her top, slipped her arms out and let it fall to the ground. Moving to her pants she undid the zip and stepped out of them. Standing in front of him wearing only her undies, she placed her thumbs under the band of his briefs, easing them down, until they fell to the floor.

That he wanted her was obvious to see, but she clearly wanted to **tease** him. Slipping her own briefs over her hips she let them fall. Holding his gaze, she moved her hands round to the catch on the back of her bra then slowly unhooked it but before she could let it drop his hands came up and held hers.

"I think I can take over from here." His voice was husky as he spoke.

With a smile she moved her hands, leaving him holding the open ends. Slowly he let the bra drop exposing the hard, erect nipples. Dropping the last item on the floor he pulled her close until he felt her breasts pressing into him. The feel of her soft body against his skin was pure heaven. They needed to move, the entrance to the room was no place for what was intended. Picking her up, for he was certain she wouldn't be able to walk, he carried her through to the bedroom. Throwing back the covers with one hand he laid her on the white sheet and stood over her, taking in every detail of her body.

"Well, wife, I guess you had this planned?"

"You did say later, and it is later now," she said, grinning at him.

Climbing onto the bed alongside her, he pulled her on top of him, his hands caressing her back. Her skin feels like velvet, he thought as teeth nibbled at his neck and ears. "Sarah, you're killing me," he groaned.

Laughing, she sat up, straddling him. He held her there, enjoying the sight of her naked body above him. Feeling his desire reaching toward a point of no return he gently eased her backwards and lifted her up so he was poised to enter her. He heard her gasp and halted. "Am I hurting you?"

She shook her head. "You make me do and want things I should be ashamed of," she whispered.

"There's nothing to be ashamed of, darling. We're two people in love, who, thankfully, happen to be married to each other. So stop talking, Sarah, and let me make love to you."

Arching his body, he moved deeper inside until she begged him to let go. Quickly turning so she was underneath, he took them both to the heights of desire, before bursting inside her and taking her with him as they fell, spiralling out of control, back to earth.

They lay with her legs wrapped around his hips, both gasping for breath.

"Wow," he said, "you keep surprising me, Mrs Saunders, not that I'm complaining. I'm really enjoying this second honeymoon, it could even be better than the first."

"Don't say that. The first one was special. It had to be, since it was the first time we made love. You took my virginity that night and I will never forget how gentle you were, or how wonderful it was. I have never wanted anyone to make love to me, but you." The words were spoken softly but sincerely.

"Sorry, I shouldn't joke. I know it was special. I can still remember it as well. I'd waited a long time for that moment and it will always be special. And for the record, I've never wanted anyone else but you in my bed. But now I seem to have a wanton hussy on my hands and I'm going to have to go some to keep her satisfied."

They both laughed at his description of her, neither of them in any hurry to move from their present position. Some time later, they stirred themselves and made use of the extra large Jacuzzi in the bathroom, taking time to wash each other playfully in the hot soapy water.

The next morning, Sarah slipped out of their room, with the intention of going to reception and enquiring if there was a post office nearby. She had a letter to send to Annie. Following instructions she took the escalator down a floor and was surprised to find a shopping mall together with a large food court. Having dealt with the letter she quickly scooted around the food area, a mischievous thought coming into her head.

Jeff allowed her to pull him away from the direction of the hotel restaurant, dutifully following her down the escalator. She laughed at the look on his face.

"Come on, Jeff. Surely you haven't forgotten how we would meet in places like this?"

He grinned and shook his head. "Are you sure about this, darling?"

"Definitely. It's great. I love the simplicity of it," she said, looking around. The area was full of tourists and people meeting with friends. Choosing from one of the many outlets they found a table and began eating with the plastic cutlery. She laughed at the expression on Jeff's face. But to Sarah it was fun, and she laughed and talked as they ate, then dashed into Tim Horton's, returning with two lattés. Setting them down on the table, her eyes sparkled with laughter as he shook his head, not in dismay, but remembering the other times they did this.

"Is this a walk down memory lane, Sarah?"

"Perhaps, or just a reminder of how the simplest of things would please us."

He reached across the table and took her hand. "They still do, and no amount of money can replace memories. But money we have, we can't escape it, but we can still enjoy the things we used to. And yes, this is good, sharing something simple with the person you love. And as long as I have you, darling, I won't want anything else."

"Oh, I…"

"What, Sarah, didn't you expect that declaration?"

She shook her head.

"Good to know I can still surprise you. Now drink your coffee before it gets cold," he said aiming the straw at her lips.

Afterwards, they took the escalator back to the hotel lobby where Jeff told her they had some very serious shopping to do. "You are badly in need of a new wardrobe, sweetheart."

Being used to buying her clothes from chain stores or charity shops, the Boutiques he took her into scared her, particularly when she heard the price of some of the items.

But Jeff wasn't listening to any arguments, and by the end of the day she had acquired at least six dresses, the same number of smart pants and casual pants. Tops and blouses that would last her years, together with accessories she was sure she would never get to wear. Shoes, she usually hated shopping for shoes, but the styles that were brought out for her were a delight. Dainty strappy sandals, smart high heels, and casual shoes all in wonderful colours, all carefully chosen to match the newly bought clothes. It had been hard at first to let go of her thrifty attitude, but one look at Jeff's face told her this was non-negotiable.

Finally, Jeff took her to a lingerie boutique and, after telling the salesperson what they wanted, said he would leave her to choose. "That way they will all be a surprise for me," he whispered. Telling her that he would be back shortly he left her to the tender mercies of the sales person who, Sarah was sure, must have thought all her birthdays had come at once and was probably already totalling up her commission before Jeff had even left the store.

Exquisite bras and briefs, the likes of which she had never seen, except in glossy magazines, left her breathless. The silk nightgowns with matching robes were chosen with Jeff in mind. Although she doubted they would be on long enough to be fully appreciated. Finally, just before he returned she selected a number of sheer tights to wear on special occasions.

Sarah was horrified at the number of items they had bought, but Jeff had taken it in his stride, settled the various accounts, before arranging for them all to be delivered to the hotel. Leaving the shop, Jeff took her by the hand and they walked along Robson Street strolling in and out of the various shops. "Just in case you have missed anything," he teased.

By late afternoon, Sarah was shattered and said as much to Jeff. Hailing a cab they went back to the hotel. By the time they were ready to go out for dinner all of the packages had arrived.

She selected a simple deep blue silk dress with a wrap around drape effect and coupled this with a pair of nude heeled shoes. A cream coloured light jacket finished off the look and would be just right to keep out the evening chill. Glancing across the room at her husband, dressed in mid cream smart trousers with a pale blue shirt, the sight of him made her heart flutter. Bringing home, again, that this was all real.

Jeff picked up the room key and held out his hand to her. Walking out of the hotel into the waiting cab, Sarah was excited and wondered where they were going. The cab stopped outside the Harbour Centre and they took the lift up to the revolving restaurant. "I took the opportunity of making a reservation," he whispered as they followed the waiter.

Sitting at the table next to the window, she was able to look out over the city and the harbour as they slowly revolved, so slow she could hardly tell they were moving. Jeff pointed out various places to her and, as the sun set, the lights of the city came on and the view took on a whole new concept. The lamps in Gas Town made the area look like a wonderland, although according to Jeff not far from there was an area of a much different character. The experience for Sarah was out of this world, she was so happy she could have cried. Arriving back at the hotel she was oblivious to anything but her husband and the light touch of his arm around her shoulders. All she wanted now was to spend the night in his arms, something she knew she could depend upon.

The following morning breakfast was delivered to their room. Wrapped in matching hotel bathrobes they sat at the table, set by the waiter, next to the window enjoying the view, and watching the helicopters and float planes taking off from the inlet as they ate.

Watching the almost childlike excitement on her face brought a smile to his lips. Things could so easily have turned out differently. From the moment he saw her he knew his feelings hadn't changed, perhaps one day he would confess how scared he'd been that she might not feel the same.

"Hey, you look serious." Sarah's voice interrupted his thoughts. "Are you okay?"

"Darling, I am more than okay. I was just thinking, and enjoying the view." Leaving her to decide which view he meant.

As this was their last day in Vancouver, they went to the top of Grouse Mountain and then stopped off at the Capilano Suspension Bridge on the way back. Jeff had no qualms, and laughed at her fear of going on, teasing her from a distance while he was walking out.

"I don't care what you say, Jeffrey Saunders, there is no way you are getting me out there," she said laughingly. She loved him, but this was one journey she was not going to take with him.

Tired, relaxed, and happy they returned to the hotel, then after changing, made their way down to the hotel restaurant for an early dinner.

"I thought we could leave early in the morning and make a stop after a couple of hours for a late breakfast?"

"That's fine with me. You're the one driving, so whatever you think best." Once back in their suite, she took the opportunity of packing, so they were ready for an early start.

Loading the car the next morning took a bit longer with all the extra packages but, with the help of the porter, this was soon done. Driving out of Vancouver, Jeff turned onto the highway and soon they were heading back in the direction of Banff. They stopped in a small town that night and set off again early next morning reaching the outskirts of Banff in the early evening. Turning into the driveway, Sarah was struck by the beauty of the house as it stood bathed in the early evening sun.

Jeff turned to her and smiled. "Welcome home, Mrs Saunders."

Leaning toward him, she placed her hand on his and returned his smile. "I am home whenever I'm with you."

"I feel the same way too, darling. All we have to do now is to bring our wayward son back into the fold.

Chapter Sixteen

Waking the next morning, it took a few minutes for her to remember where she was, but the warm body next to her was enough to remind her that it didn't matter what bed she was in as long as he was with her.

They had both been tired the night before, particularly Jeff, making her realise she really needed to do something about driving again. She couldn't rely on Jeff to run her about. It was a long time since she had driven any real distance, and Jeff's car was a lot bigger and much more powerful than the small mini she was used to. But she could decide about that another time. Snuggling into his back, she wrapped an arm around him, then felt her hand grasped, as a husky voice wished her good morning. He turned and drew her into his side. They lay there, reminiscing about the last couple of weeks until eventually she made the effort to get up and greet the day.

Having phoned Tom, Jeff was pleased work didn't need him today. Tom had assured him that Corey had been pulling his weight and that he had, in fact, gone to see him the day he had gone away.

"I think he realised that he'd gone too far by not turning up for the meeting. When he found out you had gone away he was genuinely shaken, and I have to admit, Jeff, I felt sorry for him."

"Good. It's about time my son learned he can't have it all his way all of the time. Sorry if that sounds harsh, Tom, and I know you must be aware there is something wrong. The only thing I can say at present is that I will explain it all to you before too long. All I ask for now is that you keep an eye on him, he's got a lot of soul searching to do, and he's got to do it on his own."

As he put the phone down, Jeff knew Tom would be curious. But he couldn't say anything more to him at this time. He'd given enough indication to let him know this was something more serious than a simple disagreement.

Having completed one call, Jeff phoned Laura at work. She sounded pleased to hear his voice, but sorry to tell him that things hadn't really changed apart from the fact that she saw Corey coming out of the guest bedroom one day.

"I thought perhaps he'd opened the cases, but when I checked, nothing had been disturbed. They were exactly where you'd left them, and were still unopened."

"Thanks anyway, Laura, for the update. I can only say again how sorry I am for making life so difficult for the two of you."

"It can't be helped, and to be honest, Jeff, I'm starting to get mad at Corey for being so stubborn about the situation. He was really shocked when you went away without saying anything to him, especially when you were away for Canada Day. I think it may have started him thinking about things, but at present he's sticking to his guns. He's just carrying on as if nothing is wrong and it's really frustrating. I've come so close to telling him about his grandma and me because I know it would change his mind…"

"No, Laura, don't do that. I really need him to work this out himself."

"I know you do, that's why I've kept quiet, and I will as long as you want me to."

"You're a star, Laura, and I will make it up to you as I've said before."

Leaving the den, he went in search of Sarah, and found her outside looking at the garden. She appeared deep in thought so he waited patiently. Eventually, Sarah turned to him.

"Do you think we could get some large pots to put on the patio and some plants to go in them?"

He smiled at the request. She was seeking to put her own mark on the garden and make it her own. "Whatever you want, Mrs. Saunders. You only have to ask."

Shortly afterwards, he drove them to an out of town nursery. On the way there he told her of his call to Laura and that things were still the same with Corey. She went quiet and he heard the soft sigh, so squeezed her hand. "He'll come around, darling, things will work out given time. Trust me." He only hoped his last words were not wishful thinking.

To take Sarah's mind off what was happening he allowed her free rein at the nursery to choose what she wanted. He patiently followed her until she was satisfied she had everything she needed, before handing over his credit card and then driving home.

Unloading the purchases from the car, they carried them round the side of the house and through the gate into the garden. Following instructions as to where each was to go, he left the soil and plants on the patio, telling Sarah she could play with them the next day, while he was at work.

After waving Jeff off to work the following morning, Sarah looked forward to planting up the pots. It was a small step, but it made her feel a part of the house by contributing toward the garden. Hopefully she would have them finished by the time Jeff got home. Changing into a pair of old shorts and sandals, she pulled on one of her old tops, one that had seen better days, then wandered outside into the sun.

She worked steadily all morning but remembered Jeff's parting words, to drink plenty of water. Breaking for lunch, she surveyed her handiwork, pleased with the two pots she had already completed. Working on through the afternoon she finished the remaining pots and cleared away the mess from the patio. Admiring her finished handiwork, she was delighted. The pots gave a lift to the patio and separated it from the lawn area with a burst of colour in each. This is my garden now. More work was needed to add softer colours to bring the areas of greenery in the borders to life. Oh, she was going to have such fun doing it all. Pulling the hosepipe out from the wall connection she turned on the water and carefully watered each newly planted pot. Walking across the grass she began to water the borders, spraying the water left and right, making sure everything got a good soaking.

* * * *

Jeff was glad to be heading home. He had attempted to speak to Corey on the phone about business, but whenever he rang he was told he wasn't there. Knowing full well he was there made him angry. Enough was enough, something needed to be done to shake Corey out of his comfort zone. Phoning Tom, he made sure of his facts about Corey's whereabouts that day and, satisfied that he had been avoiding him, instructed Tom to send him out to Canmore for a couple of weeks to work under Steve.

"Are you sure that's the best thing to do?" questioned Tom.

"No, but I'm running out of options, and perhaps the drive there and back each day might give him time to think and come to his senses."

Tom didn't argue. "When do you want me to send him there?"

"No time like the present, so as of tomorrow. I'll have a quick word with Steve but I'll leave you to work the finer details out with him and inform Corey of the arrangement." Putting the phone down, he felt bad at drawing Tom into the battle of wills he was having with his son. But he needed to take some constructive action, and hoped that this was not the wrong move.

Having made the decision, Jeff felt both guilty and relieved. He needed to have things sorted out; not being able to bring Sarah into town for fear of bumping into Corey was getting him down. They were living a normal married life at home, but he couldn't extend it beyond there. He wanted to show Sarah off, to let people know they were a couple and to do the normal things that married couples do, go out for dinner, go shopping. More than anything and he wanted to show her the hotels, and all that he had built up in the years they had been apart. But most of all, he wanted people to know that she hadn't deserted him and their son. That she had always been a loving wife and mother. But until Corey accepted the situation, Jeff wasn't able to do any of that, so hopefully forcing things somewhat, might have some effect. Arriving home he let himself in. Seeing Sarah still busy in the garden he went upstairs to change before joining her.

Sarah wasn't quite sure when she realised she wasn't alone, and turned quickly around, forgetting the pipe in her hand, spraying water as she did. As he walked across the lawn, Jeff got a soaking he didn't expect.

Clasping a hand to her mouth, she said, "Sorry," as she tried hard to contain a burst of laughter.

"You will be," he replied, with a glint in his eyes.

Moving backward, she could only do one thing and sprayed water in front of his feet as he moved toward her. Laughing nervously, she kept backing away but knew it was useless, he just kept advancing with a determined look on his face and a mischievous grin. She was going to get soaked. Should she surrender now or try running away? But to run could prove difficult as she was now running out of lawn. She took a chance, darting off to the side still spraying water as she did.

Jeff watched her eyeing up an escape, and was ready. As she tried to run past him he grabbed the hosepipe from her, getting a soaking as he did. With the pipe held firmly in one hand, he managed to grasp her around the waist with the other. She was almost hysterical with laughter, begging him to let her go. Dropping the hosepipe, he swung her around, lifting her off the ground, and was about to bring her lips down onto his when he felt her stiffen in his arms and her laughter stopped. She was looking beyond him, over his shoulder toward the house.

Fearing that Corey was behind them, he gently put her down and turned slowly around. It was a relief to find Laura standing in the doorway. The bemused look on her face told him that she had been watching them. He looked beyond her but couldn't see anyone else. Realising that this was a potentially awkward situation he decided to play it cool, calling out,

"Hi, Laura, want to come and join the fun?"

Laughing, she declined. He wasn't surprised, she'd been caught up in water fights with him and Corey before, but his comment had broken the awkward silence.

Taking Sarah's hand he led her back toward the house knowing that this meeting was inevitable. He could see from the look on Sarah's face that she was in shock, the last thing she would have expected was to see anyone there. And that was his fault, he realised, for not securing the door when he came home. He knew what would be going through her mind. If Laura was here, was Corey with her? Well, that was something he could settle now.

"You on your own, Laura?" he asked calmly, more calm than he actually felt.

As they walked back across the lawn Jeff knew that if she was alone, he would now have to draw Laura into this secret, and ask her to keep Sarah's presence to herself for now. Something he hadn't wanted to do considering the other secret she was already keeping.

* * * *

Laura was still coming to terms with the sight that had greeted her. She'd heard the shouts of laughter while walking across the hall, and had stood back watching them from the kitchen. They were clearly enjoying each other's company. The playful banter between them left her in no doubt that they were together as a couple.

She recognised the auburn haired woman as the same one with Jeff the day they came back unexpectedly, even though she had only caught a fleeting glimpse of her. Watching her, she saw where Corey had inherited some of his mannerisms from, he laughed in the same way, throwing his head slightly back. Seeing them today and the way they were together just confirmed her suspicion that this was Corey's mom. The realisation brought her thoughts back to Jeff's question.

"Yes, it's okay. Corey had to stay late for a meeting with Tom so I thought I would take the chance to drop by and see you, find out how the trip went, but I didn't know you had a visitor." Why did I say that? I know perfectly well who this is and I don't think she's just visiting. Having said the words she couldn't take them back and waited for Jeff to reply.

Reaching the patio, Jeff let go of Sarah's hand and leaned forward to hug his daughter-in-law. Moving back, he placed his arm around Sarah's shoulders and moved her to his side.

"I guess introductions are in order. Laura, I'd like you to meet Sarah, my wife and..."

"Corey's mom," she finished the sentence for him.

"Yes, how did you know?"

"I just did. I knew there was something the day we arrived back unexpectedly and saw you together. There was a closeness between you that struck me as odd, and also I have never seen you with a woman before."

"Hey, Laura, don't let Sarah think I've been a monk."

"Yeah, okay, so what do you want me to say, that you've had a parade of females, because you and I both know that's not true."

"Okay, the truth's out. I've been pining for Sarah all this time." He laughed as he spoke and hugged Sarah to him.

Laura looked serious for a moment. "Yes, I think you have." Then smiled suddenly. "But going back to what I was saying....When Corey told me what you had said to him about his grandma I knew who it was with you that day, and just now watching you together, it was so obvious. I felt like I was watching Corey and me and, looking at Sarah, I can see Corey has inherited some of her mannerisms."

"I only wish he had inherited her ability to forgive," said Jeff wryly.

Throughout this, Sarah stood looking at the young woman in front of her, who was her daughter-in-law, listening to the banter between her and Jeff, and wondering how she should re-act. But before she could decide Laura took the initiative and stepped forward.

"I guess I can hug my mom-in-law. If that's okay?"

With a feeling of relief, Sarah moved forward. "Of course you can, Laura. I'm only too happy to meet you at last."

Jeff suggested they adjourn inside. "While I turn off the water before the garden is flooded," he said, frowning jokingly at Sarah.

Leading the way into the house, Sarah asked Laura if she would like a drink, then realised that she probably knew the house better than she did. Opening the fridge she lifted out a jug of juice, poured three glasses, and then carried them through to the lounge. Jeff called through that he was going to change into something dry, emphasising the word dry for Sarah's benefit.

Watching, Laura saw how Sarah laughed when he said that, but also noticed how her hand shook slightly as she lifted her glass. Wanting to put her at ease she leaned forward.

"It's okay, Sarah. I understand what has happened and how."

Sarah gave a relieved smile. "I know you do, Laura. Jeff told me what had happened between you and Corey's grandmother. I'm just sorry that you had to go through that. But at least things worked out for you both."

"Yes, thankfully. But it was awful at the time," said Laura. "I hate the way things are at present. It's almost as if Sylvia is still here and manipulating everything again. I just wish Corey would listen to what his dad has told him."

"I'm sure he will in time," she said with more conviction than she felt. "How is Corey, otherwise?"

"Stubborn and infuriating at present."

"He probably gets that from his grandmother."

"Who's stubborn?" asked Jeff, walking into the room and sitting next to Sarah. Draping one arm behind her, he took the offered glass from her and waited for a reply.

"Corey is, apparently," replied Sarah.

"Yes, well I've done something to try and resolve that. Look, I'm sorry, Laura, but the meeting he's having with Tom at present is to tell him he's going to Canmore for a few weeks. I thought perhaps the drive back and forth might give him some time to reflect on things."

"He won't like that," said Laura. "You know how he prefers being in Banff where he knows everyone."

"I know he won't, but he's brought it on himself by deliberately avoiding my phone calls. I really thought by the time we got back from holiday he would have moved some way toward accepting what I'd told him, but the fact that he hasn't is making me more annoyed as the days go by. I've never lied to him before and I can't understand why he would think I'm doing so now. Apart from that, I'm sick of hiding Sarah away in the house, or skulking off to out of the way restaurants where we won't be seen, just to avoid bumping into him or anyone who knows him."

Seeing the frustration and annoyance in Jeff's face Laura understood why he was doing this. "Well, as I said, he won't like it but if you think it may help then I'm fine with it. I just want it to be over and for us all to be able to have a normal relationship."

"Thanks, Laura, that makes me feel a bit better about doing what I am, and I know Sarah and I will be glad when he comes to his senses. It's about time he got to know his mom," he said, giving Sarah's shoulder a squeeze. "Anyway, tell us how you both are and how you're settling in to married life, and we'll tell you all about our trip, or perhaps I should say our second honeymoon." He looked mischievously at Sarah, watching her blush.

Driving home, Laura couldn't help but reflect on what she'd discovered. If only she could confide in her own mom about what was going on, but knew it was impossible until it was all sorted out. It was hard trying to keep up the pretence of agreeing with what Corey was doing when she knew it was wrong. If only he could see his mom and dad the way she had seen them today he would realise they belonged and deserved to be together after everything they had been put through. In all the years she had known Jeff, she had never seen him look at anyone the way he looked at Sarah.

Pulling up outside their apartment, she noticed Corey through the lounge window. Darn it. She had hoped to get back before him. Climbing out of the car she waved as she walked toward the door. He raised his arm in reply. Opening the door for her, he planted a quick kiss on her lips.

"You'll never guess what Tom's just told me, and I know it's come from dad, although Tom wouldn't say that."

"What?" she asked with a sigh, knowing full well what he was about to tell her.

"I've been banished to Canmore."

He sounded so dramatic Laura had to turn away to stifle the laughter that rose in her throat. Keeping her back to him she walked into the kitchen, poured a glass of water, took a long sip, and then went back to join him.

"What do you mean banished?"

"I've got to go and work with Steve for a few weeks, something about them being extra busy. But I know its dad's doing."

"Why would he do that?"

"Because he's ticked off that we're not speaking at present and that I won't believe what he's told me. I've a good mind not to go."

Sighing, she said, "Corey, look, I know how you feel about what your dad has told you but have you stopped to think this through properly? And how is not going to Canmore going to help?"

"What do you mean properly?" he queried, his voice rising.

Realising she was going to have to say something constructive to avoid an argument, she took another sip of water and thought carefully before she replied.

"Well ask yourself this; have you ever known your dad to lie to you before about anything? Have you ever known him to take one person's word about anything before having it checked out properly, particularly something as serious as this? And why would he tell you something he knew would upset and hurt you if he wasn't certain it was true?"

"So you're on his side?" he flung back at her.

"No, I'm not on anyone's side, and there are no sides anyway." Laura could feel herself getting annoyed with her husband. "All I'm saying is look at it logically, try and get some perspective on it. Why would your dad lie to you? To be honest, I'm fed up with you and your dad not speaking, I hate it. I hate us not being able to go and see him, and I hate seeing you so miserable. We've just come back from honeymoon and instead of being happy and looking forward to each new day together, I'm worrying all the time about what's going to happen next. It's got to stop, Corey, because I've had enough." There, she thought, I've said it.

Looking at his shocked face she wondered if she had gone too far. He was just staring at her, looking visibly shaken by what she had said. She never lost her cool and no doubt this had shocked him. For a moment she felt sorry and was tempted to apologise. But that would serve no purpose and her outburst was something that had been growing for weeks. So perhaps it was best that he saw how she felt.

"I'm sorry, I had no idea. I guess I've been so wrapped up in the situation with dad that I didn't give a thought as to how it was affecting you."

Shrugging her shoulders, she said quietly, "No, I guess not. Corey, you are a kind, sensitive and wonderful person, but sometimes you are too stubborn for your own good. I know what your dad told you about your grandma was a dreadful thing for you to hear, but if it is true, have you really stopped to think how he must have felt finding this out and realising what he had lost all those years ago, and then knowing that he was going to have to tell you?" Taking a deep breath she continued. "If what he told you was true, then he and your mom were forced apart and she didn't desert either of you. Can you, for one minute, imagine how she must have felt knowing that she couldn't go back to her husband and baby? Please, darling, you have got to open your mind to the possibility that it could be true for everybody's sake, particularly your own."

Fearing that she had finally said too much she stopped there and waited for his reaction. Having spent the last hour with his parents she wanted nothing more than for them to be reunited as a family but didn't dare let him know that, well not yet anyway. Not getting any reply she turned and walked through to the kitchen. She would give him time to digest what she had said.

He watched her retreating back, not knowing what to say. But hearing Laura's words and knowing how she felt about the situation made him feel sick to his stomach. She was right, they should be enjoying this special time together, but it was all messed up. It was his dad's fault, but in the back of his mind a small voice was whispering something different. Whatever he thought, he wasn't going to have Laura unhappy. Walking through to the kitchen he stood for a moment watching as she rinsed the glass before placing it on the top. Then moving toward her, wrapped his arms around her and held her close.

"I'm sorry. I just don't know how to deal with it."

She held him tightly. "I know you don't. You and your dad have never fallen out like this, darling. You need to listen to your head as well as your heart on this one and, if you do that, you will know what you have to do next."

Corey listened, knowing that what she was saying was right. Her words made him ashamed of how he'd let this situation come about, but he wasn't ready yet to try and face up to things. What he did want to do was to make amends to Laura right now.

"Look, sweetheart, how about we go out for dinner since I'm likely to be late home for a while as I'll be working in Canmore.

Sitting in the restaurant later, she watched him as she sipped her wine. It was almost impossible to believe how bad things had been these last few weeks. She felt tired and more than a little sad. As if reading her thoughts, he reached for her free hand and squeezed it. Meeting his gaze she wondered if anything she had said had penetrated enough for him to do something constructive about it. Giving him a smile she squeezed his hand back.

"Why don't we get the check, then have coffee and dessert at home?" he suggested with a grin.

Noticing the glint in his eyes, she knew exactly what he meant by dessert. A flash of her previous annoyance came back at his suggestion, as if that was going to solve everything. Seeing his expectant face, she suddenly realised that perhaps she did have some leverage in the present situation. It wasn't something she would particularly enjoy but it might help bring about some kind of resolution a bit quicker.

Leaning across the table, smiling into his eyes, she said very quietly, "That kind of dessert is off the menu. So if you want dessert I suggest you have one here." Still smiling, she leaned back in her seat.

He looked as if she had hit him and felt a twinge of guilt, but the remark had gone home. His jaw tightened so she knew he was angry, or was that frustration, she thought. Glancing around the room while she finished her drink she could see the attractive females ogling at him.

She glanced back at him, he'd been watching her and, as if to teach her a lesson, he smiled broadly at a very attractive blonde a few tables away. Laura found it amusing, so turned and smiled at her as well, causing the poor girl to blush and look quickly away. Realising that he wasn't going to win he called for the check much to Laura's amusement.

They walked home in a somewhat uncomfortable silence. Laura did allow him to hold her hand, thankful that he had done so. She didn't want open warfare, or even an argument, but was determined to stick to what she had said. Jeff was taking some action to try to resolve matters, this would be her contribution.

Lesley Field

Arriving home, Corey made coffee and handed a mug to her. Switching on the television he checked out the weather for the next day. Sitting on the sofa together with his arm draped around her shoulders, he figured that she had been joking earlier, so ran his fingers up and down her bare arm to test her reaction. When she didn't stop him he started to nibble her ear and the side of her neck. Venturing further, his hand moved across to her breast and still she didn't stop him. Deciding everything was okay between them he suggested they have an early night.

Laura had quickly escaped into the bathroom. What he had been doing was torture. Her body had responded to him but she was determined to fight against it. After splashing her face with cold water several times she went into the bedroom. She was going to have to resist his attempts to seduce her, and knew from experience that he was very good at that. Having now seen his mom and dad together she knew exactly where he got it from.

Climbing into bed, she avoided direct eye contact and immediately turned off her bedside light. Responding in the same way he settled down and turned toward her. Before she could turn away, his hand came across her stomach and he began moving in to kiss her. Well, she thought, kissing isn't prohibited, so responded to his kiss, but then immediately turned in his arms, setting her back to him. Very quietly, she said goodnight. He wasn't one to give up easily but after a few minutes, he turned away. Offering a silent prayer of thanks, she didn't know how long she would have held out. Closing her eyes, she willed herself to sleep.

He moved carefully out of the bed so as not to wake her but couldn't help but see her tanned back where the covers had pulled back. He longed to run his hands down her body but was certain he would get a cool response. Anyway, he needed to get ready for the drive to work.

Laura had felt the movement. Turning over she opened her eyes and looked across at him. "Hi, husband."

"Hi yourself," he called back as he headed for the shower.

Laura chuckled. The slight exposure of her breast as she turned was no accident. She just wanted to remind him of what he was missing. She could quite enjoy this game, although she hoped it wasn't going to last for too long.

By the time Corey came out of the shower and was dressed Laura had prepared coffee and toast for them. As they sat at the breakfast bar she couldn't resist allowing her short robe to fall open as she crossed her legs, displaying a tanned leg for his benefit. She saw his jaw clench and bit back the smile.

"I'm going for my shower. You have a good day, and drive carefully." Slipping her arms round his neck she whispered, "I love you, Corey Saunders, and don't you forget it." Placing a kiss on his lips she felt him try to take control, but she pulled back reminding him he would be late. "I'll see you tonight," she said as she slipped from the chair and disappeared into the bathroom, with the intention of having a cold shower. She didn't know how much of this shunning she could keep up. Corey needed to come to his senses, and quick.

Chapter Seventeen

Driving out of Banff toward Canmore, Corey was cursing the fact that he'd had to leave so early. He may have been able to persuade Laura back to bed if he'd had more time. She was playing with him and while part of him was quite enjoying the teasing, he would prefer the ending to be somewhat different. Keeping an eye out for early morning animal activity on the road he switched on the radio but wasn't really paying much attention to it. His mind kept going over the things Laura had said last night, and what his dad had told him. By the time he got to Canmore he was more confused than ever and glad to switch into hospitality mode for the rest of the day.

The next few days followed the same routine. Work and home and, if he was honest, he was beginning to prefer the time at work. Laura was still playing the temptress with him leading him on, which was something he wasn't going to turn down, and then closing the door on him at the last minute. He'd had more cold showers in the last few days than he'd had during his teen years, but he knew she was feeling it too. She couldn't disguise the trembling when he kissed her, but this game was of her making, so he was prepared to wait. He wondered how long she would last before surrendering to him.

Driving back and forth to work gave him too much time to think. Although he still didn't want to believe what his dad said about his grandma, he had reluctantly accepted that his dad had never lied to him, nor did he suffer fools gladly so would have checked out what he'd been told. He hadn't discussed the matter with Laura at all since the night they had what he supposed was their first marital argument.

He was tired tonight, and the drive home seemed never ending. It had been a particularly busy day with a lot of people checking out who'd been staying for the Calgary Stampede. His drifting thoughts were brought sharply back into focus when an elk suddenly appeared at the side of the road. For a moment he thought it was going to cross and was ready to react, but it lowered its head and started grazing. The incident made him recall his grandmother's accident, reminding him how quickly one's life can change. The thought made him shudder. Now, he just wanted to get home to Laura.

Arriving home, he'd forgotten Laura had invited a few of her girlfriends. By the time they left he was tired and grumpy. Helping her clear away the dishes, he tried to pull her toward him. He wanted to tell her he loved her, but as he reached out he knocked a plate out of her hand causing it to smash on the floor.

"Now look what you've done," she snapped.

"Sorry. I've had a really tough day and all I wanted was to hold my wife."

Laura immediately regretted what she had said. She hadn't meant to snap but this sex ban she had imposed was getting to her, and spending a night with her girlfriends pretending all was wonderful had been a strain.

"I'm sorry as well. I didn't mean to snap. I'm tired too. You go on through to bed, I'll clear this up."

"Are you sure?"

"Wouldn't have said it if I wasn't. You go on, I won't be long."

She didn't need to tell him again and watched as he quickly disappeared into the bedroom. By the time Laura climbed into bed he was asleep. Leaning across, she gently kissed him on the forehead, told him she loved him, then turned over pulling the covers around her.

When she woke the next morning, Corey's side of the bed was empty.

* * * *

Jeff was becoming more and more annoyed, and frustrated at Corey's continued silence. It had been well over six weeks since he had told him everything that his grandmother had done, and over a week since Laura had been to the house. After his initial storming out, Jeff had expected him to come to terms with what he'd been told by now, but still nothing, only silence. Laura had been keeping him updated on Corey's frame of mind, but there was no change. He was still adamant that he didn't believe his grandmother would have done such a thing to them. Jeff was glad that he had taken Sarah away from the situation for a couple of weeks, in truth he'd been glad to be away himself, but disappointed they had come back to the continued silence. He'd told Sarah that Corey would come around in his own time, and they just had to be patient, but his own patience was wearing thin.

As well as looking after Saunders, Jeff was keeping an eye on Mountain View when Tom wasn't there, since Corey was still effectively banished to Canmore, until he saw fit to bring him back. The way things were looking hell would freeze over first. With all the events of the past few weeks running through his mind he was finding it difficult to concentrate on work and sitting in his office staring into space wasn't helping. The ringing of the phone brought him back to the present. Any hope that it would be Corey was dashed. Although, it was the Canmore hotel, it was Steve, the manager.

"Hi, Jeff, is Corey with you?"

"No. I haven't seen or spoken to him. Why?"

"Well, look, I don't want to worry you but he took some corporate clients to the airport. They'd had a problem with their transport and Corey offered to drive them, but they left just before seven this morning, it's now after two and he's not back. I've tried his cell phone but it just goes to voice mail. I've rung the airport and they've confirmed that the passengers checked in so I know he got them there, but he just seems to have disappeared, and it's not like him."

"How was he before he left?" asked Jeff, with a growing sense of unease.

"I must admit he didn't seem his usual self and he was in very early this morning. That's one of the reasons why I'm worried. I know there's some personal things going on, you know what the hotel grapevine is like for gossip. I didn't want to phone Laura and worry her so figured it was best to call you."

"Good decision, Steve. Last thing we want is Laura in a state and then finding out that Corey is sitting at home. Look, I'll go round to the apartment now and see if he's there. If not, I'll come back here and wait until Laura is home from work. If he's not surfaced by then, I'll go and see her. Look, just keep things under wraps for now. I'll let you know when we track him down, but if he turns up there let me know."

"Okay, Jeff. I'll speak to you soon."

As he put the phone down, Jeff's mind was racing. He didn't want to let on how worried he was, but this was certainly out of character for his son in any event, without the added complications of the last few weeks. Telling the reception he was going out for a while, he walked round to Corey and Laura's apartment. Corey's car wasn't there, but he would still check. He knocked on the door but got no reply, so using the spare key let himself in. The place was deserted, he knew the moment he stepped inside, but he still called out. No answer so he quickly left.

Back at the hotel, he checked there had been no road accidents before deciding the best course of action was to wait and see what happened, if anything, by five o'clock when he knew Laura would finish work. If there had been no news by then he would have to go and see her. He decided against letting Sarah know what was going on until he got home.

Watching the hands on the clock moving past five, Jeff picked up the phone and called Canmore, but Steve hadn't heard anything.

"I've tried calling him again, but just keep getting voice mail."

"Thanks, Steve. There's nothing I can do now but drive round to see Laura. I'll let you know when we hear anything."

Putting down the phone he sat for a moment. Where the hell are you, son? Sighing, he pulled on his jacket and set off to see Laura. Reaching the apartment, he noticed Laura's car but Corey's was still missing. Laura looked surprised to see him.

"Corey's not here," she said as she let him in.

"I know he's not, Laura, that's why I'm here."

Laura swung round. "Oh no...oh God please...please don't tell me he's had an accident?"

Seeing her white face Jeff quickly assured her that as far as he was aware he was okay but he had simply gone AWOL. "I know he's not been in an accident, Laura, because I've checked with the

RCMP and the hospitals. But we just can't find him. How was he this morning before he left?"

"I didn't see him; he'd gone when I woke up. But he wasn't happy last night and, to be honest, we'd had words," she admitted reluctantly.

Not wanting to pry, Jeff made no comment and continued speaking. "I know the revelations about his grandma have really knocked him and he's having a hard time coming to terms with his mom turning up, but just disappearing is totally out of character."

Nodding her head in agreement she said, "I know it is, and we had a bit of a bust up about things the day I'd been to yours and met Sarah. I really got annoyed with him about it and about him not looking at things properly. I told him how you have never lied to him before and why would you lie now. I thought that I was beginning to make him think." She paused, and looked at him. "Just a minute Jeff, I wonder..."

She quickly went to the bedrooms and opened the door to the guest bedroom. "You'd better see this, Jeff," she called out.

Jeff went through and, looking over her shoulder, saw the floor was strewn with parcels from the cases he had left with Laura. Some parcels had been opened and, picking up a small truck, Laura turned to him.

"What are they, where did they come from?"

"They are presents and cards that Sarah sent to Corey over the years. Things that my mother kept from him."

She stared at Jeff. "They weren't open yesterday because I was in here. He must have opened them sometime during the night, or early this morning. Oh, Jeff, what kind of a state must he be in?"

Seeing Laura close to tears he pulled her close. "Don't worry, Corey is sensible, well most of the time he is, and he'll work this out. All we can do is wait, at least we now know the reason for his disappearance."

Before leaving, Jeff made Laura promise to let him know as soon as Corey got home, no matter what the time was, even if Corey didn't want her to. He felt bad leaving Laura, but he needed to get home to Sarah, but how could he tell her what had happened. "I know you just want him home safely, Laura, and knowing Corey, he won't want you worrying. My guess is he'll be back soon. The fact that he has looked in the cases is a breakthrough, and hopefully a good sign. Look, if you need anything, give me a call."

Driving home, Jeff was more worried than he had let on to Laura, and he was still reluctant to mention Corey's disappearance to Sarah. Perhaps it would be best to wait and see what developed over the next couple of hours. Greeting Sarah with a hug and a kiss he felt guilty but knew he would have to do his best to hide his anxiety.

* * * *

Sarah wasn't stupid. She knew something was wrong the minute he stepped into the house. The small frown and the worried look in his eyes gave it away, but she said nothing, deciding to wait until he was ready to tell her. Patience is supposed to be a virtue, she thought, but by the time they had finished coffee she couldn't wait any longer.

"Okay, you told me there would never be any secrets between us again, but something is clearly wrong. So will you please tell me what it is?"

"Is it that obvious?"

"Yes. I knew from the moment you came home. Your eyes gave it away, not to mention the frown. So you had better tell me or I'll be thinking the worst."

Taking a deep breath Jeff said, "Corey's gone AWOL."

"What do you mean, AWOL?" A chill swept through her.

"Exactly that," and he proceeded to explain to her all that had happened that day from the first call from Steve to his visit with Laura, and what they had found out.

"You mean he's opened the parcels I sent to him over the years, and that's made him disappear?" There was no disguising the panic in her voice.

"No, darling, it's not like that. He's only opened some of them, and one can only hope that he's realised I was telling him the truth about what his grandmother really did. I have no doubt that he's extremely upset and has needed some time to come to terms with it all, hence the disappearing act."

"It's still all my fault that he's upset."

"No, it's not, Sarah," he said sternly. "If it's anybody's fault it's my mother's for ripping this family apart. And I'm not going to allow her to make you feel guilty. All we can do is wait. Laura is going to phone as soon as he turns up, and turn up he will. I know my son...sorry, our son, and he will work this out, but only in his own time."

They spent the evening trying to watch some television to take their minds away from listening for the phone. By eleven, Jeff insisted that Sarah go to bed but she was determined to stay up with him. By eleven thirty, Jeff had got to the stage of pacing from the lounge to his den. He was on his way back to the lounge when the phone rang. Picking it up he heard Laura's voice speaking quietly telling him that Corey had just come in, he was okay, and she would phone him tomorrow. The call was so short Jeff knew she had phoned without Corey's knowledge, and was grateful for her doing so. Relaying the message to Sarah he saw the relief in her eyes.

"Come on, Sarah. This day's drama is over. Let's try and get some sleep, then see what tomorrow brings." They walked slowly up to their room. Jeff went to the bathroom, and Sarah began to undress. Too tired to shower she fell into bed, her mind in turmoil. What was to happen now? Would their son let her back into his life, or...? No, she didn't want to think on that. She wasn't prepared to lose her family again. She would not let Sylvia win this war. She needed Jeff tonight. Needed to have him hold her. A tear ran down her cheek followed by another.

Having made a quick call to Steve, Jeff came back into the bedroom. Looking across to Sarah, he saw the tears rolling down her cheeks.

"It's not your fault, Sarah. Things will work out, trust me."

He pulled back the covers and lay beside her, then pulled her close, her naked body moulded to his. Looking directly into his eyes, she held her arms open.

"Make love to me, Jeff. Please?"

"You know you don't have to ask. I have great difficulty keeping my hands off you, but are you sure. With all that's happened tonight I would understand."

"I know you would but I need you more than ever tonight."

"As long as you're sure." Seeing her nod, he turned into her waiting arms.

* * * *

While Sarah and Jeff were making their own peace, Laura was trying not to be angry with Corey for what he had put them all through. When he'd walked in the door he had looked terrible, forcing her to stop being mad with him. Taking his jacket and steering him into the lounge, she calmly suggested that she make coffee for them both. He had said very little since he came in, except to mumble that he was sorry he was late. Now back in the lounge Laura handed a coffee to him and sat on the floor facing him.

"Okay, look, I know things have been really difficult over the past few weeks, but have you any idea how worried everyone's been? You've been missing most of the day, and not answering your phone. Your dad didn't tell me until this evening to spare me hours of worry, but he's been going out of his mind for most of the day. Where have you been?"

"I'm sorry, Laura. I just had to go somewhere to clear my head and when someone needed to be driven to Calgary airport it gave me the opportunity to do just that."

"Yes, but that was this morning, where have you been all these hours?"

"Sitting in a parking lot near one of the lakes, trying to make sense of it all."

"And have you?"

"I'm not sure, but I think so."

Looking down at her he leaned forward and took her hands in his.

"I woke up last night after you had come to bed and couldn't get back to sleep. I guess I was still upset about last evening and everything else, so I got up in the early hours. I don't know why but my curiosity about the cases dad left got the better of me. I know I said I didn't want to see what was in them as it would make no difference, but I suddenly felt a need to open them." Taking a deep breath he continued. "Do you know she wrote to me, and every birthday and Christmas sent me cards and gifts, but my grandma kept them all from me? I didn't think she loved dad or me and that was why she left, but reading her letters all those years ago, telling me how much she loved and missed us, I was wrong. Why would grandma do that to us?"

Looking at his face Laura saw the tears in his eyes, and although she wanted to hold him she needed him to finish telling her what had happened, so she just held his hands tightly, and waited.

"How can I face her after all the things I said to dad when I first found out. She must hate me now."

Pulling one hand free she reached up and touched his face. "No, darling, she won't. She's your mom and no matter what you do, or say, she will always love you. Believe me, I know that from experience and the things I have said to my mom over the years. A mother's love is unconditional."

"I hear what you're saying, Laura, but I'm scared. I don't even know where she is. Is she still here, and will she want to see me, and dare I go and see her?"

"She's probably more scared than you are, darling," she said, deciding not to answer the question about his mom's whereabouts.

Wiping a hand across his eyes Corey stood. "Come with me." She allowed him to lead her into the guest bedroom where they sat together on the floor while he opened every one of the remaining letters, parcels, and cards.

They cried a lot that night and Laura hoped that the tears would wash away some of the hurt that had been caused over the years. Now that Corey had accepted his grandma for what she was, she knew that it was now time to tell him the last piece of information, which may help him to understand why his mom had been manipulated in such a way. But that could wait until the morning, there had been enough emotion today and she didn't think either of them could take any more.

Waking next morning, Laura rang Jeff while Corey was still asleep and told him that she and Corey needed some space today, but that everything was going to be okay and confirmed that what he'd found in the cases was what had caused his disappearance. "And, Jeff, he's opened everything, he knows what his grandma did and he's accepted it. Well, perhaps not fully accepted it yet, but he's coming to terms with it." She made him promise to tell Sarah that everything was going to be fine. Before ending the call Jeff said that he had something else that she and Corey should see promising that it would help him. Laura hesitated. "I don't know if he can take any more, Jeff."

"He can this. I promise it will help, Laura. Trust me."

"Okay, are you going to bring whatever it is here?"

"No, I think me putting in an appearance right now wouldn't be the best thing to do. But I'll bring it to Saunders, and can get someone else to bring it round or, you could call to collect it?"

"Okay, but I think I'd better call. I'll try and call in sometime this morning."

She then had to phone work and tell them that she wasn't feeling well, something she hated doing, but it wasn't really a lie and there was no way she was going to leave Corey on his own. They spent the morning sorting through the contents of the cases.

"You know, we should keep these things, Corey. When we have a family they can have them and that will make them even more special."

He smiled. "I'd like that. I would hate to think that they were never used, or worn."

As they worked they talked and this gave Laura the opportunity to tell him how his grandma tried to break up their own relationship.

As Laura started talking he remembered how they had broken up for a couple of months. "I remember. It cost me a fortune in flowers and telephone messages trying to persuade you to give us another chance." He would have said more but the look on Laura's face stopped him.

"Your grandmother told me you were just sowing your wild oats with me and that nothing would come of our relationship as she would make sure that it ended. She told me I wasn't good enough for her grandson and for a time, Corey, I believed her. Then you kept pestering me and I thought if you only wanted a casual relationship why were you still chasing me. My friends all thought I was crazy to keep turning you down, and eventually I realised that I must be good enough for you as you obviously thought so. That was when we got back together and I can tell you now that your grandmother wasn't pleased when she found out. If I hadn't had the support of my folks, who now knew what was going on, I would have been tempted to walk away again. Her snide and cutting remarks really hurt, but you know what, eventually they made me more determined to show her that we were meant to be a couple. But if your grandmother hadn't had her accident she may still have managed to split us up, so while I was sorry that she was dead, in a way it was a relief. I'm sorry if that hurts you but it's what I felt at the time, and it's how I still feel."

Corey listened to what Laura was saying with growing horror. He didn't know what to say to her so just sat while she talked on.

"If I had been in your mom's position I think I would have ended up doing exactly what she did. It took a lot of courage to come back to see you, or rather us get married. She didn't know your grandmother had died but she risked her anger, and goodness knows what else, in coming back. If your dad hadn't seen her in the church she could have left without anyone knowing that she had even been here, and no one would have ever known what had really happened. And that would have been a tragedy for you, and for your dad."

This final tale about his grandmother was too much, he felt sick to his stomach. "Grandma was always so good to me. Always looking out for me. How could she have done what she did? It feels as though she controlled my life, deciding who should and shouldn't be in it. I'm so sorry, Laura, I had no idea."

"I know. No one did except my parents, until I told your dad a short time ago. I wanted to tell you about this earlier but your dad asked me not to. He wanted you to reach your own decision about your grandmother and your mom without being influenced in any way. While I wanted to tell you, I had to agree with him that it was best left unsaid until the right time, and that time is now."

Holding his wife in his arms Corey realised how his grandmother's actions had destroyed, and almost destroyed, so many lives. He had to face up to the truth of it all, and face his dad, then find out where his mom was. He needed to see her, no, he wanted to see her, to tell her he was sorry.

The fact they'd had nothing much to eat gave Laura the excuse of going out to get something for lunch, and also to call at the hotel to see Jeff. Walking back home, she wondered how she was going to explain the package Jeff had given her for Corey. Jeff had been so adamant that they see it she hadn't the heart not to take it.

Arriving back at the apartment she quickly put the package from Jeff in their bedroom and called Corey for lunch. Afterwards as they sat talking in the lounge, Laura admitted that she had been to see his dad while she was out, and also told him of her visit to Jeff's house a few days earlier, although she was careful to omit any mention of Sarah being there.

"I don't want you to think I was going behind your back seeing your dad, because I wasn't. But I felt that I needed to keep the contact with him, for both your sakes. Today, I called because he asked me to. He gave me a package and said that you needed to see it."

Walking back into the lounge she handed the package to him. "I don't know what's in it, but your dad says it's important that you see it."

Taking the package from her he opened it and was surprised to see it contained an album. Turning to the first page he realised that it was a record of his birth. Seeing what it was Laura suggested that he might want to look at it on his own but he shook his head and patted the floor next to him.

Sitting alongside she looked on as he slowly turned the pages seeing his parents, his mom pregnant, and himself from the moment he was born. Then information about his first tooth, when he first talked and walked and alongside him in these photographs was his mom.

"I've never seen these before, Laura."

She put her arm along his shoulders as they continued to watch the early years of his life unfolding in photographs. "That's my mom. She looks happy and so does dad."

"Of course they were. They had you and they loved you, and each other."

"So why did it all change?"

"It didn't. It was changed for them, as you now know."

"She looks beautiful. No wonder Dad fell for her."

Without thinking, Laura said, "She's still beautiful." Then realising her mistake, waited for him to say something, but her words hadn't registered with him yet. The moment passed.

They laughed at some of the photos that were obviously taken in a moment of fun but for Corey it showed him a part of his life he'd never seen before.

By the time he closed the album he realised that he owed one hell of an apology to his dad, and he felt nothing but bitterness toward his grandmother who had stolen his family life and made him grow up without his mom. Wiping the tears from his eyes he asked Laura how he was going to be able to face his dad.

"It won't be easy for you but he will understand, and he will forgive you. If I were you I would go and see him in the morning after you've had a decent night's sleep, and feel more up to facing him."

He nodded. "I don't think I could face him right now."

Deciding that he should know the final part of the story she said, "There is something else I think you should know."

He turned to face her. "I don't think I can take any more, Laura."

"Well, I think you can cope with this." She then revealed that his mom had been at the house the day she called to see his dad, and that she had met her.

"You'll love her, Corey, and if you could see them together you would see how much they love each other. In fact, you have seen them, remember the day we returned from our honeymoon?"

Laura waited for his reaction to what she said, and saw the look of amazement on his face.

"You mean that was my mom with dad, and she's been staying with him at the house?"

Smiling, she replied, "Not staying, darling, she's living there. They're together as a couple, and I've never seen your dad look so happy."

This was a revelation he hadn't expected but was surprised to find it didn't shock him. "What's she like?"

"Just like her photos but a bit older and any more information you will have to find out for yourself. One thing I can say is that I think...no, I know you will get on famously. I like your mom and you'll like her too. I promise you will."

Feeling happier than he had in weeks he turned to Laura and kissed her. "You know, I'm really glad grandma didn't chase you away."

Snuggling up together later in bed, they were both glad to have called an end to the sex ban. Their lovemaking was gentle and passionate, the tensions of the last few weeks had finally disappeared. Now they could concentrate on building their own new life together, one that would include Corey's mom and dad. But first of all he had to make his peace with them both.

Returning from work that day, Jeff confirmed all the updated information he had already given to Sarah over the telephone and was able to tell her what Laura had said that everything was going to be okay.

"I gave Laura the baby album for them to look at. It's the last piece in the puzzle for Corey, as he's never seen it before."

"Never?" queried Sarah.

"No, I didn't see any need to upset him with photos of a life I thought was a lie, but now he knows the truth, and he needs to see how it all started. I'm sorry I hid them away, darling, perhaps if I hadn't things would have been different."

Sarah rested her hand on his. "It's alright. I can see why you did it and it made sense at the time. But what happens now?"

"We wait," he replied, covering her hand with his own. "The next move is Corey's."

She nodded. "I'm just glad it's over. I was so worried I was about to lose everything again."

"What do you mean?"

"I couldn't come between you and our son. I would have left rather than do that."

"Sarah," he said sternly, "there is no way on earth that I would have let you go. I would have dragged Corey here by the neck if necessary to get this sorted. Our lives have been ruined once by someone else, and I'm damned if I would have let our own son do it this time. So you can forget any thoughts of being anywhere else but here with your family."

For both of them that night it was as if a black cloud had been lifted. They fell asleep content, holding one another.

Chapter Eighteen

Preparing breakfast for them both, Laura was pleased to see Corey almost back to his old self, although a little quieter.

Coming into the kitchen, he sighed. "I guess I'd better face the music sooner rather than later."

She gave him an encouraging smile as he picked up the phone and walked into the lounge.

He phoned Steve first, apologising for his absence the day before but said that he needed to see his dad so would be late in. Then after breakfast he drove to Saunders on Banff and, after parking the car, walked into reception. Checking that his dad was free he went through to the office. He stood outside the closed door for a moment, took a deep breath, and then rapped on the wood before walking in.

Jeff was in the middle of checking paperwork and looked up expecting to see someone from reception but was surprised to see Corey in the doorway looking very sheepish. If the situation hadn't been so serious he would have laughed. He looked just the way he did when he was a youngster and had done something wrong. He had the same look on his face, but this time he wasn't a youngster he reminded himself; he was a married man. He put the papers down on his desk and sat back, continuing to look at his son, waiting for him to say something.

Closing the door and walking across the room, Corey placed the package containing the album on the desk, then sat down opposite his dad. He was uncomfortable, something he had never felt with his dad before. But then they'd never been in this kind of situation before.

He coughed nervously. "I guess I owe you an apology, dad. I thought I should bring the album back and also say sorry."

Not intending to make things easy for him, Jeff leaned forward. "Sorry for what?"

Fidgeting in his seat, Corey took another deep breath. "For not believing what you said, for losing it, for using the language that I did, and for not speaking to you. And for making everyone's life hell for the last few weeks." God, I hope I've covered it all, he thought, as he waited for his dad to speak.

Keeping eye contact with his son, he calmly asked, "What about the disappearing act?"

"Yes, I'm sorry about that as well."

"You know if you were younger I would have expected that reaction but I thought you were old enough and wise enough to understand. Have you any idea what you have put everyone through over the last few weeks? How you could believe that I would lie to you, and to hear you use the language that you did was unbelievable. I didn't raise you to use words like that against anyone, let alone family." His voice rose as he spoke.

Seeing his son's stricken face he realised that he needed to cool things down. He was angry with

Corey, even now while he was apologising, but he needed to remember that they'd all been through hell and none of it was their fault. Lowering his voice he put his hands on the desk.

"Look, son, I realise that it was one hell of a shock learning what your grandmother had done. It was the same for me, and also for your mom. I guess I also feel partly to blame for letting your grandmother have so much influence over you, so much so that you found it hard to accept what I told you. But I was really hurt that you could think I would lie to you about something as serious as that."

Getting up, Jeff walked across to the side table and poured them both a coffee. Handing one to his son he sat back down again.

"Why don't you start talking to me, Corey, let me try and help you to understand anything that is still causing you some doubt."

Shaking his head, he looked at his dad. "I don't think I have any doubts...well, not since Laura told me what happened between her and grandma. If I'd had any doubts that information certainly wiped them away. I just want to try and explain to you why I acted like I did."

Seeing how upset his son was he tipped his head. "Go ahead," then sat back in his chair and let him talk.

Listening to what Corey was saying Jeff began to understand his son's reaction and fully appreciate just how big an influence his grandmother had had on him. Hearing how she had been the one he looked on as a mother figure while growing up, and had never really questioned why he didn't have a mom around.

"You know I never really wondered why there was no mom and just a grandma, except when one of my school friends told me his mom was really sick and he was scared she was going to die. I asked grandma if that was what had happened to my mom, but she told me no. She said my mom just stopped loving us and didn't want to live here anymore so she'd gone away. Told me it didn't matter because she was there for me instead, and she loved me more. I guess in my mind I figured if my mom didn't want to live here and didn't love us then I didn't have to love her. So I just closed my mind and tried not to think about her. When you told me what you did I just couldn't accept it, not after what grandma had told me. But when I saw all the presents and cards she had sent over the years, I realised she did love me. But it was hard opening my heart to someone I had shut out all those years ago, and to accept that the one person I thought I could always rely on had lied to me and deceived me."

Looking at his dad he again told him he was sorry for the pain he had caused over the past few weeks.

"I just want things to go back to how they were, dad."

"That's something that can't happen, Corey. As you know your mom is back but more importantly, she's also back in my life."

"I know. Laura says you are together as a couple and that it was her with you that day when we first got back."

Nodding, Jeff thought, That's one hurdle over. "So is that going to be a problem for you?"

Corey shook his head. "No. Not now I know the truth."

"Good, because nothing will change that fact. I lost your mom once and I have no intention of losing her again."

Having finished his coffee Corey poured them both another mug before sitting back down again. "Why did you never talk about my mom? And why never show me the album before now?"

Realising that he owed his son some kind of explanation he began to explain.

"I was hurt and angry when I heard she wouldn't come back, but I also had a very sick young boy. I put all my energy into looking after you and getting you well again. I think I always hoped that she would come back, but then as time went by I had to accept that it wasn't going to happen. I left all the sorting out to your grandmother but, as I have now found out, that was clearly a big mistake. Your mom had given me the most precious thing she could, you. I owed her for that, and at the time I still loved her and hoped she would come back one day, which is why I made payments to her over the years, or at least I thought I had. In reality, your mom has struggled since she left while we have enjoyed the best of everything, but you know she's not at all bitter about it and that's so typical of her. As you got older there didn't seem any point in telling you about her. My reasoning for that was why should I cause you any pain by telling you about things I couldn't change."

When his dad had finished Corey asked if he would tell him about his mom now.

"Where do you want me to start, son?"

"At the beginning."

Settling back in his chair he looked at him and smiled. "Do you remember how you felt when you first realised you loved Laura?"

Grinning, Corey said, "Yeah, like I'd been kicked in the stomach by an elephant."

"Yes, well that's how it hits you. I was a couple of years younger than you and doing a stint on reception when I looked up and found myself staring into the greenest eyes I had ever seen and from that moment I was lost."

Looking at his son's eager face he knew he was ready to hear the rest of the story so continued telling him about their life together as a couple and then as a family. By the time he had finished Corey understood why his mom and dad were back together.

"You must have really loved each other to be able to put everything that has happened behind you?"

"That's what you do when you love someone. The moment I saw your mom again I knew I still loved her, and thank God she felt the same. There's no point in ruining the future for what happened in the past, especially when none of it was our doing and we'd both been manipulated."

"So she came back to tell you what had happened?"

"No, she came back for you. She found out you were getting married and wanted to see you. She thought we were divorced and I had married again."

Realising he was going to have to tell him about the deception over the divorce papers he continued on with his story until Corey knew about the further lies his grandmother had told.

"Why would Grandma have divorce papers with her?"

"I've tried to figure that out and I can vaguely remember her making remarks about grounds for divorce before she went to England, but I wouldn't listen to her. I can only assume she took them with her with the intention of using them if she possibly could. I never had any intention of divorcing your mom."

Telling his son about this was hard, and even harder was admitting that he had signed the papers without knowing, that his grandmother had been clever enough to have them witnessed by someone whose name Sarah would have recognised, thus making them seem legitimate.

Waiting for his reaction to all of this he saw no point in telling him about the baby they had lost but hadn't reckoned on his son's continuing curiosity.

"Couldn't she...mom, have come back even if she thought what grandma had told her was true? She could have put up a fight for us, for me!"

Sighing he realised he had no option but to tell him the rest. "Perhaps she might have done so but your grandmother made some pretty convincing threats to her particularly about losing any custody claim for you, and there was another reason. I didn't really want to tell you this, son, but as a result of her mom dying and probably your grandmother's visits, your mom had a miscarriage. We didn't know she was pregnant when she left, but when she lost our baby she felt as though she had let me down and couldn't face coming back, particularly when she thought I didn't want her. She wasn't well for some time after that and when you're away from the people you love your mind plays tricks with you and you start to believe what you have been told. So she accepted the situation as she believed it to be, tried to get on with her life but she never forgot us, especially you."

"I know that now. I've seen the gifts she sent. Have you seen them?" he asked.

Jeff shook his head. "No, they're yours and your mom wanted you to be the one to open them."

Looking at his dad he asked, "Do you think she will want to see me after all I have said about her?"

Smiling, he looked at his son. "She's just waiting for the moment and, if it's any consolation, she's probably as scared as you. Why don't you go and see her?"

Looking worried, he asked, "Will you come with me?"

Jeff shook his head. "No, son, this is one meeting that you need to do alone."

"Where is she now?"

"At home, son, waiting and worrying about what will happen next."

"When's the best time to go do you think?"

"There's no time like the present. The longer you put it off the worse it will seem, and there's really nothing to be worried about."

Getting to his feet he held out his hand. "Are we okay, dad?"

Looking at his son's worried face, and hearing the uncertainty in his voice, Jeff stood and walked round to the front of the desk. Ignoring the outstretched hand he pulled his son toward him into a bear hug.

"We are now, but don't you ever put me through anything like this again, son, and don't ever use language like that to me again or I won't be responsible for my actions, despite your age."

"I won't and I'm really sorry. I've missed you, dad."

Standing back he noticed the relief on his son's face. "And I've missed you too. But there is someone else who has missed you for a lot longer. So you need to go and do what's necessary."

Leaving his dad's office, he drove along the familiar route to his old home. He couldn't help but notice his hands shook slightly as he hit the cruise button. He felt worse than he had when he was in trouble as a teenager. Pulling up outside, he walked toward the door then hesitated for a split second, should he knock? No, he'd never knocked before. Pushing the door open, he walked across the hall toward the kitchen from where he could hear movement. A female voice saying damn stopped him short of the doorway and he looked inside. She was standing with her back to him wearing a pair of dark blue cargo pants with a pale blue top. His mind switched back to the times he had come home from school, but unlike his school pal's homes, there had been no mom waiting to greet him. Before he could stop himself he started to speak.

"You know, sometimes when I came home from school I wondered what it would be like to have my mom waiting in the kitchen for me with a glass of milk and a cookie."

He saw her jump when he spoke and saw her hands grip the worktop, but she didn't turn around.

* * * *

The sound of his voice made Sarah start. She held onto the worktop for fear of falling. The muffins she had just managed to save from the oven were on the top in front of her. Hearing his words, made her want to cry, and tears welled behind her eyes. She needed to turn around but was scared to move in case her legs gave way. There was a silence in the kitchen that was deafening. Taking her hands away from the top, she turned to face him, taking in every detail of his face.

He was so like his father. Long gone was the chubby little boy she used to scoop up in her arms and hold high above her head until they both collapsed in giggles, but that little boy was still there, she reminded herself, inside the handsome young man standing in front of her. Neither of them seemed to know what to do but Sarah realised that what happened within the next few minutes would lay the ground for their future relationship. Biting her lips together to stop the tears from spilling, she took a step forward.

"I can always do a glass of milk and a cookie, but you might prefer a cold beer and I can offer an almost burnt muffin?" Feeling her face break into a nervous smile she waited for his reaction.

His mouth started to twitch and the smile she had waited to see again for so many years spread across his face.

He said one word, "Mom." Sarah moved the same time as him and they held each other tightly. Tears were running down her cheeks, or was that Corey's tears, she wasn't sure and didn't care, all she knew was that she had her little boy back in her arms where he belonged.

Some time later when they had managed to stop holding and touching each other, they sat in the kitchen, Corey with a beer and Sarah with a juice. He took up her offer of a muffin declaring it quite edible. "Almost as good as Laura's, but don't tell her I said that."

"Tell that to your dad," she said, laughing. "He goaded me into making these because he knows baking isn't my strong point, although I have improved a bit over the years." She knew she was gabbling because she was nervous.

She stopped when she mentioned the years bit, fearing she might upset him but he just smiled. "It's okay; I know all that happened wasn't your fault. I know what grandma did, although I don't fully understand why. And anyway, we can't not mention the last eighteen years, we have a lot of catching up to do."

However did I manage to produce such a thoughtful and gorgeous son, she wondered, and all the worries of the last few weeks were suddenly forgotten.

They sat talking for ages, discovering what they could about each other in the short time until Corey realised he would have to go before he was in more trouble with Steve.

"Being the boss's son doesn't buy me any favours," he told her.

"Why don't you and Laura come over for dinner tonight, if you're not doing anything else, that is?" Sarah waited anxiously for his reply. She didn't want him to go she wanted this special time together to last.

She waited as he pulled out his phone and his fingers worked away on a text to Laura. It amazed her how much the younger generation relied on this form of communication. She didn't even have a cell phone, although Jeff said he would get her one in case of emergencies. But Jeff much preferred her to phone and speak to him, telling her it brightened his day.

A few minutes later, he received a reply. Smiling he confirmed they would love to come for dinner. "And Laura said to say hi." Hating to leave her he kissed her and held her close. "I think I'm going to enjoy having my mom around."

"I hope so, darling," she said, tentatively using the endearment. "I love you so much and I always have."

"I know that now. I'm just sorry it took me so long to get my head around it all."

Walking to his car with him, she noticed he had a four-wheel drive, smaller than his dad's, and she smiled when she read the license plate, 'Saunders 2.'

Waving until he was out of sight, Sarah turned back into the house and almost ran to the phone.

Jeff picked up immediately when he saw it was home calling. It took him several seconds to make any sense of what Sarah was saying but eventually he grasped that Corey had been to see her and it had gone well. In fact, all she kept saying was it was wonderful. She was so excited she nearly forgot to tell him Corey and Laura were coming to dinner that night.

"Why don't I book a table for us all?"

"No, I want us to have a proper family meal at home. I've waited such a long time for this, Jeff. I don't want to sit in a restaurant with strangers."

"Okay, darling. I understand, a home cooked meal it is. Do you want me to pick anything up?"

"No, just don't be late."

Jeff had sat Sarah down at least half a dozen times before Corey and Laura arrived. She had declined a glass of wine saying she was so excited it would go to her head and she didn't want to be tipsy when they arrived.

"No, better not create a bad impression," he said, laughing. "I'll keep the alcohol until later." He heard her laugh and the sound was intoxicating. He had never seen her look so stunning. Her face was radiant and her eyes sparkled with excitement. This was his Sarah, this was the young girl who had captured his heart and held it safe all this time. If Corey and Laura were not expected he would have swept her into the bedroom now. But they were expected, and were about to have their first dinner together as a family, something he had never thought would happen.

He sighed, he would be on his best behaviour when they arrived. But they weren't here yet. He moved his hand so it rested around her waist, allowing his thumb to brush lightly against her breast. He thought he was being discreet until she turned and gave him a mischievous grin, telling him not to even think about it. Hearing the car pull up outside they both walked toward the door. Sarah would have run but Jeff kept a firm hold on her waist until the door opened and the kids entered.

Jeff had waited a long time to see his son in his mom's arms again and he wasn't disappointed. He couldn't begin to imagine what it was like for Sarah, holding her son again, when the last time she'd held him he'd been a toddler. All those wasted years, he thought, all the hell we've gone through just to satisfy a cold-hearted woman's desire to control everything within her grasp.

Shaking the thoughts from his head, he turned his attention back to what was taking place. When he finally managed to tear them apart, he hugged his son. "I guess I've slipped down in the pecking order now?"

"Never, but you will have to share with mom," said Corey hugging him back.

Turning to his daughter-in-law he waited until Sarah had finished embracing Laura, and then bent down to hug her too.

"Come on, kids, let's go through to the garden. It's too nice a night to be indoors."

After declaring that he was cooking, Jeff broke open a bottle of champagne, handed a glass to the others, then announced that he wanted to make a toast. But before he could, Sarah spoke up.

"If you don't mind could I make a toast first?"

Tilting his head toward her in acknowledgement, Jeff waited and watched her face as she raised her glass.

"To the two most important men in my life, and my lovely daughter-in-law, to my family."

Seeing the tears about to flow, Jeff put his free arm around her shoulder and added, "To our family, may it never be apart again."

Having drunk the toast Laura shooed the men outside to start the barbeque while she and Sarah got to know each other a bit better.

Settled around the table later Laura asked if it was okay for her to tell her parents all that had been going on and what had happened in the past.

"My mom knows something isn't right, particularly since a certain person was moody when we were visiting with them last week."

"Well of course I was moody, you had that ban thing going on."

Jeff and Sarah looked at the young couple wondering what on earth he was talking about.

"Dare we ask what ban thing?" enquired Jeff.

Corey didn't answer and waited for Laura to say something, but she just raised an eyebrow, leaving him no option but to briefly explain to them about Laura's ultimatum to sort the matter out, and until he did, certain benefits were off the menu. The blush on Corey's face said everything. Jeff threw back his head and roared with laughter followed closely by Sarah who, despite her desperate attempts not to, started to giggle.

"I bet it was fun when you made up though, son?"

"Jeff," said Sarah, scolding him, "don't tease."

"No...sorry, son, I know exactly how you feel. I had eighteen years of it and that included a lot of cold showers, but the making up is definitely fun," he said, winking at Sarah.

"Too much information, dad, thanks."

"Probably so," he replied as he continued to laugh. "Anyway, referring back to Laura's question, I think it's only right that her parents are put in the picture. They need to know exactly what happened and whose doing it was."

That agreed, Jeff turned the conversation to a happier subject and the light hearted banter continued for the rest of the evening. It was late when the young couple finally tore themselves away, but not before Corey managed to get his dad to agree that he could finish the week out at Canmore and then return to Banff.

"Okay with me, but you'd better check with Steve and Tom."

"Yeah, right, as if they make the decisions," he said jokingly when he saw the smile on his dad's face.

Loading the dishwasher, Sarah couldn't stop chattering. Jeff eventually stood back leaning against the unit waiting for her to catch her breath. When she finally realised she was doing the loading herself she stopped and stared at him.

"What?"

Shaking his head, he took the last dishes from her, put them in the machine and switched it on. She stood in the doorway, arms folded across her chest.

"What?" she repeated, refusing to move as he walked toward her.

"I'll tell you upstairs."

"No, tell me now."

Not hesitating, he picked her up, switched off the lights, and carried her upstairs. "I said upstairs and upstairs I meant."

Settling down in his arms she allowed herself to be carried into the bedroom and dropped onto the bed.

"Have I done something wrong?"

"On the contrary, everything has been perfect. I never realised until tonight how I've longed to see you and our son together again. I can't begin to imagine how emotional it's been for you, darling. The last time you held him was in the airport when he was just a toddler. Tonight, seeing you together, was surreal but wonderful.

"And you couldn't tell me that downstairs?"

"Yes."

She looked puzzled. "So what it is that you need to tell me upstairs?"

He smiled. "Not tell you, show you. You see tonight was perfect except for one small minor detail."

"What's that?"

"Nothing serious, but I realised this evening that from now on I will have to share you. So for now your husband would quite like your undivided attention." To prove what he meant he very quickly shed his shirt and the rest of his clothes, and walking to the bed, proceeded to do the same with hers.

Lying back naked, watching as he completed his task, she shivered in anticipation of the lovemaking that was to come. Holding open her arms, she waited while his body came down on top of hers. He pushed the hair back from her face.

"There are days when I sit in the office and think of you at home waiting, and it feels like a dream. Then I usually phone you, just to prove that it isn't. You hear people talking about love, but you never know what it is until you feel it. That our love for each other has survived all the years apart, proves that there is such a thing as true love. I fell in love with you, Sarah, the moment I saw you and I love you more today than ever. Seeing you and Corey together tonight was all I could ever wish for, but something I never thought would happen."

His words meant so much to her. Putting her hand up to his face she drew his lips down onto hers then gave her mind and body to him. Their coming together was gentle and beautiful with a depth of passion almost beyond words. Sarah slept like a baby that night and, waking the next morning, made a wish that they would always be as happy as they were now.

Chapter Nineteen

Now that the situation with Corey was resolved Jeff was determined that he and Sarah would enjoy married life to the full, and that included introducing her to the staff at the hotels. Having announced his intention the following evening, Sarah enquired how he planned on doing this.

"Quite simply, darling, by taking you into town with me tomorrow and telling people. I would have done it today, but figured you needed a day to get over the meeting with Corey."

"Well, I'm grateful for that. But wouldn't you rather leave it for a couple more days?"

"Nope. The sooner the better. I want to be the one to tell people, I don't want it getting out on the grapevine. And our son is not going to keep this to himself for long."

Phoning Saunders before they left, he asked for the team leaders of each department to attend a short meeting in the conference room at ten. Sarah was nervous but tried not to show it as she and Jeff walked into the hotel. The curious eyes of the reception desk followed them as they made their way through to the conference room. She had tried to walk behind Jeff but he had pulled her forward and held her hand firmly.

Opening the doors to the conference room, Jeff glanced around noting that everyone was present. "Sorry to call you away, guys, but there's something you need to know. I won't beat about the bush, I want to introduce you to someone who will be in and about the hotels from now on, my wife, Sarah."

The small gasp of surprise was audible to them both, but Jeff continued speaking as he pulled Sarah to his side explaining that they hadn't just got married, but they had been married for a long time, and that Sarah was Corey's mom. He had no intention of going into details about his mother's deception but simply said that due to circumstances completely out of their control Sarah had been living in England, but she had now returned to Canada. Having finished this brief explanation he quickly introduced Sarah to the various people and the meeting was at an end.

Whisking Sarah into his office he promptly kissed her, told her she had been brilliant, and then took her on a conducted tour of the hotel and its facilities. Sarah was enthralled by the simple but beautiful décor in the hotel as they walked round. "I hope I can make use of some of the facilities it offers?"

"I hope you will. The sauna can hold more than one person," he said, grinning wickedly at her.

"I'm ignoring that comment, Mr Saunders."

Having shown her around Saunders on Banff, Jeff took her on the short walk to Mountain View, knowing Tom would be on duty, since Corey was still at Canmore. He couldn't wait to see his reaction.

Jeff was delighted to see that Tom was actually behind the desk talking to the receptionist when they walked in. They both looked up when they heard them and Jeff could see the look of surprise on Tom's face when he noticed him holding hands with the woman at his side.

Watching as the older man looked at Sarah he saw the recognition slowly dawning on him and the look of delight on his face when he realised that it was really Sarah.

Coming from behind the desk, Tom walked quickly toward them. "Sarah, it is you...isn't it?" he said, somewhat bemused.

"Yes, Tom, it is."

The older man hesitated, as if unsure how to act. No such thought entered Sarah's head. She walked and part ran up to him, throwing her arms around him.

"Oh, Tom, it's so good to see you, and so good to be back."

"I knew you'd come back one day, I always had faith in you." He cast a quick look in Jeff's direction as he spoke.

Jeff suggested that they move the discussion into Tom's office, which the older man was only too happy to do. Having known Tom since he first started in the Company he knew that he would need to give him a fuller explanation of what had happened, not only because he felt he deserved it, but because he had always had a soft spot for Sarah ever since she started working in the hotel, and he'd often covered for them when they had been dating.

Once in the office Jeff explained to Tom that he wanted him to let the staff at Mountain View know of Sarah's presence. "I don't feel the need to call a staff meeting, Tom. I'm sure you can deal with this in your own way." He explained what he had told the staff at Saunders and suggested that he give the same explanation. "Although, I feel sure that the hotel grapevine is already passing the news around."

"Well you'd probably be right there."

"As for you, trusted friend, you deserve a proper explanation."

Once they were all seated, Jeff proceeded to tell him all that his mother had done.

As she listened to Jeff, Sarah watched Tom's eyes grow rounder and his mouth fall open, and felt sorry for him. Leaning forward she took his hand in hers, holding it until Jeff had finished speaking.

Tom had tears in his eyes when he finally spoke. "I always knew you wouldn't just desert Jeff and Corey. I saw you two together since the day you met and watched as your relationship developed and none of it ever made any sense to me. But who was I to question what I was told. I take it with all that's been going on you had trouble convincing Corey about his grandmother though?"

"Yes, that's what caused the disagreement between us but he's finally come to realise just what she did and he's more than happy to have his mom back in his life."

"So you two are back together as husband and wife?" The question was asked hesitatingly, but the hope in his eyes was clear to see.

"Most definitely," replied Jeff, taking hold of Sarah's hand. "And that's the way it's going to stay."

"That's the way it was always meant to be," said Tom. "Do you want me to keep the full story to myself?"

"Well, I've already thought about that Tom and I don't expect you to keep it from Mary."

"You know my wife, Jeff. Once she knows the full story the chances of her keeping it to herself are pretty slim. The mountain telegraph between her and the other ladies in her various groups is faster than a flash of lightening."

"I know," said Jeff, with a laugh. "But in a way that might be a good thing. I don't want to have to explain to people what happened, or what kind of a person my mother was, but I don't want Sarah being subjected to recriminations from anyone. So if the right people know what really happened it would make life a lot easier."

Nodding in agreement, Tom said, "You leave that to my Mary, she'll sort it out and I won't have anyone saying anything against Sarah."

Turning to Sarah he patted her hand. "Don't you worry, Sarah. People will know soon enough what really happened."

Sarah, touched by Tom's concern, hugged the older man as they got up to leave.

Saunders – Lies and Deception

Having done the tour of both the Banff hotels, Jeff drove along the highway to Canmore. For Sarah this meant another chance to see her son, even if it would only be a brief visit. However, she had reckoned without Jeff's planning, and discovered they were to have lunch together in the restaurant, after which she was to be given a conducted tour by their son while Jeff had a short meeting with Steve.

This surprise meant everything to Sarah, it was just as families should be and she made sure that the two men in her life knew this.

The next few weeks passed in a haze of happiness with lots of loving as well. She met Laura's parents and they had been to their home for dinner with Corey and Laura. The lawyers had already confirmed that there was no problem with her remaining in the country as she was married to a Canadian citizen and already had citizenship. Jeff had been certain there was no problem, but he wanted to be sure that nothing could spoil what they now had. She had also been having driving lessons. Although she could drive, Jeff had insisted that she have a course of lessons to refresh herself with the Canadian laws, pointing out that she would need to know these. She had applied for a Canadian driving licence and Jeff was making arrangements for her to take her driving test.

Annie had been a wonder throughout it all, dealing with the selling of Sarah's car in England, giving notice on her flat, and had also packed up the few belongings she wanted to keep. They had already been shipped out to her. Her whole life had changed. She was so grateful to her late grandparents for making her find out about her son, and to Annie for persuading her to fly out to Canada. Without them she would not have regained everything she had thought lost.

Although everything was perfect there was one date looming on the horizon, but Sarah didn't know how to mention it, and in the end she decided to wait and see what happened.

Waking up that day, she found Jeff already up and dressed.

"Sorry, darling, I need to be in the office early as I have a meeting. I'll phone you later," he said, handing her a cup of coffee, and then he was gone.

Sitting in bed on her own she thought, Well, happy fortieth birthday, Sarah. For a moment she felt sorry for herself, but then accepted it was her own fault for not saying anything to anyone. Showering and dressing, she ate a solitary breakfast in the kitchen. The days were getting cooler and she knew the snow would soon come. By lunchtime, she was bored and thought to phone Annie, but it was too early due to the time difference. She could have done lots of things, but because it was her birthday didn't feel inclined to do anything in particular. Oh, why hadn't she said anything to Jeff?

She'd found a card from Annie in the mailbox a couple of days earlier and had kept this in the drawer so as not to draw attention to today. Now, that didn't seem to have been such a good idea. She had hoped that Jeff would have remembered but this morning's rushing off to work dashed any hopes of that. Annie's card was now sitting all alone on the dresser in the bedroom. Watching the clock, she waited until the hands showed two o'clock and immediately phoned Annie knowing her friend would be up. But there was no reply.

Feeling really down in the dumps now she wandered into the lounge and picked up a book and started to read. She must have fallen asleep because the next thing she heard was the front door closing and footsteps coming across the hall. Jumping up from the sofa she ran to the doorway and a chorus of 'Happy Birthday' rang out.

She just stood there with her mouth open as she took in the scene before her. Standing in her hall were Annie and Bob, and behind them Corey and Laura and Jeff. She couldn't move, but then Annie suddenly rushed forward, breaking the spell and they hugged and hugged each other until Jeff threatened to hose them down. Greeting Bob in the same way she looked at her husband, son and daughter-in-law grinning and knew they had all been plotting behind her back.

Throwing herself into Jeff's arms she couldn't stop saying thank you and then scolded him for letting her think he had forgotten her birthday.

"Sorry about that, darling, but everything had to be carefully planned and I needed to get to the airport, then we had to meet up with Corey and Laura."

Lesley Field

Telling her to take their guests through into the lounge he and Corey took the bags up to the guest bedroom. When they came back Sarah had made drinks for everyone, then excused herself and made to go upstairs. Following her, Jeff caught her in the hall.

"Where are you going?"

"Beds, the guest bed needs making up."

He started to laugh. "Hey, I'm not useless. What do you think I was doing yesterday while you were having your driving lesson?"

"But you were at work?"

"Not all the time, sweetheart. Come on back to our guests, everything else is in hand."

This was the best present Sarah could have ever wished for. She spent the next couple of hours talking non-stop and opening cards and presents. She opened Annie and Bob's present first, and then Corey and Laura's. Finally, there was Jeff's card. She wished she could have opened this with just the two of them but that would have looked odd. Pulling the card out of the envelope the writing alone on the front, dedicating the card to a wonderful wife, and the words he had written inside were enough to start Sarah crying again. She didn't question the lack of a present because she knew that he had given her the best present possible, to celebrate her special day with her family and her best friends.

When Sarah remembered about dinner she discovered Jeff had arranged for a special meal to be prepared by the chef at Saunders and it was being delivered to the house, so all she had to do was to change. Looking at her husband she didn't think she could love him any more than she did right now. The look she sent him conveyed that more than words could say.

* * * *

Lying in bed later, Sarah continued to let him know how much she appreciated and loved her surprise. Not wanting to spoil his wife's wandering hands, he settled back and let her take charge of their lovemaking at least until it reached a crucial point when he deftly took over.

Sarah was up before Annie and Bob next morning, and after waving Jeff off to work for a few hours she set about preparing breakfast. Later, sitting in the kitchen watching them tuck into eggs and ham, she began to tell them all about her life here and how wonderful everything was, apart from the fact that she missed seeing them. Annie assured her that they could speak on the phone whenever they wanted and they also had the web cam, and that her happiness was all that mattered.

"What you have now, Sarah, is a far cry from the life and the small flat back in England. You've had years of heartache, and you deserve this new life. But it shouldn't have been a new life, this was the life you were meant to have. I was watching you last night, seeing the interaction between you and Jeff. I can see how much he loves you. I have to confess I was worried at first, but once the truth was out, I could tell from the way you both spoke that this was meant to be. You're like a younger sister to me and we are both just so happy that things have turned out the way they have."

"If it hadn't been for you two nagging me to follow up the information we found on the internet I probably would never have come to see Corey and none of this would have happened. Do you know I thought Jeff had remarried, and he let me believe that for weeks, but all the time we had never been divorced?"

The mention of Jeff's name made Annie ask where he was and Sarah explained that he had to go into work for a couple of hours but would be back soon and they planned to take them out for a drive around the area if they weren't too tired.

"No, we're dying to see everything."

True to his word, Jeff returned just before lunch and, loading everyone into the car, they set out on a sightseeing trip. When they finally got home, Sarah was surprised to see a strange car on the drive, but the front door opened and Corey came out, so assumed it was one he was using. Greeting her son she was about to follow the others inside when Jeff held her back. He asked Corey to see to their guests before he turned to Sarah and handed a small box to her. Holding it in her hands she looked quizzically at him.

Smiling, he said, "You didn't think I'd forgotten to get you a present, did you?"

"I thought Annie and Bob were my present?"

Saunders – Lies and Deception

He shook his head and suggested she open the box. Lifting the lid, she saw a key, and frowned, looking at Jeff in confusion. He had the biggest grin on his face as he stepped to one side and pointed to the blue four-wheel drive. "Happy birthday, darling."

Sarah's mouth fell open and she rushed forward to look closer at the car. She saw the customised plate that said, 'Saunders 3' and it gave her a thrill. The car was smaller than Jeff's, for which she was grateful, and looked similar to Corey's. She'd driven Jeff's car on a few occasions but found it a bit heavy and big, but this looked just perfect. Turning, she threw her arms around him. "Does this mean I get to go out on my own soon?"

"I guess so. Your instructor says you are good to go and that's good enough for me. You have your test lined up in a couple of weeks, so after that you can go solo. Sorry you have to be number 3 on the Saunders plate."

"I wouldn't want to have it any other way. The two men in my life will always be number one and two," she said as she ran to the side of the car. Opening the door she climbed in behind the wheel and was delighted with what she saw. Joining her in the passenger seat Jeff suggested she take them for a short drive, and secured his seat belt. Buckling up, she started the engine and put the car into drive. They didn't go far, just to the end of the drive and then a short way up the road before turning back. Switching off the engine, she leaned across and thanked her husband with a very passionate kiss.

"I hope that was only a taster of your thank you?" he joked.

"You'll have to wait and find out."

Finding the others in the house she took them out to see her present, not forgetting to thank her son for his part in the surprise.

The next couple of weeks were spent showing their guests the local area and doing the touristy things, even managing a couple of nights at the lodge in Radium. But all too soon Annie and Bob's visit was over and they were driving them to the airport. Watching the plane take off, Sarah's feelings were mixed. Happy to have had this time with Annie and Bob, but sad knowing it would be a long time before she saw them again.

Chapter Twenty

As the days shortened and became colder, Sarah settled into a very comfortable family life. She took advantage of the facilities at Saunders, particularly the Yoga classes, the one luxury she had afforded herself in England, and soon became a regular sight downtown. Having passed her driving test, she now had the freedom of being able to come and go as she pleased without dragging Jeff away from work. She had also been invited to join various groups and had very kindly thanked but declined their invitations saying she wanted to spend time with her family and hoped they understood. Since the grapevine in the town was very active, thanks to Tom's, Mary, there were not many people who hadn't come to hear exactly what had happened and what the late Mrs Saunders had done, so nobody took exception to the refusals.

Sarah made new friends, whom she met on a regular basis for lunch or coffee but always made sure she was home when Jeff came back from work. In time she hoped to help Jeff in some capacity in one of the hotels, but for now she needed to re-connect with her family. It was still difficult at times relating the grown up Corey to the infant she'd held in her arms when she'd left. And still shed the occasional tear at the lost years, but never when anyone was around. She had no intention of letting her family know. With time she knew the loss would ease.

She also formed a close friendship with Laura's mom, Julie, who had thought it hilarious that Sarah had believed she was married to Jeff. But the thing she loved best was being a wife and mom.

Sarah had just had coffee with one of her friends, then browsed around the shops for a while, before deciding to see if Jeff was free for lunch. Walking into Saunders she was greeted by reception who told her that Jeff was in his office. Tapping on the door she opened it and walked into the room, smiling at her husband as he rose from behind his desk. The next thing she knew the floor was coming up toward her and could hear Jeff's voice in the distance calling her name, before everything went black.

She could hear distant voices which were becoming clearer and louder. Raising her hand she put it to her face and opened her eyes. The first thing she saw was Jeff's anxious face bending over her. "What happened?"

"You collapsed, darling. Don't move. I've arranged with Laura to take you down to the hospital straight away to get you checked out."

She tried to sit up. "It's okay. I'm fine, or I will be in a moment. Please don't fuss, Jeff. I'm embarrassed enough as it is."

"Sorry, I'm not taking any chances. You're going to see Dr. Hall and there's not going to be any argument about it, Sarah."

Seeing the shock on Jeff's face she decided it would be pointless to argue, not that it would have mattered because before she could say another word he had lifted her off the sofa and was carrying her out to his car.

"Put me down, Jeff, I can walk. You're embarrassing me even more."

"You are not walking anywhere until I know you're okay."

With one of the staff walking ahead to open the doors, he put her in the passenger seat. Taking the key he climbed into the car, then pulled out of the car park and drove to the Community Hospital.

Arriving at the main entrance he insisted on fetching a wheelchair, despite her protests that she felt fine. Wheeling her inside, he registered at reception before leaving her in the capable hands of Laura who had been watching out for them to arrive. Instructing her not to move while he went to park the car.

"Honestly, Laura, I'm fine. It was probably just the change in temperature, coming in from the cold into the warm."

Laura looked sympathetically at her mother-in-law. "Sarah, you might want to argue with Jeff, but I have no intention of doing so because it's an argument that only he will win. So if I were you I would just sit back and let him manage things."

"Okay," she said with a resigned sigh. "But do something for me. Don't tell Corey, I don't want him worrying over nothing"

"Well I won't tell him until after you've seen the doctor, but after that I'm not promising anything."

Realising that was the best offer she was going to get from her daughter-in-law, Sarah reluctantly agreed.

Within a short time she was sitting in the doctor's office answering a whole list of questions. Jeff was listening intently to everything that was being said. Dr Hall was probably in his late fifties but very friendly and immediately put her at ease. Having answered his questions he suggested that Jeff might like to wait outside while he examined Sarah. Reluctant to leave he hesitated.

"Jeff, for goodness sake, go. You are only holding matters up," she said, giving him a smile to take the edge out of her words.

Lying on the examination couch she waited until Dr Hall had finished checking her over.

"I can't find anything really wrong. It could have been the sudden change in temperature as you suggested but, can I ask you something, Mrs Saunders. Could you be pregnant?"

She was sure that the look on her face told him that she had never thought of the possibility, and the heat she felt come into her cheeks only confirmed that it was a definite probability.

"I take it that it is possible?" he said with a smile.

Blushing, she remembered the way she and Jeff had been, the saying 'at it like rabbits' came to mind, and could only nod her head.

"I think we'd better do a test so we can find out for certain if that's what we are dealing with."

"I never thought it could be that." She felt embarrassed but excited at the same time. "Can we keep this possibility to ourselves, until we know for certain?"

"I think we can manage that. I guess this has come as a bit of a shock. But don't worry, patient confidentiality is everything."

Taking a blood sample he disappeared from the room saying he would be back shortly, but in the meantime perhaps she would like to avail herself of the washroom adjacent to his consulting room, then handed her a home pregnancy testing kit.

"I always have a few of these handy, the instructions are quite simple and the blood test will just confirm matters."

Leaving her staring at the packet she heard him talking to Jeff outside, suggesting he grab himself a coffee while he was waiting. Going into the washroom, she followed the instructions on the packet and waited the allotted time before looking at the indicator. Oh. My. God. She couldn't believe what she was seeing. She was pregnant. She was having Jeff's baby. Feeling faint again, this time from shock, she made her way back to the couch, her mind in a whirl.

Why was she surprised? Why hadn't she thought of it? They hadn't taken any precautions. She had never thought to do so, and they had certainly been making up for the lost years. She felt a sudden surge of excitement as she remembered how she'd felt when pregnant with Corey. The thought of feeling that way again, of her and Jeff having another child, was overwhelming.

She couldn't stop smiling and thought Dr Hall was never going to come back, but eventually he did.

Taking in Sarah's flushed face and bright eyes, he smiled. "I guess we have both got the same result?"

Sarah nodded, "I'm pregnant."

"You certainly are, I would say at least three months. We'll need to get you fixed up with antenatal appointments, but I think for now we'll leave things and you can come back another day when we can sort that out."

"Thank you," said Sarah. "Could I ask that you don't let Laura see the results? I know she's your PA but I would really like to tell the family myself first."

"My lips and paperwork are sealed until you tell me otherwise. Now, I just want to check everything is okay with junior before I let you go out to our expectant father."

Sarah dressed quickly and, leaving the wheelchair with Dr Hall, preceded him out into the waiting area. Jeff was anxiously pacing the floor and came straight over to them.

"Nothing to worry about, Mr Saunders. Your wife is the picture of health. I suspect it may have been the sudden change from cold air to hot that just unbalanced her for a short time. But all is well now as you can see and you can safely take her home."

Thanking the doctor, Jeff put his arm around Sarah and guided her outside; failing to notice the wink Dr. Hall gave to her as they left.

Chuckling to himself, Dr Hall returned to the reception area where he found Laura waiting anxiously. "Nothing to worry about, Laura. Mrs Saunders senior is in perfectly good health."

Driving Sarah straight home, Jeff called the office and told them Sarah was fine but he wouldn't be back for the rest of that day. He then called Corey and told him what had happened, but assured him his mom was okay and there was no need to come rushing over.

Having had her jacket and shoes removed and firmly placed on the sofa when they got in, Sarah lay watching her husband. She was so excited and hoped he would be pleased. Well he had better be she thought, after all, it's his fault, well partly.

Bringing her a blanket to put over her legs he fussed around asking if she wanted anything. Deciding to enjoy the situation a bit longer she thought perhaps he could get her a slice of that lovely lemon cake they had and maybe a cup of hot chocolate would be nice to go with it. Biting back laughter she watched as he dashed off into the kitchen. How long could she keep this up, she wondered.

She was bursting to tell him, although a part of her was a little concerned about his reaction. Perhaps having raised Corey virtually on his own he wouldn't want to do that again. But no, she told herself, they had always talked of having a larger family, and this time he wouldn't be on his own. It wasn't long before he was back with the cake and drink. Looking at his worried face she realised she couldn't keep this up any longer.

Putting the drink down, she looked very seriously at him. "Do you know what I really fancy, a peanut butter sandwich with jam."

He was about to turn to go back to the kitchen when she saw the puzzled look that came across his face. "You don't like peanut butter."

"Not normally, but I have a real craving for it that could probably last for about six months."

He looked even more puzzled. "Sarah, what are you talking about, are you sure you didn't hit your head?"

She couldn't keep it up any longer and burst out laughing. "Didn't you hear what I said...six months...?"

She watched him staring at her and knew what he was thinking, that she had lost it. Then suddenly his face changed as what she said started to dawn on him.

His face flushed. "Are you saying what I think you're saying?"

Nodding, she smiled. "We're pregnant, and I hope you're pleased?"

She watched as he put his hands up to his head and then spun around before turning back to look down at her. "How, when?"

That did it for Sarah, she dissolved into a fit of giggles. If he didn't know how then she certainly wasn't going to remind him.

He burst out laughing. "Stupid question," and then gave a whoop of joy before picking her up and kissing her until she begged him to stop. "God, Sarah, this is fantastic. Are you okay about it, and when are you due?"

Nodding, she nestled into his chest. "I'm ecstatic, what do you think? We'd always planned on more than one child. As for junior, well he, or she, should put in an appearance in about six months. I only hope Corey will be pleased about having a new brother or sister."

"He'll be delighted. But there's going to be one hell of an age gap."

"I know. But how will he feel seeing me with a young child and knowing that he missed all of that?"

"He'll cope. I know he will. So when do we tell them?"

"Well, sooner rather than later. Perhaps we could invite them for dinner tomorrow night and tell them then?"

Jeff couldn't do enough for Sarah and for the rest of the day she let him fuss over her as much as he wanted. Tomorrow, she thought, we are getting back to normal. I'm not ill, just pregnant. As they lay in bed that night she smiled as he kept running his hands over her stomach, as if unable to believe his child was in there.

"I can't believe it, Sarah. It's just as we planned all those years ago, to have more children. And now it's happening."

"It certainly is. And this time everything will be okay because we are together. But I hope this doesn't mean that making love to your wife is out of bounds for the next six months?"

Smiling he answered, "Definitely not, I seem to remember we managed quite well when you were expecting Corey. Although we were somewhat younger then, but I don't think we'll have a problem."

The next day, they told Corey and Laura. To Sarah's relief, they were both delighted at the news. She had worried that having just got her back into his life Corey may have been reluctant to share her with another sibling, but her worries were unfounded.

The days shortened, snow blanketed the grounds, and Sarah delighted in the changing shape of her body. Her world was perfect.

Their first Christmas together as a family was magical. Sarah insisted on having a huge tree in the hall as well as a tree in the lounge, but she also wanted Jeff and Corey to do the special things they had done together over the years, as well as introducing new traditions for the future. The weeks leading up to Christmas she spent working on her present to Corey. With help from Jeff, she had carefully copied each of the photographs from Corey's baby album and had bought a new album for him inserting the photos, each with the appropriate description of what it was and where it was taken. Jeff had suggested that she put them on a disc but she said it wouldn't have been the same. This was to be her special present to their son. Buying joint presents for Corey and Laura was a thrill for Sarah. They each wanted new snowboards so there was no problem in deciding what to get.

The young couple had arrived late on Christmas Eve and stayed over so present opening took place before brunch. Watching them unwrap their gifts on Christmas morning was wonderful and a tearful Sarah told everyone so. Sarah was given a special gift from her son and daughter-in-law, a silver framed photograph of them on their wedding day. "Oh, darlings, that's wonderful. It will have pride of place so I can look at it all the time." She said tearfully.

Corey and Laura looked at each other. "Look, mom, dad, we didn't know what to get for you both, so we've made up a selection of things that we think you will want." Handing over a large package they both looked sheepishly as Sarah and Jeff undid the wrapping.

Sarah was the first to start laughing when they opened what was clearly a baby box, containing everything from safety pins to clothes and toys, together with a book especially for the older parent, which immediately became the subject of great hilarity.

"Look, son, we've both dealt with a baby before, it's like riding a bike you never forget."

Teasing them, Corey replied, "What don't you forget, dad, the baby raising or baby making?"

"Corey," said Jeff, with a hint of reproach. "You're making your mom blush."

"After that comment," said Sarah, "I don't know whether you deserve your special present." But she handed him the album carefully wrapped in glittery Christmas paper. She watched as he opened the package, waiting eagerly for his reaction. She didn't have to wait long before his face broke into a huge smile and he jumped to his feet, wrapping his arms around her.

"Mom, this is perfect. In fact, this is the first Christmas that everything has been perfect."

Before he sat down she handed him an envelope telling him it was for him and Laura. Passing the envelope to Laura to open he watched as her face changed from a smile to one of shock. Looking at him, she handed him the envelope and piece of paper. Taking it from her he saw it was a cheque for fifty thousand dollars.

"We can't take this, mom."

"Yes, you can. It was part of the money your dad had been sending to me over the years, money I'd never received. Your dad insisted on putting it in an account for me, but I don't need it all, and I have more than enough left. Look upon it as a belated wedding present. It will give you both a start to your married life."

Corey looked to his dad for guidance but Jeff just smiled.

"It's what your mom wants and it's fine with me. Anyway, who's prepared to argue with a pregnant woman? Certainly not me."

Opening the rest of their presents the snowboards proved a big hit, and it wasn't long before they were enjoying a late brunch. Laura's parents were arriving early afternoon to share Christmas dinner with them before Corey and Laura went back to Canmore for a short visit. Jeff had taken charge of the kitchen so Sarah was able to enjoy this first Christmas with her family. Next Christmas, their family would have an extra person and the magic of a child at Christmas was something Sarah couldn't wait to share with them.

It was late when Corey and Laura left following her parents' car through the snow. Sarah was tired, but overwhelmed with happiness. After all the excitement they were only too ready to fall asleep, but before going upstairs Jeff disappeared into the den and returned with a small box that he placed in her hands.

"Happy Christmas, darling. I wanted to give this to you when we were alone."

Opening the box she found the most beautiful green and blue ammolite pendant in the shape of a heart in a gold setting. She could only stare at the beauty of it.

A long time ago, not long after they had been married, she remembered looking at the ammolite necklaces in one of the shops in the town site and recalled how Jeff had told her that the gems were in fact the fossilized shells of molluscs called ammonites that had been buried for millions of years. She had been amazed that something so beautiful could come from a fossil, but he had promised that one day, when they could afford it, he would buy one for her. She couldn't believe that he had remembered that promise. Lifting it out of the box he turned it over so she could see the inscription on the back, To my darling wife, before fastening it around her neck. Wiping the seemingly ever-present hormonal tears from her eyes, Sarah could only take his face in her hands and kiss him before thanking him for being the most wonderful husband in the world.

Not to be outdone she quickly pulled herself together and disappeared, returning with her own package neatly tied with a ribbon.

"It seems we both had the same idea about opening our own presents to each other," she said, handing the package to him.

Sitting down she watched as he carefully opened the gift and lifted the gold watch out of its box.

"I didn't know what to buy the person who has just about everything, but I thought this would keep a part of me with you when you are away from home. There's an inscription on the back."

Turning the watch over, he read the words, Time belongs to us, followed by their initials intertwined. Kneeling in front of her, he pulled her forward and kissed her gently on the lips.

"I love you, Mrs Saunders, and have done since the day I first saw you. I can't believe how I let my mother try to make me think otherwise and made us waste all those years."

"Hush," said Sarah, putting her finger against his lips. "It's in the past; the future is ahead of us. We are together now as a family, an expanding family," she said, patting her stomach, "and nothing is more important than that."

Smiling he sat next to her on the sofa and draped his arm around her as she nestled into his shoulder with a contented sigh.

As the months went by the staff at Saunders couldn't fail to notice Jeff's disappearance when Sarah was in the hotel Spa at her weekly class. Standing near to the closed door he would watch through the glass as she took up the yoga positions, taking pleasure in seeing her growing stomach. He knew she was aware he was there, but she wouldn't look around, much to his amusement, and kept her eyes firmly on the instructor.

Sarah was content, cherished and loved. Her world was one of complete and utter happiness.

Maddison Ann Saunders kicked and screamed her way into the world on a rainy day in April. Jeff and Sarah were overcome with emotion as they looked at the little wrinkled bundle the nurse had just placed in Jeff's arms. Sarah wanted to capture the moment forever in her mind. Bending down and placing their daughter in her mom's arms he leaned forward and kissed Sarah on the forehead.

"Thank you, darling, for the second most beautiful thing you have given to me."

They had declined to know the sex of their child so to have a daughter with fair hair and blue eyes so like her brother was a moment of intense happiness for them both.

Laura had been kept informed by the nurses as to how matters were progressing. When things were imminent she had phoned Corey who had dropped everything and rushed over. Having allowed the parents a few minutes together with their new daughter the nurse allowed an excited Corey and Laura into the room.

Corey was besotted with his little sister from the moment he set eyes on her, and Sarah could see the couple getting broody as they took it in turns to hold her. Having assured them all that she was okay but tired, Sarah insisted they go and celebrate and pass the news on to their friends. But there was one person she needed to speak to. Jeff dialled Annie's number, had a few words with her then handed the phone over. Sarah quickly assured her friend all was well, waved to Jeff as he and the others left, and then settled down to give her all the details of the new baby.

Word of the birth circulated the hotels and town in record time, and they found themselves inundated with cards, flowers, and gifts from well wishers for days. It seemed that everyone was happy to welcome the new addition to the Saunders family into the township.

Epilogue

Watching her family together as they celebrated their daughter's first birthday was something Sarah could never have imagined in her wildest dreams when she first arrived back in Canada. This had been a double celebration as they had waited until yesterday to have Maddison, or Maddie as the family called her, christened since Sarah wanted Annie and Bob to be there to share it with them.

Now they were all gathered to celebrate the first wonderful year of their daughter's life. To say she was a delight would be an understatement. She had her moments though, and had the same stubbornness as her dad and brother, but the cherub-like face with blonde curls and blue eyes could melt an iceberg. Miracles do happen, she thought, as she saw her husband walking toward her carrying the birthday girl in his arms.

As they got close, Maddie leaned toward her mom and in her baby words called, 'Ma ma'. Taking their daughter she tickled her until she giggled.

"Who was on the phone?" asked Jeff.

"Oh, it was nothing, just about an appointment."

Nodding, he dropped a kiss on his daughters head and then on her mom's.

"I see I come second now," she said, grinning at him.

"Never, except for today, but I'll make it up to you later."

The look in his eyes told her exactly what he meant by that and she shivered in anticipation.

Walking back into the lounge, she put Maddie down on the rug watching as she promptly rolled herself around until she reached the chair and then proceeded to try and pull herself up. Watched by her parents and godparents, they had chosen Annie and Laura as godmothers and, of course, Corey had to be godfather, she stood upright against the chair and held her little arms up to Corey, calling, "Orey Orey."

Sweeping her up in his arms, her brother swung her high above his head as her delighted giggles sounded through the room.

Watching her son and daughter Sarah was thankful that her family had been able to come together despite the interference in their lives in the past. Looking across at her husband, their gazes locked and a shared smile told her that their thoughts were the same.

Placing her hand on her stomach and gently stroking it she knew that today belonged to their daughter, but later when the house was asleep and she was lying in her husband's arms, she would tell him about the other new life already growing inside her.

****

Saunders – Lies and Deception

Saunders Series–Book 2

"Saunders: Endings and Beginnings"

Corey Saunders had grown up with everything he wanted, except one thing, his mom. The revelation of the lies and deception which had destroyed his family had turned his world upside down. But they were now in the past, an unpleasant, but not forgotten memory. His mom was back in his life and she and his dad were happy, and they were all learning to adjust to their new family.

His own life was good. He was married to Laura and they now had their own family. Everything was perfect. Too perfect.

When life kicks you, it kicks you hard as he found out. Nothing he could do, no amount of money could change things. All he could do was face up to life, and move on.

But when moving on annoyed the hell out of him, drove him to distraction, what could he do. And what would he do when he discovered things were not as he thought? Lies and deception had torn his family apart once, was he prepared to take a chance. Was he able to forgive and see beyond it?

Could he forget the past and risk everything for happiness?

Lesley Field

About the Author

Lesley Field grew up on Teesside. She enjoyed riding and reading and later spent most of her working life pursuing legal cases. When retirement came, she kicked off the restraints of the law and discovered her real self.

Lesley writes contemporary fiction which is set in Canada, and historical fiction set in the Regency period in London. Her first historical novel, "Dangerous Entrapment," was shortlisted for the Romantic Novelists Association's Historical Novel of the Year 2016. She came into the Romantic Novelists Association under the New Writers Scheme and has now progressed to full membership and is also a member of ROMNA.

Following publication of "Dangerous Entrapment," her second historical novel, "Dangerous Deception," was published in November 2016.

Her first contemporary novel, "Betrayal," was published on the 27th February 2018. Again this is set in Canada, on the outskirts of Calgary.

Now comes the Saunders Series, a trilogy of contemporary novels set in Canada. The first in the series, "Saunders–Lies and Deception," was released as an e-book on 29th May 2018. This will be followed by "Saunders–Endings and Beginnings," and finally, "Saunders–Sisters and Lovers,"

Happily living on the North Yorkshire coast with her husband she spends her days enjoying life and writing.

Lesley Field

If you enjoyed Saunders – Lies & Deception, please help spread the word about Lesley Field It's as easy as:

   •*Recommending the book to your family and friends by -*
•Posting a review
•Tweet and Facebook about it
Thank you

Follow me on my website:
www.lesleyfield.com
Facebook
Twitter: and also on Goodreads
For details of future releases
and more!

Or contact me on lesley_field2@btinternet.com if you want to ask any questions or post any comments.

Also by Lesley Field

Contemporary Novels
Betrayal

If Jessica had known that her life was about to be shattered she would never have returned home early. Betrayed in the cruellest of ways, and disillusioned with her legal profession, she abandons the life she thought she had.

Staying with her cousin in another city, circumstances force Jessica into a hotel for a few nights. There, she meets *Grey*, and she abandons her inhibitions in a one night stand – a night of passion where she discovers a connection between them that can't be denied. But she leaves before he wakes, knowing she will never see him again.

Settled into a new job, in a new town, the one person she thought never to see again comes back into her life, and offers her a new start, but a discovery threatens to destroy any future happiness.

Has she been betrayed again? Can she trust again? And what will she do when the one person she wants is in danger...

Lesley Field

Historical Novels
Dangerous Deception

Lady Caroline (Callie) Sutton has known Nathan, heir to the Dukedom of Craven all of her life. His family's estate borders that of her family and he is best friend to her brother, James. Her childhood has been idyllic brought up away from the restrictions and trials of society.

As she grows from child to maiden, the feelings between herself and Nathan change. A touch, a smile and a kiss, promise future happiness. When he leaves to tour the Americas with James, there is an unspoken agreement between them. But events destroy her idyllic life, snatch her away from that she had expected, and push her into a life she does not want. Unable to fight the forces now controlling her she vows to seek one last moment of the life she was destined to have, before bowing to the life she must now live.

But into that life she takes a secret so dire that if it were discovered her very life could be at risk.

Will she be able to maintain her deception? Will she be able to re-capture the happiness she once knew, or is she doomed to the fate that was thrust upon her...?

Dangerous Entrapment

Shortlisted for Historical Romantic Novel of the Year 2016 by the Romantic Novelists Association

"I do know what I am saying. I want rid of this stupid virginity before it causes me more problems".

Lady Isobella Rothbury believes herself to be on the shelf at 21 having suffered the humiliation of being cast aside in her coming out season. Now needing to help her cousin she seeks assistance from the Duke of Carlisle.

Richard Duke of Carlisle was intending to take a new mistress but is intrigued by Isobella's approach and finds himself developing a growing interest in her. How he moved from considering a mistress to contemplating matrimony comes as some surprise.

Harry Duke of Exmouth was duped into marriage and plots to capture the virgin he let go. He will bed and breed from the un-named lady he boasts to his friends.

Overhearing the plan Richard realises that the lady is question is Isobella and he has no intention of allowing the lady he desires to end up as mistress to a scoundrel.

If he saves Isobella will he discover the passion she can bring to his bed? And will Isobella find out that to prevent the man you love from seeking a mistress, you should take on that role yourself?

Lesley Field

CPSIA information can be obtained
at www.ICGtesting.com
Printed in the USA
LVHW041821240120
644725LV00003B/524

9 781724 927484